Black Widow
and the
Sandman

L.L. Reaper

This is a work of fiction. All of the characters, events, incidents, names, organizations and places portrayed in this novel are either products of the author's imagination or are used fictitiously. Any resemblance to actual persons, living or dead, business establishments, events or locales is entirely coincidental.

Print ISBN-13: 978-0-9829673-0-0

BLACK WIDOW AND THE SANDMAN

Copyright © 2011 by L. L. Reaper

Printed in the United States of America

First Edition; First Print Run

Library of Congress Control Number: 2010937931

Cover Artist: Keith Saunders
Developmental Editor: Sidney Rickman
Copy Editor: Lynel Washington
Proof Reader: Zena Gainer
Typesetter: Jim Brown – jimandzetta.com

All rights reserved. Except for the use in any review, the production or utilization of this work in whole or in part in any form by any electronic, mechanical, or other means, now known or hereafter invented, including xerograph, photocopying and recording, or in any information storage or retrieval system, is forbidden without the written permission of the publisher, Hourglass Unlimited™.

Acknowledgments

First and foremost, I'd like to thank God for giving me the talent, drive, patience and opportunity to share this project with the world. Among the countless people who have supported me over the years, I'd like to thank my family for their continued love and support.

Special thanks go out to Sharon Wright, owner of Carol's Books in Sacramento, California. Thank you for always being there in my times of need. I am forever indebted to you.

To my fans, there's no way I can express how much you mean to me on this page. Instead, I'll use the positive energy I get from you and put it into my future works, ensuring you more lively and entertaining reads. Thank you for everything.

I'd like to bid a special farewell to the finest Marine I have ever known, the late Richard Daniel Muse. Enjoy your stay in Heaven, my friend. *Sempre Fi!*

Chapter One

Cuba...

"The flesh rotted down to the bone abnormally fast. I've never seen anything like it." Dominic Ortega handed one of the photos to his long-time friend, Lincoln Mallard. "This guy here died less than forty-eight hours ago."

"And you say all twelve victims lived in a secluded area here in Cuba?" Lincoln swiped his large, battle-scarred hand across his sweaty brow as he looked at the photo of the dead man.

"Yes. These symptoms are...I don't know." Dominic removed his wide-brimmed straw hat and ran his chunky fingers through his mostly gray hair. "I'm at a total loss. Unfortunately, most of the victims were unable to make it to the hospitals until they were nearly dead."

Lincoln sorted through the photos Dominic had given him. Death was nothing new to him, but this? The ruined face of a little girl just about made him puke. Suddenly the eighty-degree heat of the December day felt like eight hundred degrees. "So the scientists you have working on this agree it's not some natural infection, infestation, allergic reaction?"

"We've had some of the best scientists on the planet work on it. They all agree it's definitely man-made." Dominic walked over and sat on one of the stone benches in front of the Nuestra Señora de la Asunción Cathedral.

Lincoln adjusted the collar of his white polo shirt, walked over and sat next to Dominic. The shade trees that surrounded the benches were a blessing. He tore his dark eyes from the photos of the dead and stared at El Yunque, the large flat-topped mountain in the distance. "And you say something like this happened in Baracoa not too long ago?"

"About a year ago, five children died in a similar fashion."

Lincoln ran his hand over his salt-and-pepper hair and massaged the back of his neck.

"What's going through your mind, Linc?"

"It's just a gut feeling."

"That gut feeling has gotten many out of a tight situation. What are you thinking?"

Lincoln drew in a deep breath and released it slowly. "I think someone is using your citizens as guinea pigs." He tapped the photo of the decomposed little girl. "And it seems the bastard is targeting children."

"I pray you're wrong."

"There are no chemical plants anywhere near the areas where these victims died. Not even a damn gas station. The first set of victims lived far from the beach, so you can rule out a chemical spill at sea washing up on shore. This has got to be some sort of targeted study."

Dominic leaned over with dry heaves.

Unsettled, Lincoln waited for Dominic to calm. "I have to know everything. What aren't you telling me?"

"My granddaughter, Vanessa, has lesions on her leg. The doctors are baffled. She visited with her cousins in the same area of Las Tunas this second set of victims came from. What if...?" He recomposed himself. "Do you think this is some kind of attack?"

Five-year-old Vanessa's face appeared in Lincoln's mind's eye. He remembered the day she was born; he and Dominic had to cancel their deep-sea fishing trip off the coast of Manzanillo.

They made it back just in time to watch Vanessa enter the world. He felt for Dominic, but knew there was nothing he could do to make his friend feel at ease. Nothing except find a cure.

Lincoln reached into the pocket of his white shorts and removed a pack of spearmint gum, wishing it were a shot of Tanqueray over ice. He held the pack out to Dominic. "Want a piece?"

"No, thanks." He stared into Lincoln's eyes. "You know I trust you with my life, but I have to ask you one thing. Is America behind this?"

Lincoln removed a stick of gum, unwrapped it and placed it in his mouth. "No...I know my government and yours are far from fuck buddies, but I promise you, if we were behind it, I would know."

Dominic's body relaxed slightly. "That's the first good news I've heard since these deaths began. Concealing this from the World Health Organization has been a full-time job."

"You can't keep something like this hidden. It'll get out. And it should."

"Our tourism industry is just picking up. Something like this will ruin us. The problem is contained."

"You have no idea when or where this will pop up again. Cuba needs to be seen as protecting future visitors from any hazards that might be on the island."

"I know." Dominic sighed. "But my hands are tied."

"Tied? You're the freakin' head of the Cuban Toxicology Agency," Lincoln snapped.

"At times like these I feel like more of a figurehead. You have no idea the risk I'm taking bringing you in, but I can't stand by and do nothing." He took a report out of his briefcase and flipped through a few pages. "I can't believe none of these scientists have been able to find a cure."

Annoyed Dominic hadn't seen fit to seek Lincoln's special brand of outside help until his grandchild was affected, Lincoln held out his hand. "Let me see your list." He scanned the dozen or so names. "Why do you have this name checked?"

Dominic looked at the sheet. "We were not able to get in touch with that particular scientist. We left several messages, but received no response whatsoever. She was our best option." He shook his head. "I wish we could have gotten her."

Lincoln checked the dates they had tried to reach the scientist. *Should have known she wouldn't be available.* "What do the scientists you used know about who commissioned them?"

"Nothing. Not even the location of the outbreak." Dominic took a pack of cigarettes out of the pocket of his light-blue Guayabera shirt, tapped one out and fired it up. "Each was paid enough not to ask questions or divulge any information on what they were hired to do. All but the one checked on the sheet has top security clearance in their respective countries. We provided each of them with samples of the tissue and stressed to them the serious repercussions if any of them were to discuss what they were working on." He pointed at a name on the list. "Escondido was a little different. He was one of our top choices, so we gave him vague information about our location and need of his expertise, but he declined our offer. We thought the money would draw him in."

"You were probably too cloak and dagger. When did the last death occur?"

"Before this one, about two weeks ago."

Lincoln spat his gum out in disgust. "Dammit!" He glanced at the dead little girl again, then handed the pictures back to Dominic. "I wish you had come to me after the first incident. We might have stopped this by now. How many have to die needlessly?" Then realizing that pointing out the obvious would get them nowhere, he checked his emotions and lowered his voice. "That being said, I am grateful you contacted me. I'll do all I can to help fix this mess."

"You're the only person I can trust to get things done." Dominic dropped his cigarette and ground it out with the heel of his sandal. "Waiting for these fucking politicians as they fight over bureaucratic bullshit will only lead to more deaths."

Lincoln could have pointed out that Dominic had been just as big a contributor to the bureaucratic bullshit as the rest of the politicians, but held his tongue. There were lives to be saved. The bells of the cathedral rang out, letting them know it was three in the afternoon. Both men sat in silence as the bells tolled and reflected on the odds of finding a cure with so little to go on. Lincoln stood up, took the pair of dark shades out of the pocket of his shirt and slipped them on. "You know the deal. Don't tell anyone I'm working with you, not a soul."

Dominic stood and shook Lincoln's hand. "You don't have to ask. I've worked with you long enough to know the routine. I just pray the connections you have will be enough to get to the bottom of this plague."

Lincoln took the keys to his rental car out of his pocket and stared at the cross erected on the grass in front of the gigantic church. *All right, Lord, I get the message. Guess it's time to pay what I owe.* He watched Dominic pack up his briefcase. "I think I know just the person to help. I'll contact you with details."

~~~~~~

Though physically at the hotel, mentally Lincoln was still at the Nuestra Señora de la Asunción Cathedral, looking at the photo of the little girl. By no means did Lincoln consider himself a saint, but damn. He had accidentally taken innocent lives, but this bastard had targeted the most innocent of all—children. This animal deserved an immediate, cruel death.

He walked onto the balcony of his fifth-floor room, sat in one of the multicolored lounge chairs, Tanqueray over ice in one hand, a folded piece of paper in the other. He took a gulp of his gin, then put it on the circular glass table next to him. He unfolded the list of scientists and reviewed it again. As the last ray of sunlight bounced off the ice cubes in his glass, he rubbed his tired eyes. *Had to be your hard-headed ass, huh, Black Widow?*

The scientist they'd wanted most was the one they hadn't

been able to contact, Jeanette Mason, or Dr. Jeanette Stone as she was known in official documents. Of the countless doctors, scientists, biologists and other brainiacs his forty years of top-level government access had acquainted him with, none was as brilliant—or deadly—as Ms. Mason.

Lincoln thought back to the reason he'd selected her alias. He had been following her, considering whether to approach her about joining his team. Her intelligence and beauty were obvious, but did she have the umph, that special "it" it took to kill if needed? Then he had witnessed her dump the body of a lover, and he no longer had any doubt. The Black Widow had been born.

Over the following decade, he had called on her to eliminate four "impossible to reach" targets—all males she'd been able to gain access to. Unfortunately for the males, meeting Jeanette had been a death sentence for each: two heart attacks, an aneurysm, and a severe allergic reaction.

Lincoln spotted a United States C-130 transport plane in the distance headed toward Guantanamo Bay. *Be a lot more of those in the air if I can't find a way to clean up this shitstorm.* He went inside and sat at the laptop on the desk. Of his twenty operatives, only two were qualified to handle the high-risk operation he had in mind—the two who worked for him unwillingly.

He reached for his glass of gin, but realized he'd left it on the balcony table. Instead of preparing a fresh drink, he focused on the picture of Jeanette on his laptop screen. Disguised as a gardener at the Westhampton Bath and Tennis Hotel, he had snapped the photo a year ago.

The picture showed Jeanette in a red and black tennis outfit, tossing a tennis ball into the air, preparing to blast her opponent with a vicious serve. He knew he needed her for this mission, but controlling her had become quite difficult of late. That was why, aside from keeping an eye on her from afar, he hadn't contacted her in over a year. He didn't want to push her to the point where she didn't give a damn who he told her secrets.

Instead, he had allowed her to enjoy life again, return to normal. At least normal for her. She was such a recluse. His intention was to give her time to become attached to things she wouldn't want to lose, such as her freedom.

Colin will use my nuts for pool balls if he finds out what I've turned his baby girl into. He and General Colin Mason, now CIA Director—the Black Widow's father—had literally joined the army on the same day. After a long, bloody fistfight in boot camp that ended in a draw, the two exhausted men had laughed at each other's weak punches. From that point on, they had been inseparable. One difference between the two outstanding soldiers was the way they showed their commitment to their country. Although both men loved their country, Colin wrapped himself in the American flag while Lincoln preferred to wear his flag underneath his leave-me-the-fuck-alone cloak. As one of the best snipers the army had ever seen, Lincoln preferred to work without supervision. This made some foolishly question his loyalty to his country.

Hard to believe I changed a few of her diapers. He grinned at the thought of the nickname he'd given his little caramel goddaughter after a particularly full diaper: Stinkbottom. By the time she was a toddler, he had slipped into the shadows of her life, out of sight, out of mind. A few years earlier he had left the military to create his own team of mercenaries, and business was good—too good.

Ten years of guilt ate at him. He had betrayed his best friend and godchild. Originally, it had been easy to justify making her a part of his team. How could he let her skills slip through his fingers? But now...Now he saw himself as the worst opportunist ever.

Damn. Memories of another's diapers he had changed came to mind, but he quickly shoved those memories away and focused on Jeanette.

Her photographic memory and 191 IQ amazed him. Her list of accomplishments also wowed him. She had obtained doctorates in microbiology, chemistry and genetics, all before her twenty-third birthday. Skipping to college from elementary school had helped. Highly skilled in several forms of martial arts and kickboxing, she also had "it." The same "it" he was cursed with. It was that inexplicable and rare ability to kill quickly and efficiently with no remorse. There was another who possessed "it" also.

Don't even wanna think about him right now.

His mind returned to Jeanette. He couldn't release her now. Too many lives depended on her.

The ringing of his satellite phone broke the silence in the room. He answered, "Deckard, what's the word?"

"Good evening, sir. We have the bird fueled and ready for your trip. When will you be arriving?"

Lincoln checked his watch. "In an hour or two."

"Will you be flying alone, sir?"

He minimized Jeanette's picture and pulled up another photograph. "Yes…just me. Tell your crew to plan on spending the night at Moffet Field. I want them ready to fly me back to Florida tomorrow morning." He snapped his fingers. "Oh, I need you to have a few things ready for me when I arrive in California. I'll e-mail you a list."

"No problem, I'll take care of everything."

"I'll give you a call when I'm en route." He ended the call and placed the phone on the bed. Looking at the picture of the amber-colored, dark-eyed man in the camouflage kill suit on his laptop screen, he exhaled deeply. "Let's see where you are, soldier." Lincoln opened a special tracking software program on his laptop. *Should be done with the assignment I gave you.* A satellite launched by Lincoln's former no-name government department rotated and began to home in on Roman's signal. The screen showed a map of the globe. He selected a few tabs and watched a red dot beeping in the western United States. He clicked on the magnification and the red dot showed up in southern California, indicating the location of his second operative who had "it."

Time to visit the Sandman...

A groan escaped him. The Sandman had the needed connections, could quickly adjust to whatever the situation called for and be lethal if necessary. Unfortunately, the Sandman was the second operative who wasn't following orders so willingly.

With each of the kills ordered by Lincoln, Sandman had left a little message. With his first mission on Lincoln's behalf, he'd left an hour glass. With the second, a broken hour glass, the third and subsequent, grains of sand. The assassinations were at various locations in the world, so no one saw any connection. Lincoln knew the Sandman even better than he knew the Black Widow because the Sandman was a younger version of Lincoln. In a way, he considered them his children—his two bad-assed children. The messages were the Sandman's way of telling Lincoln his time would come.

Maybe his time *had* run out. He knew his threatening to tell the Sandman's beloved mother about all the lives he'd taken wouldn't keep the Sandman in line forever. Lincoln was tired of the life he led, the guilt he carried. He would never have peace. If he ever let down his guard, Black Widow and the Sandman would be there to make him pay for his sins.

The decomposed face of the little girl in the photo haunted him. This situation was bad. Much larger than a few unexplained deaths in Cuba. He felt it with everything he had in him. Having the Black Widow and the Sandman join forces to stop the looming catastrophe might be the only way he could make amends for his sins. Once they joined forces, they would be unstoppable—even by him.

Chapter Two

Los Angeles, CA...

The familiar odors of gunpowder, blood and death seeped into Roman's nose. He looked through the two new holes in the privacy screen and saw Father Irvin Kline slumped against the wall of his confessional booth with a pair of bullet wounds in his head.

"Thanks for seeing me on such short notice."

Roman had reluctantly accepted the job of eliminating the corrupt priest from the mystery man who seemed to know everything about him—and his family. This wasn't the first time the mystery man he referred to as Shadow had blackmailed him into working for him by threatening to tell his mother what her son really did for a living. To find out her only child was a killer would devastate her even more than the fact that her only child had walked out of her life. Shadow paid him well for the assignments, and he would have taken them anyway because the targets all deserved to die, but the idea that Shadow had anything on him pissed him off.

Shadow had told Roman that Father Kline used his "faith" to conceal his gun smuggling trade, most of which placed weapons in the hands of gang members. The police and local government officials had turned a blind eye to the man of God's misdeeds, but Shadow hadn't.

Roman, as usual, carried out the assassination perfectly. He'd studied the church for weeks, noting the habits of the surrounding community in relation to the church. He knew when it would be best to strike, when he could have a personal session with the good Father.

Roman unscrewed the silencer from his pistol, tucked it and the pistol into his jacket pocket and exited the booth. He opened the dead man's booth door and watched as the white of Father Kline's collar slowly turned red. Blood streamed from his ruined head, down his neck. Expressionless, Roman removed his tight leather gloves and reached into his pocket. He removed and opened a small vial of sand and sprinkled a tiny bit on the priest.

After picking up the spent shells, he pulled a packet of cinnamon-flavored toothpicks out of his pocket, put one in his mouth, left the deserted church and drove his stolen Honda Civic to the train station. He preferred to travel by train, bus or car when he could; it made it easier to transport the "tools" of his profession.

~~~~~~

"How are you tonight, sir?" The Amtrak train conductor stepped into the bedroom compartment.

Because Roman suffered from claustrophobia, he always booked the largest compartment available on the trains he rode. His current one was designed to accommodate four to six adults.

He stretched his long, muscular arms and legs, then handed the conductor his ticket. "I'm good, just a little tired."

The conductor punched the ticket and handed it back. "Well, you'll have plenty of time to rest. We won't arrive in Oakland for another ten hours, Mr. Ross." He nodded his head in farewell and moved on to the next roomette.

Roman smoothed down his goatee and adjusted the ponytail

that touched the bottom of his neck. *Damn, don't remember the last time I used my real name.* Roman Tate closed and locked the door of his private roomette. One of the world's best assassins, most assumed he had earned the moniker of Sandman for his flawless record of putting targets to sleep— permanently. Only Roman and Shadow were aware of the real meaning to his nickname.

The train pulled out of the Los Angeles station. Roman removed the black, silencer-equipped *HK USP* compact .380 pistol from the custom-made pocket sewn into his black leather jacket. Since the pistol had been recently fired, the smell of gunpowder lingered. He broke down and cleaned the gun. Finished, he leaned back in his seat and ran his golden-honey hands over his wavy hair. *I need a serious vacation.*

Roman unpacked his laptop and used his wireless Internet connection to check his e-mail. In the midst of sending a job completed e-mail to his client, the satellite phone next to his briefcase rang. After reading the number on the caller ID, he smiled. "Well, long time, no speak, chick."

"What did I tell you about calling me 'chick?' You know I hate that term."

He finished the e-mail message, "Jack fell down and broke his crown," and sent it via his specially configured, encrypted, five thousand hop, anonymous routing system to Shadow. "You didn't mind me calling you that while you were under me in Russia a couple of years ago."

"Yeah, you think about that. What other woman do you know would up and fly all the way from Las Vegas to Russia just to spend a night screwing you on your birthday?"

He put the phone on speaker, picked up his pistol and inspected it. "I bet you got a nice write-off out of it for your corporation."

"Of course I did, business is business...but you know I can't get enough of you."

"I'm impressed. It's been over two years since we last... touched."

"Enough bullshit. Where are you these days? When are you coming to see me again?"

He logged into his private server and reviewed the three new assassin jobs he'd been e-mailed. "I'm not sure. You know how my photography business keeps me movin'."

"You need to come take some pictures of me in this new flamingo-pink bikini."

Roman imagined her fabulous, bikini-clad body. Remembered how good that body felt against his. The swelling in his slacks ceased once he recalled how insanely possessive she was. "I'll have to check my schedule and see if I can squeeze you in."

"Squeeze me in? Is that how you see me, as just another job?"

He set the pistol down and rubbed his eyes. *Ah, shit. Here we go.* "It's time for me to go."

"Don't you hang up on m—"

He ended the call. "Crazy broad." He returned to his computer screen and reviewed his new job offers. He hadn't heard from Shadow since receiving his last assignment.

Bet that won't last long.

~~~~~~

Jeanette lay diagonally across her king-sized bed with copies of scientific notes, textbooks, and journals all around her. The Christmas carols emanating from the television commercial in the background seemed oddly out of place in the warm December Miami afternoon. She picked up the universal remote and turned off the annoying holiday advertising in exchange for a CD. The song "No Air" by Rissi Palmer, her favorite singer, poured from the Bose surround sound.

"That's more like it." She bobbed her head. "Country music is so under-appreciated."

She picked up her half-eaten Snickers bar and refocused on the work at hand. An acquaintance had asked for her assistance in identifying a lethal toxin of unknown origin. This colleague had been commissioned by a non-identified government source to find a way to combat the toxin. Several top scientists had been working on the project for months, but had found next to nothing and had little hope.

She rolled off her platform bed, walked over to her balcony window and stared out at the handful of residents in the pool. Ready to crack the toxin mystery, all sorts of unanswered questions rambled through her mind. What was this toxin? America's chemical warfare? Had someone used it against American troops? How did the victims ingest it? How many victims were there and where? Why had someone created this? She finished off the Snickers bar and tucked the wrapper into the pocket of her red satin robe. The main question she was concerned with was how to stop it. If she could only obtain fresh samples. The tissue sample she had been given was nothing more than a few cells...nowhere near enough.

The person who had created this toxin was yet another example of why she had given up on much of humanity. Many would call her insane for her beliefs, but she knew she was the sanest of them all. People like the one who created this toxin did not deserve to live. She used one of her bare feet to scratch the other. Anyone who would use or create such an agent deserved to die. That individual was nothing more than a bug that needed exterminating.

Distracted by her phone, the ring tone shifted her mood from disgust to anger. It had been at least a year since she'd heard from the asshole. She'd hoped he had figured out she was tired of playing his game and would leave her alone. She snatched her earpiece off the nightstand and put it on. This year of freedom from him had given her time to think, to decide she couldn't live like some damn marionette with him being the master puppeteer.

"What do you want?" she said into her headset.

"Glad to hear your voice also. I have an assignment for you—"

"Don't even finish. I'm done working for you. Go to the

police, FBI, CIA. I don't care anymore. I'm through."

Silence filled the line. Before she could disconnect, he calmly said, "You'll change your mind for two reasons. First, this mission relies completely on your scientific abilities, and secondly, if you refuse, I'll have to let your father know what you've been up to. Just because you gave up your family doesn't mean you gave up the most important tie to them, your love. What will he think of your extracurricular activities?"

A genius, Jeanette entered college after junior high. Only twenty-two by the time she completed her third doctorate degree, her family couldn't be prouder of her. Her shame was what initially kept her away from her family. She'd murdered a man. She had just been so hurt, so angry and wasn't thinking clearly. Now she didn't regret killing him, but did regret killing him without a clear mind. If she had, this asshole on the phone wouldn't have had any way to blackmail her into being his personal executioner.

She pushed a lock of her thick hair out of her face. "I'm not a little girl anymore. My father is a top CIA official and would make sure my record stays clean." The possibility of jail was the least of her troubles. Sadness encompassed her as she paced the cream-colored carpet. How could her father have allowed her to walk out of his life? Over the years, she had tried to bury the pain, but the hole she dug was never deep enough.

Acting as if he hadn't heard her, Papa, as she not so affectionately called him, told her about the assignment without giving her a chance to say no. She quickly realized this was the same toxin her associate had asked for her help with. She couldn't stand this arrogant asshole, but had to admit that he'd never ordered her to execute someone who didn't deserve it. Then there was the toxin. How could she pass up the chance to crack the mystery?

She walked into her living room and sat on the overstuffed sofa. "I'll find a cure and track down whoever is responsible."

"Tracking isn't your specialty. You'll need assistance with this one. I'm teaming you up with—"

She jumped off the sofa. "Hell no! It's bad enough you know who I am. I don't want anyone else having anything to *try* to use against me. No."

"First off, you won't be killing anyone. You're a scientist and that's all he'll ever know unless you tell him otherwise. I'll tell him he's to assist you in any way you need and protect you."

She looked at her unusually sharp fingernails. "I don't need protection."

"I know you don't. But he won't expect a scientific nerd to have your...your special abilities, Black Widow."

"I still don't need him."

"You have a cure to find. He can do the footwork and remove any obstacles in your way. And, hell, who knows how many will need to be eliminated. My man was made for this. You do your part and allow him to do his."

She hated to admit it, but she had no idea how to track anyone down. She walked into the kitchen, removed the candy wrapper from her pocket and tossed it into her stainless steel trashcan. "Fine, but if he steps out of line..."

"Do not kill him. Do you hear me?"

"If he steps out of line, he's a dead man."

~~~~~~

"We touch down at Moffet Field in fifteen minutes, sir."

Lincoln moved his wide leather seat back to the upright position. "Thanks, Major." He peered out the window of the fast moving jet and watched moonlight reflect off the cloud cover below. He picked up his laptop from the seat next to him and checked on the bleeping red dot on the screen. He zoomed in on it. The movement was way too slow for him to be flying. He studied the highway arteries and train tracks along the dot's path. "So the Sandman is riding Amtrak. I swear I love nanotechnology." Many years ago he had heard about a crew of snipers caught in an avalanche during a cold-weather training mission. Once informed one of the missing men was Roman, he immediately got involved.

After tracking the homing beacons in the men's backpacks, he found them. The only survivor was Roman, who was clinically dead for thirteen minutes before doctors were able to restart his heart. *Scared the holy hell out of me. If I had lost him...*He'd had an epiphany and breathed a sigh of relief once he heard Roman would survive. Before Roman could regain consciousness, Lincoln went to his office, opened his safe and removed an opaque vial and syringe from its sealed metal case. The vial contained a saline solution with thousands of micro-sized computer chips. The so-called "nanotechnology" of the day had been discovered decades before the public even heard of the term. Lincoln, always being in the loop of the newest technologies, was fascinated at the possibilities of nano science. He had worked with several of the military's best nano experts and had them create micro beacon chips that could be implanted in a human.

After Dr. Yamoto showed him the tiny chips under an electron microscope, Lincoln found it hard to believe they would work. Yamoto went on to tell him that not only would they work, the chips would use the body heat of the subject to generate power. The chips were designed to travel to the spine, assemble as one unit and anchor themselves there. The synthetic coating on the chips fooled the body into thinking they were part of the bone structure. The chips had an estimated useful life of fifteen years. Once their energy was spent, the chips would detach and be ejected by a sneeze, out of the tear ducts and as Roman urinated. While looking in on the still unconscious Roman, Lincoln waited for the nurse to leave, then loaded the contents of the vial into his syringe and injected his protégé with it.

Lincoln braced himself for the landing of the jet. *Time flew by too quickly.* Once the red dot disappeared, so would Lincoln's ability to track Roman. Lincoln took comfort in knowing he'd crafted the Sandman's core training program, yet was disquieted by the unknown possibilities of what his student had learned since. The Sandman's connections couldn't be surpassed.

He departed the hypersonic jet, stepped into the drizzling rain and hopped into the unmarked white minivan he'd requested. He set up his laptop on the passenger seat and monitored the dot's progress. *Three hours before he arrives in the Bay Area.* Lincoln recalled the places where the red dot had shown up during routine monitoring of his most deadly solider.

He opened his briefcase and tested the power on the handheld tracking device inside. Without time to visit all of Roman's hangouts, he settled for what his instincts told him. He drove through Oakland, California, until he came to the area with the highest concentration of Roman's visits over the years: an elevator shaft in the parking garage of the West Oakland Bay Area Rapid Transit light rail station.

He parked, got into the back of the van, found a duffle bag, and unzipped it. *Good job, Taylor.* Inside he found a pair of B.A.R.T maintenance worker coveralls and ID, a uniform cap, fake beard and glasses, flashlight, Glock pistol with laser sight, two spare clips loaded with armor piercing rounds, a cell phone, sealed manila envelope and a pair of leather gloves. After donning the coveralls, cap, beard and glasses, he put the gun in the large front pocket of the coveralls and the portable tracking device in the duffle bag. He carried it with him and took the elevator down to the basement parking level. After checking the coordinates on the portable, it took him a few minutes to spot the Sandman's entrance. Chuckling, he walked over to the dusty AUTHORIZED PERSONNEL ONLY door behind the elevator shaft. He inspected the door and saw broken cobwebs around its perimeter.

"Knock, knock, Sandman."

Lincoln used a set of lock-picking tools identical to Roman's and easily opened the door. Five steps inside the damp, dimly lit room, he checked for cameras, found none nearby, then pulled the flashlight and gloves out of the bag. He put the gloves on and directed the beam of the flashlight over dust-covered change machines, a long tool bench, and spare elevator parts.

He heard the intermittent hum of the elevator motors. *Where do you go from here, Sandman?*

He set the duffle bag down, retrieved the portable tracking device, and powered it up. The red dot was still far enough away for him to complete his mission, but he didn't have time to spare. He played the flashlight beam on the walls in all directions. Minutes later, he spotted a door partially obscured by a huge, dust-caked, obsolete ticket machine. *What's behind door number one?* He placed all of his weight on the machine to push it out of the way. The machine rolled away smoothly, causing him to almost lose his balance. He shined the light on the bottom of the machine and saw someone had placed it on a pair of relatively dust-free piano dollies.

He inspected the door and found a dingy sign: DANGER! DO NOT ENTER! CONDEMNED AREA. The lock was very old, but well lubricated. He inspected the door for alarm triggers and found none. He readied his pistol and then picked the lock. Inside, utter and complete darkness swallowed his light beam. A constant musty draft of air ran up his pant legs and over his face. Ten feet across the concrete floor, he saw an opening in the floor with the rails of a steel ladder growing out of it. *This is definitely the place.* He opened the duffle bag and put the spare clips of ammo in his pocket. Dust and darkness greeted him. He cautiously inspected the tiny room for traps. A family of rats squealed and ran from the light. Cockroaches scattered into the darkness. He approached the manhole and saw a filthy, barely readable sign: SAFETY HARNESS MUST BE WORN WHILE ON LADDER.

The moment he shined the light down the hole, a chuckle escaped him at the thought of Danny Glover's line from the movie *Lethal Weapon:* "I'm too old for this shit." Thirty feet below, the beam of light found the filthy, concrete floor of the tunnel. He inspected the rusting metal ladder mounted to the crumbling concrete tunnel wall. It had definitely seen better days. He saw no signs of alarm devices and began his descent. After stepping off the last rung, onto the dirt-covered floor, he felt a small bump under his foot and heard a muted *click* in the silent darkness.

"Shit!" Heart beating rapidly, he shined the light around his foot and saw nothing but dirt. The buildup of dirt on the concrete floor concerned him.

A bead of sweat formed on his wrinkled forehead. He followed the dirt with his light and saw it was spread only in a five-foot radius around the bottom of the ladder. Satisfied he wasn't standing on an anti-personnel mine, he eased his foot up. He bent over and brushed at the dirt. Three inches below the surface, his fingers brushed against a rubber, pressure sensor mat. *Son-of-a-bitch!* He continued to wipe away dirt and found a pair of wires running up the wall, wrapped around an old conduit pipe, disappearing into the darkness.

"Great going, Lincoln, you just tripped his alarm system." He re-covered the mat in dirt and scrambled back up the ladder. He ran to his bag, checked the red dot and saw it was considerably closer to Oakland. He packed up his goods and exited the door. Before rolling the ticket machine back in front of the door, he went into the duffle bag, removed the manila envelope and cell phone. He put the phone against the door, pulled an ink pen out the breast pocket of his coveralls, and wrote a note on the envelope before putting it next to the phone and repositioning the ticket machine. Nerves on edge, he headed for the garage. "I'm *definitely* gettin' too old for this shit."

Chapter Three

"Happy holidays!" the undernourished security guard said to Roman as he departed the train station.

"Same to you," he mumbled in return as his watch beeped, signaling it was half past eleven. He looked out the huge glass windows of the station as the light rain danced in the luminescence of the streetlights. He adjusted the shoulder strap of his laptop bag and tightened his grip on his black briefcase. *Be glad when all this holiday bullshit is over.* He pulled down the bill of his silver Oakland Raiders cap and stepped out into the night.

For the past twelve years, after leaving home to join the U.S. Marines, holidays always put him in a grumpy mood. Growing up, holidays were special in his home even though he'd never known his father. His mother told him that when he was three months old, his father had gone camping in the mountains and never returned. His Jeep had been found at the bottom of a deep ravine, burned to a crisp. A body was never recovered. It was assumed he had been ejected and his body consumed by the abundant wildlife. A year later, Roman's mother petitioned the courts to declare him dead. Six months later, they did.

After graduating from high school, Roman joined the U.S. Marines against his mother's wishes. She detested people who took other people's lives—even soldiers. No matter how much he tried to justify the military's need to sometimes take lives, she refused to listen. "I will *not* have a murderer for a son!"

He had stormed out after the last of their many heated conversations and gone to boot camp. Although he checked on her periodically, without her knowledge, he hadn't spoken to her since leaving home. That bothered him more than he cared to admit, but due to the dangerous nature of the lifestyle he had chosen, he could ill-afford to contact her.

Dodging water-filled potholes, he crossed the street and entered the Amtrak parking lot. His vehicle looked undisturbed in its parking spot at the rear of the parking lot. He took his keys out of his jacket pocket, pointed the alarm remote at the gray-primered ex-highway patrol car purchased from an auction a few years ago. He opened the driver's door and then popped the trunk. After he placed his briefcase and laptop in the trunk, he checked the large blue bottle of nitrous oxide mounted on the trunk floor. "Almost time for a refill." He closed the heavily armored trunk lid and got inside the car. The car growled to life after he started the engine. The extra couple hundred horsepower he'd put into the engine begged to be unleashed.

He lowered the bulletproof and tinted window, spit out his toothpick and left the parking lot. Silver and gold tinsel draped the light poles of downtown Oakland. Rainwater dripped from the oversized Christmas ornaments that hung from street signs and most of the trees that lined the sidewalks. A bus with an enormous wreath tied to its grill passed Roman going in the opposite direction. His wipers squeaked in protest against the dry windshield as the light rain let up. By habit, he drove several extra blocks to make sure he wasn't followed. He paid for monthly parking at garages all over the Bay Area. Tonight, he needed to return to his underground hideaway he referred to as his "basement."

Although he had amassed enough money to live anywhere he pleased, he chose to live his life underground—literally. A year after being booted out of the military, he'd hacked his way into the database of Oakland's light rail system in order to discover how to print his own train tickets. As a bonus, he'd discovered a mile of tunnel that had been excavated and abandoned after geologists discovered it was too close to the San Andreas Fault line to be deemed safe. Instead of wasting taxpayer money to have the tunnel filled in, they'd decided to just seal it off.

Late one night, Roman stowed away in one of the tunnels until the trains had stopped running. He then found a door sealed with a rusted padlock, which lead to the abandoned section of the tunnel. He picked the lock, descended the metal ladder into the dark tunnel, and found his new home. He discovered a dusty electrical panel, crossed his fingers and threw on the main breaker. To his delight, one hundred yards of the mile-long tunnel illuminated. He found several empty offices, tollbooths and even a working restroom. The thick layer of dust on the floor told him he was the only person interested in the condemned tunnel.

After several late night trips to his haven, he discovered a plastered-over door that served as an emergency exit for the workers who helped dig the tunnel. He sledge hammered away the plaster, followed the emergency tunnel and found it ended inside the elevator shaft of a working section of the B.A.R.T. system. Instead of opening the exit door immediately, he waited until the following day to investigate where it led. Luckily, the door exited into an underground commuter-parking garage. Once he picked the lock and made himself a key, that exit became his new front door. The train repair yard, located a few blocks away, was his secondary entrance. The tunnel the trains traveled through to get to the yard was unguarded, but he had to go a quarter mile through the tunnel to get to his back door. With the danger of approaching trains and only three feet of clearance between the train and the tunnel wall, he only used that entrance if he had to. He feared the tight enclosure more than an approaching train. Four years later, he'd converted the abandoned tunnel into his own assassin's lair.

He parked in his rented stall, in a garage two blocks away,

then walked to the West Oakland B.A.R.T. parking complex. After making sure he was alone, he took the stairs down to the basement parking level and used the key he'd made for the elevator-shaft maintenance entrance. He entered the tunnel, pushed aside the ticket machine blocking the entrance to his "basement" and froze at the sight of a manila envelope and cell phone at the bottom of the door.

"What the fuck?" He set his laptop to the side, opened his briefcase and removed his gloves. He cautiously got on his knees and inspected the envelope, making sure it contained no lightweight explosives. His blood pressure went off the charts after reading the name on the envelope: Sandman. Only one person would have the audacity to enter his home. He grimaced and read the short note on the envelope:

> Sandman, I dig your cozy home! I started to wake you up, but I didn't have time to disarm all the booby traps I'm sure you've installed. Instead, I decided to leave you this note. I'm sure you know who I am, and are wondering what I want. I have a new job for you. I'd intended on giving you a much-needed break, but something's come up. I'm calling the phone I left you at 1:00 A.M. I expect you to answer. Don't disappoint me. I'd really hate to send your sweet mother pictures of your victims.

"Oh hell naw!" A quick check of his watch indicated he had only twenty minutes before asshole's call. He put the envelope and phone in his briefcase, picked up his laptop and made haste to his lair. After descending the ladder, he walked twenty feet to his right and shined his pen light on the six breaker boxes mounted on the wall. He opened the dusty cover of one of them and punched in his thirteen-digit pin number on the keypad he'd installed, disarming the system. He pressed a few more numbers and a quick diagnostic was run. Eight seconds later, he saw the words, "alarm activated" and a blinking number 1, indicting the number of times the alarm had gone off.

"Fuck!" He pressed another set of numbers, and it showed the time and date of the last alarm. "That bastard was here just a couple of hours ago." He flipped another switch in the breaker box, and a string of low-watt bulbs illuminated the one hundred yards to his hideout.

He walked until he came upon the metal door with no knob or keyhole that served as his secret entrance. Another bank of ancient breaker boxes hung from the wall next to the door. He pulled on one of the boxes and the entire box swung open. The high-tech hand scanner he'd installed blinked on. He pressed his palm against it, and seconds later, a green light flashed. Following that, he heard the click of the magnetic lock disengaging and the sealed door popped open three inches. He closed the faux breaker box, opened the door and stepped inside.

Motion sensors tripped and bright fluorescent light filled the large room. His forty-by-forty room had originally been designed to warehouse parts for the B.A.R.T. trains. After four years of hard work, he had transformed the room into an elaborate lab/living quarters. Putting his briefcase on the long wooden table that served as his tool bench, he removed the cell phone and waited for the call. He pulled a seven-inch long stainless steel throwing knife from the leather sheath around his shin and stared at the angry face reflected in the blade.

The memory of being kicked out the military for "allegedly" shooting at a general resurfaced. *General Stallworth...I can still see the look on his old, leathery face.*

He recalled how at the age of eighteen, fresh out of high school, he had enlisted in the marines. He went on to become one of the youngest gunnery sergeants and best sharpshooters they'd ever seen. He won numerous awards and competitions en route to becoming one of the most lethal snipers in marine history. *Still considered a hell-bound murderer in my mother's eyes.*

After years of faithful service, he had been given a

dishonorable discharge for refusing to kill an African warlord. He refused to take the kill shot after the Warlord picked up his infant daughter and kissed her before he got in his armored car and drove away. With his positioning, he would have had to kill them both. It didn't help Roman's cause when he threatened to give his sergeant a forty-five caliber suppository for questioning his refusal to take the shot. His disdain for authority was legendary among the ranks. A day after General Stallworth called him a "fucking coward" for refusing to take the shot that would have killed the child also, the general's coffee mug mysteriously exploded in his hand while he took a sip in front of the officers' club.

Upon investigation, they found a bullet in the wall of the building the general was standing in front of. After a massive investigation, they found half a boot print and some unusual depressions in the dirt. They concluded that the depressions came from a stand used to support a sniper rifle. They measured and found the shooter was over half a mile away. The only person accurate enough to make that shot was Roman. Without enough evidence to send Roman to prison, they settled for kicking him out of the marines.

Ever since his discharge, he had received communications from the unsavory man he had come to know as Shadow. Roman's inability to locate his foe frustrated him to no end. Shadow always seemed to be a step ahead of him. For the past couple of years he had tried to ease out of the business of killing, but Shadow had a way of pulling him back in. A way that went deeper than his mother finding out her son was a murderer.

He opened the envelope and pictures of his victims and him with his sniper rifle, taken at various locations spilled out, along with a few photos of dead children. *What the fuck!* The photos of his victims didn't affect him in the least, but the children...It looked as if their flesh had decomposed all the way to the bone—while they were alive. *Why would Shadow send me this shit?* He was so heated he didn't bother to look at the rest of the pictures. He put the photos aside and ground his teeth with fury.

At one o'clock on the dot, the cell phone rang. "What the fuck do you want?"

"Good morning, Sandman."

"You have no idea how much I'm gonna enjoy carving your shriveled assed heart out, you son-of-a-bitch."

"Save your energy, son. You'll need it for your new job."

"I told you I am not your personal killing machine or your goddamn son. I'm out of the funeral business."

"Bullshit. You need to quit trying to fool yourself. You were born to do this."

Roman slammed the tip of the throwing knife into the wooden tabletop. "Fuck you! You don't know me. You just know how to find me. But I *promise* once I find you—"

"Roman...calm down and listen."

Hearing Shadow call him by his real name for the first time got his attention. He backed off his anger in order to calculate what this change meant. "Talk." Shadow gave Roman a brief and vague summary of the need to find a cure for the poison and his role of assisting and protecting the professor. Roman walked over to the tank containing his pet boa constrictor, Josephine—named after Josephine Baker and her sexy, snake-like curves and sensual moves.

He opened the top and rubbed the smooth brown, black and white skin of his seven-foot-long Honduran boa. "And why should I give one fuck about a few dead Cubans? People die every day, everywhere. Besides that, I'm not a babysitter. You can find them on Craigslist all day long."

"We are assholes through and through, but we don't harm children. If you saw firsthand what this bastard did, could do again, you'd be on the first flight to Cuba. The nut job responsible for this madness must be destroyed...you're the only person I know capable of doing what must be done. I need, those children need, someone who can work outside the law in order to save them. We have to set aside our differences for a second and think about the big picture."

Shit. It irked Roman to death that Shadow was able to get under his skin this way. How the bastard had found out his soft spot was children, Roman didn't know. He closed the lid on the snake tank, walked over to his workbench and looked at the pictures of the dead children again. What these children had endured was off the "Fucked Up" scale. "I can refer you to a few people who can handle this for you possibly cheaper than I—"

"Do I need to remind you about your mother? As much as I would hate to, I'm sure you know I will—"

Brow furrowed, Roman bit out, "Okay, muthafucka, okay…I'll do it…but I fully expect you to get me everything I ask for—no questions asked. And my price is now *triple* the normal."

"Done. I'll call with more details in a few hours…"

He hung up, plugged the cell phone into his computer and attempted to trace the last call with a software program called Gotcha! he'd purchased from a Japanese software encryption specialist he'd met in Okinawa. Shadow's call had been scrambled too well. The signal had bounced around the globe every two seconds, making it impossible to trace.

Chapter Four

Sitting in his customary rear seat of a Black Falcon, a hypersonic jet fighter that supposedly didn't exist, Lincoln laid his satellite phone next to his glass of gin on the tray in front of him. After last night's calls to his special operatives, he needed a morning pick-me-up. He poured himself a shot, downed it, then refilled the glass. He felt as though he had just signed his own death warrant. He had followed the lives of Roman and Jeanette for so long, he saw them as his two bad-ass kids.

Two bad-ass kids who had more sense than he ever had. They were ready to give up the killing before the guilt set in, before that special "it" they each had wore off, yet his guilt-ridden tail was the one keeping them connected with death.

This is the last time, he swore. *The last time.*

Then there was Colin, his best friend and Jeanette's father.

Unable to deal with the betrayal he'd committed against their friendship, he returned his thoughts to Roman. Lincoln saw Roman as the man he had been twenty-five years ago, a cold, calculating, highly-skilled killer. *So much like me, it's scary sometimes.* He hated having to threaten to tell Roman's mother about her son, but it was the only way he could guarantee Roman's cooperation. Money wouldn't do it; Roman needed no money. Lincoln recalled how Roman had acquired twenty-million dollars of unmarked federal money after a botched attempt by the DEA to double-cross the Sandman. In place of the money, they found an origami fantail dragon made out of a hundred dollar bill in one of the empty suitcases. They had hired Roman to eliminate a major opium dealer in North Korea, then tried to take him out with a DEA sniper.

He shook his head at the image of the dead DEA sniper found with the barrel of his rifle shoved up his rectum and the magazine emptied into his ass. The only difference between Lincoln and Roman—besides Lincoln being more experienced—was Lincoln had no parents or family others could threaten or use against him. He was an orphan. Now at nearly sixty and having spent over forty years of his life murdering for Uncle Sam, he felt a need to atone for his past.

Over the years, Lincoln had studied human nature enough to know that Roman was in denial and subconsciously using the threat of his mother finding out his misdeeds as an excuse to be the Sandman. He often wondered what would happen when Roman stepped out of denial. Would that be the end of the Sandman?

Greeted by early morning overcast, he looked out onto the tarmac of the Alameda Naval Airbase. The photos Dominic had shown him had bothered Lincoln to his core. Death was nothing new to him, but the agony in the faces of those children wrenched his soul. This was beyond cruel. There was no need for them to suffer such a horrific death.

Like him, Roman and Jeanette's weakness was children. In a way, Lincoln knew that one assassin's flaw was what kept them human. Protect the children. All three were the same in that respect. But Lincoln had not always been that way. *The lives I've taken and the lives I've ruined...Gin sure does the body good.*

Protect the children. He recalled a toddler Jeanette. Watching her grow into a woman. He took another long swallow of gin. Sending Jeanette on this mission would surely upgrade him from the first-class seat to Hell he already had to a seat in the cockpit if anything happened to her.

Roman barely got three hours of sleep after his conversation with Shadow the previous night. While compiling the list of things he would need for the mission, his mind continually drifted back to the location.

Miami.

A few months before leaving for the Russian mission, he was contracted to delete three men who turned out to be the sons of the head of the largest Jamaican gang in Miami, the Caribbean Connection. After wiring a hundred pounds of C4 to the beach bungalow the three men used to count their cash after a huge drug deal, Roman succeeded in vaporizing them.

Unfortunately, as he hurried down the narrow road leading away from the bungalow, his car was sideswiped by a Jeep carrying four members of the Caribbean Connection who were rushing to the burning bungalow. Both vehicles were forced off the road. The men in the Jeep glared at him, yelled and flashed pistols at him as they tried to get their damaged Jeep to start.

Roman's car was stuck in the sand on the side of the road. He looked over at the Jeep and saw two of the men running down the road toward the fire and the other two running over to him. One man demanded he get out. The other man pointed his gun at Roman. Roman shot him, slid across the seat, shot the other man, exited the passenger door, and ran into the thick grove of palm trees.

Hours later, while at the Greyhound station, Roman received a call from one of his underground contacts telling him to get the hell out of Miami; a picture of him was circulating throughout the underground. A million-dollar bounty was now on his head. Thinking ahead, he had already shaved his head, put in hazel eye contacts and attached a fake goatee. He caught a bus into Alabama where he boarded a train back to California. He was still pissed at himself for not accounting for the narrowness of the road. He knew he would have been sharper if he hadn't spent the previous night and morning sexually gratifying the owner of the Diamond Dust Casino, Daphne Peres.

"It seems like every time I mess around with Daphne's crazy ass, something crazy happens to me." He walked over and picked up the photos from Shadow. He put aside the pictures of himself and flipped through the rest. "I swear, if she didn't have such a good pu—" He stopped at a picture of a beautiful woman in a white smock and forgot all about Daphne. *Damn, she's one fine-ass nerd.* "Check yourself, Roman. This is business *only*."

He put the picture in a clamp on his workbench and observed the photo under his large, lighted magnifying lens. "Hmmm, this is a blown-up ID badge picture." He increased the magnification, but Shadow had cut out the identifying information. He focused the lens on her hypnotic face. A sense of déjà vu flirted with his memories. *Those eyes...know I've seen her somewhere before, but where?* He tried to read the small logo on her smock. But that too had been blocked out.

"Ah, fuck it..." He pulled a cinnamon toothpick out of the half-empty pack on the bench, tucked it into his mouth and walked over to the three racks of computer equipment against the wall. He had more computing power in his basement than all of Cal Berkeley. He sat in his cushiony, black leather chair, pressed a few buttons and his extremely high-tech, water-cooled refrigerator-sized servers came to life. It had taken him weeks to break down all the sensitive equipment into small enough pieces to transport into his basement. He'd had the parts shipped to the apartment he rented in Menlo Park, California, the heart of the world-renowned high-tech community, Silicon Valley. He rarely spent time there, telling his nosy neighbors his photography business kept him traveling.

A red light came on atop a small black box next to the monitors. "Let's see what the Miami underworld is up to." He licked the tip of his finger, placed it in a small hole in the box, and it scanned the DNA in his saliva. If a user waited more than fifteen seconds to log in, the entire system would shut down for an hour. If the user logged in unsuccessfully a second time, the one-pound blocks of C4 wired into each server would be armed with a thirty-second timer. A third failed log in, or thirty-one seconds later, there would be an explosion. The light on the box went from red to green. His twin, fifty-inch flat screen monitors then woke up and a synthesized, sultry woman's voice greeted him. It sounded amazingly similar to that of Pam Grier. "Hey, sugah. What can Mama do for you?"

He spoke toward the small microphone mounted between the monitors. "Internet. Miami. Gangs. Bounty. Dead sons."

"Here it comes, baby." Seconds later, everything on the recent activities of the Miami criminal underground popped up on the screen. He looked for who was actively running the streets and how wanted he was. He was dismayed when he found out the Caribbean Connection was still the dominant street gang and was still on the warpath because of the murder of the leader's sons. He sat back and gnawed on the toothpick. He needed someone he could trust in Miami if things got too hot, someone who wouldn't be tempted to collect the million-dollar bounty on his head.

~~~~~~

At six in the morning, the phone he got from Shadow rang. He dropped down from the chin-up bar mounted in the doorway between his lab and sleeping quarters, sixteen pull-ups short of his normal two-hundred per morning, walked over and picked up the phone. The number on the caller ID was scrambled. He pulled off his T-shirt, wiped sweat off the side of his face then answered. "Speak."

"I trust you have something to write with. I have your itinerary."

Roman grabbed a yellow notepad off his desk and an official White House ink pen he'd "borrowed" from the Oval Office years back. *Bastard acts like this is some kinda vacation cruise.* "Go ahead."

Shadow gave him directions to a secluded house on the

outskirts of Miami. "I didn't bother to book your flight. I'm sure you have special flight arrangements to make. Oh, and when you reach your destination, use your *real* social security number to enter the gate."

Once again, Roman got the eerie feeling Shadow knew a little *too* much about him. He had more fake identities and social security numbers than he could remember. "That's okay. I'll add my airfare to your bill." He didn't bother to ask him how he got his social security number. He'd been dealing with Shadow long enough to know he never divulged everything. It reminded him of the sign posted on the wall in his boot camp sharpshooter class. The sign read "D.I.E. Deception Is Everything." He'd asked his instructor about the origin of that saying and was told it had been coined by some legendary shooter decades ago. It took Roman a couple of years to understand the meaning of D.I.E. As an assassin, having to change identities, appearance, locations and sometimes loyalties, he'd learned that deception *is* everything indeed.

"One final thing. While working with the professor, you will need to exercise patience and restraint. She has a bit of a temper. I don't need you two going after each other."

Roman laughed. "The day I need lessons on taming women from *you* is the day I become a Republican."

Shadow chuckled. "I'm telling you, she's not just another pretty face. Trust me."

For a brief moment, Roman almost liked his nemesis. He caught himself and switched back to business mode. "How many casualties should I expect during this glorified babysitting job?"

Shadow sighed. "Possibly a lot."

Roman walked into the door-less, former warehouse manager's office, which he had converted into his sleeping quarters. He pulled aside the long black curtains covering the wall across from his sleeping cot. Behind the curtain was a wall full of the most lethal and awesome weapons made. Assault rifles, pistols of every caliber, knives and martial arts weapons hung in neat rows. He picked up one of the two custom-made, black HK45 caliber pistols. Since he was ambidextrous and could shoot just as well with either hand, he'd had them specially balanced for both his hands. He also had custom twenty-shot magazines made for the pistols. "You know I still have business with you once this is done."

"Yes...just like I know where to send your portfolio to ensure your mother gets it. I'll call you tomorrow."

Roman threw the phone across the room at the concrete wall and watched it disintegrate. "Call that, muthafucka!" He packed the pair of HK45 pistols, some spare ammo, one of his three-thousand-dollar digital Nikon cameras and a few other things into his duffle bag. He went to the tall safe next to the row of rifles, opened it and sifted through the stack of various IDs. He settled for a civilian California driver's license with the alias Glenn Noble and a CIA badge with the name Maxwell Bond. The name was his personal joke, mixing Maxwell Smart and James Bond together. In the picture, his hair was cut short and his beard was missing.

He reached behind his head and removed the rubber band holding his ponytail. He sighed. "Damn. This has got to go."

After shaving the goatee into a moustache and cutting his hair, he went to his lab and created a fake CIA ID in the name of Geneva Spears, and a civilian ID in the name of Monica Noble, using the picture of Jeanette he found in the envelope. *Would love to do a photo shoot of her fine ass.*

Chapter Five

Nightmares about the lives he had taken sometimes kept Lincoln awake at night. What caused him to pickle his liver with his alcohol was the soul-eating guilt from the betrayal of his chosen family—Colin, Jeanette, and Roman. Especially Jeanette and Roman. In his heart, Jeanette was an innocent before he corrupted her...and Roman...he wasn't ready to face what he'd done to Roman. Might never be. They both wanted their freedom, and he was preventing it. If he released them now, maybe they wouldn't have the kind of guilt that weighed him down.

Had to make her a part of my team. Didn't have a choice, the old familiar voice recited in his head. Now he saw he'd had a choice. He could have saved instead of condemned her. Convincing himself that he had to continue down this path had become virtually impossible.

The way she had dumped her boyfriend's body had been cold, callous. The next day she had played the surprised, grieving girlfriend better than any Oscar winning actor could have. He'd never delved into the why behind the killing because he knew there had to be a reasonable explanation. An explanation that wouldn't play into his needs. But using the photos he had of her disposing of the body had cost him his soul. He poured himself a shot of gin and took a sip.

Now he fully comprehended the price. Over the years, he'd called on her skills only four times for kills, which she'd carried off expertly, but that *only* was eating away at his conscience.

Son-of-a-bitch. He had betrayed his best friend in the worse way. He'd also betrayed Jeanette, who was the closest he would ever come to having a daughter. He had loved—still loved her, his child. Thus the betrayal was made worse when he came to the reality of what he had done, was doing. *This is the last time.* Looking back, he couldn't see how he'd justified his actions. He finished off his drink and poured another. This time was different. Too many lives were at stake. He closed his eyes against his sins and prayed for God to forgive him for what he'd done to Jeanette and Roman.

Lincoln had started his career as Colin's spotter. Colin was the best. Then Colin fell in love with a CIA agent named Ambrosia Carson. They soon married. When the love of his life died during childbirth with Jeanette, the couple's third child, Colin gave up his life as a military sharpshooter to raise his children. Losing his wife had shown him just how precious life was. Lincoln wished he'd learned that lesson earlier. *Yeah, a whole lot earlier.* Instead, Lincoln became a mercenary. His men were so well trained the U.S. government often covertly contracted them to take care of "delicate" situations.

Lincoln and Colin kept their friendship secret from everyone. Neither wanted Lincoln's mercenary activities to hurt Colin or his family. Lincoln took another gulp of gin. Now his good buddy was a top official in the CIA. A top official with a missing daughter.

More guilt simmered within Lincoln. Colin wasn't stupid. He knew why his daughter had disappeared—to become a mercenary. Colin had the connections to find her, but he also knew no one could have convinced him to take a different path in his day. He had to come to it on his own. Until Jeanette came to it on her own, he'd have to be satisfied with the occasional card he received from her.

Lincoln had watched her grow up from afar. Jeanette had

always been a distant child. It was as if she had her own world in her head and others had to deal with it. Lincoln hadn't known how Colin would raise any of his children, but especially not Jeanette. Colin loved her to death, but hadn't known how to nurture her, how to show his love in a way his little girl needed.

By the time she was a teen, the two friends joked about how she'd make the perfect mercenary. The scary part was, they weren't actually joking. This had been scary for Colin because he didn't want his baby to take that path. He, and now Lincoln, understood the consequences to her conscience later. The true remorse. Lincoln downed the rest of his drink.

He'd prefer Hell to living with this guilt. This was it. The last time he would use Jeanette or Roman. "The last time," he swore.

~~~~~~

Salmon-colored Spanish tile and stucco exterior, arched entry onto the porch, a large redwood deck out back, a few young palm trees...and nothing for miles. The small, secluded house Papa had picked pleased Jeanette. It was literally in the middle of nowhere. *Looks like it was built yesterday.*

She didn't refer to her mystery man as Papa out of love, but out of resentment. He was always telling her what to do and giving her advice as if he were her father, yet he was the reason she'd had to give her real father up. The year of freedom from his weekly nagging session had been heaven on one hand and hell on another. Heaven in that she didn't need his fatherly advice, hell in that she had actually missed the contact. She just couldn't figure him out. How could he have known her so well? He always had. It just didn't add up. The only people who knew her even half as well were her father and brothers, and they would not have forced her into this lifestyle.

Inside the cabin, she set her suitcases on the beige marble tile in the living area and did a quick visual tour. The tile made the interior feel cold and distant emotionally. Same for the leather furnishings. She walked through the home. The faint hint of fresh paint hung in the air. What she thought would be the master bedroom was actually a high-tech lab, alleviating any doubt she had about Papa having the house built recently. Or at least modified.

Oh, my God! Before her stood the autoclave and centrifuge she'd had her eyes on. *Sweeeeeet.* In true Papa-style, the lab was equipped with the latest technology. Truth be told, she was impressed.

The only fault in the design of the house was its small size. Avoiding the babysitter Papa had hired to watch over her would be impossible. Disgusted she would have to share her space with someone else, she slowly unloaded her equipment from the car into the lab.

She never forgot a face. She'd seen this Sandman before. Her photographic memory was never wrong. She could see every detail of those few moments, but somehow she blanked out the exact date and location. They were both crossing the street when their eyes connected for the briefest of moments. More than their eyes connected. There was some sort of vibe that connected the two. She didn't understand it and in a way feared it. Thinking she would never see him again, she'd allowed the incident to settle in the back of her mind.

She placed her final case of chemicals in the lab, then reached into her back pocket and took out the photo of the Sandman Papa had e-mailed her. How could this be? How had this man been placed into her life and why? Why was she drawn to him? She stuffed the picture into her pocket. *Maybe that's why you can't remember when and where you saw him. You're scared you might get caught up in Mr. Sexy.* "Bullshit." She unbuttoned her jacket. The temperature in the house seemed to have risen. Roman "The Sandman" Tate was not her focus. Finding the antidote was. Then she'd find Papa and teach him he wasn't untouchable.

Chapter Six

"Have a good day, Mr. Bond," the Spanish-accented TSA agent said after handing Roman back his fake CIA badge and clearance to board the plane with firearms.

Roman shouldered his duffle bag full of weapons and other gear. "Thank you, Agent Hernandez. Happy holidays." Once he entered Florida, his senses had heightened. The flow of adrenaline through his veins gave him a high. He didn't truly feel alive unless he was on edge. That was when he was at his best.

He bumped into loads of sun-deprived, pale-skinned tourists. *Great timing, Shadow. Right in the middle of fuckin' tourist season.* He eased into the army of incoming passengers and waited for his bags to arrive on the luggage carousel. He looked for members of the Caribbean Connection and was relieved to see none.

Thirty minutes later, he drove out of the Ft. Lauderdale airport in a rental car. The warm, late afternoon weather was in stark contrast to the damp and chilly Bay Area weather back in California. He waited at a red light to enter the freeway.

"Let's see how far Homestead is from here."

According to the navigation program in his phone, Homestead was thirty-five miles south of Miami. He tensed up after a red convertible Mustang, bumping its music way too high, pulled up behind him. He looked in the rearview mirror and saw a pair of young black men passing a joint between them.

He removed one of the two HK45 pistols in the holsters under his jacket, took off the safety and put it in his lap. After adjusting his wire-rimmed, clear lens glasses, he eased off after the light changed. The driver of the Mustang decided not to wait behind the geek in the rental car and moved over to pass. Roman looked straight ahead while his right hand lowered to the pistol. *Be cool, youngsters.*

The Mustang driver floored the gas pedal and roared past Roman, both men shaking their dreadlocks to the beat of the music. Roman lowered his visor to block the setting sun out of his eyes, then put the pistol back in its holster and read the highway signs. After a moment's thought, he veered off I-95 south and made a detour to North Hollywood Beach Park. The smell of the ocean carried to him on the warm breeze.

The coastline soon came into view. Car parked, he grabbed his camera, got out and walked onto the beach. He paid no attention to the sand scuffing his expensive dress shoes. The breeze blew his goldfish-colored tie against his dark brown suit jacket. He stared out at the boats off in the distance, then took pictures of them and the surrounding beach area. His collection of beachscapes taken all around the world was extensive. Sometimes, when he wasn't able to get to a beach, he would go through the thousands of snapshots he'd uploaded on his computer. He bent over, picked up a handful of sand, and let it pass through his fingers.

Can't wait to pay Shadow a visit. He grabbed another handful and put it in the pocket of his slacks. *Once that's done, I'll be Roman Tate again. The last anybody is gonna see of the Sandman is his footprints on a beach far, far away...*Beaches were the only place he felt at peace. The sound of the water and the feel of the sand soothed him. He would sometimes find a secluded spot on a beach after a hit and sit for hours. The incoming waves helped wash away the blood of his memories.

He took one last deep breath of ocean air and walked back to his car. His mind went to Jeanette as he merged onto the highway. Her eyes...he did not like the tingle he got in his chest when he thought about those bright hazel eyes. With all the other shit to worry about on this job, he couldn't afford to let her beauty become a distraction. He arrived at the address Lincoln had given him just after six in the evening. *Pretty goddamn nice.* He pulled onto the flagstone driveway, stopped at the black wrought iron gate and entered his social security number on the keypad.

The gate opened up to a five acre, Spanish-style home. "I have to give Shadow credit; he has good taste and always goes first class." He pulled into the circular driveway and parked behind a murdered-out, new-looking, black GTO, or goat as some car enthusiast liked to call it. Before unpacking his bags from his Altima, he walked around the high-powered car and admired the red hourglass painted on the tail of the goat. He grinned. "This is *way* too much car for a chick."

He looked at the front of the house and saw the edge of the drapes behind the large picture window move a fraction.

"Come on out, Professor!"

When she opened the door, he knew he was in trouble. His grin turned into a smile of awe. Her photo did her no justice. He immediately sensed strength under her beauty. Never had a woman electrified his senses as she did. "Nice car. Did you borrow it from your boyfriend? No way is this a *woman's* car."

She wrinkled her eyebrows and introduced him to her evil glare. "No, but I'm sure you borrowed that piece of shit you're driving from *your* boyfriend."

Her black jeans, tight red shirt and black jean jacket give him a nice glimpse of her figure eight shape. He mentally guessed what size clothes she wore to have his man fabricate her some custom body armor. "Nice combination. Bad car and bad mouth." He peeked inside the driver's side window, then up at her as she walked over to the passenger side. "Can I take it for a ride?"

Hand on her hip and head cocked to the side, she said, "Hell no! You must be out your damned mind."

Ignoring her irritation, he ran his hand over the black hood. *Bet this baby is fast as hell, but it needs a few upgrades.* He looked over the roof and into her mad, but beautiful eyes. Now he could see they contained little flecks of green in the hazel. He removed his fake glasses and slipped them into his breast pocket. "All right, let's start over. Merry Christmas, Professor Meany."

She brushed her dark hair out of her face, went into her pocket, pulled out her key ring and set the car alarm. "Whatever. Just keep your hands off my car."

Shaking his head, he walked back to his car and got his camera. *Evil ass!* "And you keep your hands off mine."

"I'll try my hardest," she said with more sarcasm than he cared for. "I have better things to do than listen to your bull."

He surveyed and took pictures of the surrounding area and was pleased to see that within at least a mile in all directions there was no place that an intruder could hide. "Hey, Professor Meany." He snapped a picture of her backside. "What's for dinner?" He let the camera dangle around his neck, then popped the trunk and grabbed two of his four bags.

She walked toward the front door. "Whatever the hell you cook."

Lugging the bags inside, he set them on the marble tile entryway floor. He looked up at the high, vaulted ceiling of the impressive home. He wasn't surprised at the top-notch accommodations Shadow had supplied them. After inspecting the windows and doors to see how much work he'd need to do to secure the place, he joined Jeanette in the living room. He watched her rise from the black leather sofa. "Nice song. Who's that?"

"Rissi Palmer. Have you ever heard of her?"

Liking the smile she *almost* showed him, he loosened his tie. "Can't say I have, but I might have to add her to my R&B collection."

She chuckled. "That would be great except for the fact she is a *country* music singer."

He raised his eyebrows. "What? That's *country* music?"

"Yes, my uninformed friend, it is." She picked up a set of keys off the smoked-glass coffee table and tossed them to him. "The alarm code is BWATSM911. Just in case that's too much for you to remember, I wrote it on a Post-it note and stuck it on the refrigerator."

He caught the keys and cringed at the sound of her saying the alarm code aloud for anyone with high power listening devices to hear. "Thanks for that." He put the keys in his pocket. "It's time to go over a few security ground rules."

They both heard a ding sound from her laptop. She sat back down on the sofa, picked up her laptop and answered her Instant Message. "Not right now, I'm busy."

Shaking his head, he walked over, pulled the yellow note off the stainless steel refrigerator, and put it in his pocket. "Can you at least tell me which room is mine?"

She typed without looking up at him. "Figure it out. The one with my shit in it is mine."

Shadow, her attitude is gonna cost you a lot more money. He gathered his bags and carried them down the carpeted hallway. He looked in an open door and saw several bags and a red satin robe neatly folded on the ivory-colored bedspread on the queen-sized bed. He entered the room, checked the windows and looked around at the powder blue walls.

This is definitely not my room.

He took the room across from hers. The huge, cranberry-colored room was a far cry from his basement sleeping quarters. Sleeping in a room with windows made him feel uncomfortable. Vulnerable. The alarm sensors on the windows were substandard at best. Any halfway decent thief could defeat them in minutes. He walked around the room, checked each window and closed the white blinds on each one while he decided how to enhance the security.

Unpacking, Jeanette popped into his mind again. Her sexy,

athletic build and attitude told him she was more than just a geek, but he couldn't figure out what else she was—yet. He took off his camera, jacket, tie and gun holsters and tossed them on the peanut butter bedspread. After he took off his shirt and untucked his wife-beater T-shirt, the cordless phone on the oak nightstand rang. After three rings, he deducted that Jeanette wasn't going to answer it. He picked up the phone. The number on the caller ID was scrambled. "What now?"

"I'm calling to see how you and your roommate are getting along."

Roman picked up his jacket, reached into the pocket, got a toothpick and put it in his mouth. "Like oil and water."

"That'll change. By the way, I'll need you to check the fax machine in the den daily. Jeanette and e-mail attachments don't get along very well, and I may need to fax some documents to her."

"Oh, so now I'm a babysitter and secretary."

"I need a reliable way to get information to her and many times the old fashioned way of doing business can be the most secure."

Roman agreed, but wouldn't tell Shadow that.

"Once you're settled in, go check out what's in the garage."

Roman heard Jeanette turn up the volume on a new Rissi song. "What's out there? Pit bulls?"

"See for yourself. I'm sure you can find your way inside. Oh, by the way, you picked a nice room."

Roman stiffened. "Say what?" Dial tone filled his ear. He looked around the room. *No way.* He walked over to the bed, pulled one of his guns out of its holster and searched the room and closet. *No way that bastard could've known what room I took!* He set the pistol on the bed. "He was just trying to fuck with my head. I didn't even choose my room."

A cell phone rang in the living room. Jeanette turned down the music and answered a call from her father. But something about the way she said "Papa" made him curious. Instead of dwelling on it, he ignored her conversation and went through the kitchen and out the sliding glass back door. He crossed twenty yards of manicured lawn to the detached, three-car garage. A satellite dish the size of a flying saucer sat a few yards behind the house. Tall twin palm trees stood on either side of the garage. The fronds rustled in the mild breeze. Brass carriage lights were mounted to both sides of the garage.

He grabbed the handle on the garage door and pulled. "I should have known it would be locked." There was no lock to be found. He chewed on his toothpick. *What kinda game is this fool playing?* Upon further examination of the door, he found an electrical outlet a couple of feet below the right side carriage light. It protruded from the wall a little more than normal. He gave the outlet a tug and it flipped open, revealing a concealed keypad. He fished the piece of paper with the house alarm code out of his pocket and entered the code. A motor hummed and the door rolled up. The interior lights came on, illuminating a shiny, forest green GMC Yukon.

Three knuckle taps to the window brought a smile to his face. "Hmmm, bulletproof glass." He opened the driver's door. The weight of it told him it was armored. He saw the keys in the ignition, sat in the black leather seat and started the engine. He tapped the gas pedal a couple of times, appreciating the growl of the engine. *Sounds like somebody put a little muscle in the motor.* A pair of remotes for the garage door and a note were clipped to the visor*: Enjoy using my truck, Sandman. Try and keep it in one piece. You'll find some gas money in the console. More info to come.*

He looked up and saw Jeanette standing at the passenger side window. He let the window down and shut off the engine. The way she'd crept up on him unnerved the hell out of him.

She opened the passenger door. "How did you get in here? I spent an hour trying to find the lock."

He handed her one of the garage remotes. "Magic."

"Dumb luck is more like it." She walked toward the rear of the vehicle.

He opened the console between the seats and found a loaded

9mm Glock, four loaded clips and a fat white envelope. He opened it and flipped through the ten thousand dollars in cash. *You owe me a hell of a lot more than this.* He heard her open the rear hatch. He put the money into his pocket and closed the console. "What you find back there?"

"Nothing. I was just being nosy, like you."

He got out and joined her at the open hatch. "Are you always this cheerful?"

She gave him a blank look. "Yes." She walked back toward the house.

The sway of her incredibly sexy hips mesmerized him. *Mmmmm, mmmm, mmmph...all that ass and all that attitude.* He pulled his eyes from her rump and continued inspecting the Yukon. He checked the rear panels and found a couple of hidden compartments. In one he found a loaded pistol-grip pump shotgun and five boxes of shells. In the other, he found rope, duct tape, a bag of twist ties big enough to be used as handcuffs and a collapsible shovel. *Yeah, I like the hell outta this truck.*

Truck secure in the closed garage, he went back inside the house. The evening news played in the living room, so he went to see the headlines. Jeanette sat on the loveseat, busily working on her laptop. She paid no attention to him or the news anchor reporting on a home invasion in Miami where the occupants had been robbed and executed. Speculation was Caribbean Connection gang members were responsible. He grimaced at a photo of a seven-year-old boy who was one of the victims. "What a bunch of low-life punks."

She glanced up and wiped a lock of hair out of her face. "Did you say something?"

"No." He checked all the door and window locks, set the alarm and went back to his room. The face of that little boy reminded him of the dead children in Cuba. *What a fucked up world.* He opened his briefcase, took out a note pad and jotted down a few things.

Using his satellite phone, he called his most trusted friend,

Abraham "Hillbilly" Hocksteader.

"Hey, Bubba! What's shakin'?" Hillbilly said.

Roman kicked off his brown loafers, sat on the bed and opened his briefcase. "I need you to do a little shopping for me." Roman used the coded language they had worked out while they were in the marines together.

"Gotcha. What you need?" Hillbilly's spotter skills were almost as legendary as Roman's sniper skills.

"I need a size eight wedding dress, some bug spray, about five hundred and forty-five pounds of beans, a bloodhound, two fireflies and a magic wand."

"Got it, Bubba. You want them sent to your billin' address or shippin' address?"

"I'll e-mail you an address later. I'll need them sent overseas express."

"Can do. I'll have your goods ready in about twenty-four hours. Hey, will you still be able to come up to the ranch and teach the fellas next week?"

Shit, forgot I was supposed to be in Oregon. "I'm gonna have to postpone the class for a few weeks. I have a real hot photo shoot that's going to have me busy for a little while. Can you make do until I'm freed up?"

"Damn...well, I guess I can move them on to advanced fishin' or sumthin'," he said, still talking in code.

"I'll make it up to you, homeboy. I'll throw in a second week of training, my treat."

"Good deal! That's my Bubba! Don't forget to send me that shippin' address."

"I won't. I'll catch you later." He took the chewed-up toothpick out of his mouth, put it on the nightstand and disconnected. Logging onto his laptop, he e-mailed his Navy Seal buddy, Heath. Roman and Heath had become close after Roman was commissioned to work a mission with the Navy Seals. Thanks to Roman, the mission to assassinate a nuclear arms dealer in Pakistan several years ago was a success. Roman ended up saving the life of the navy seal team leader during the process. Via encrypted e-mails, Heath arranged to have the items Roman needed flown from Oregon to the Fort Lauderdale naval Air Base via a special navy courier jet by tomorrow evening.

After only two years in the marines, Roman had been chosen to join the Omni Squadron. They were known by that name only to the president. To everyone else, they didn't exist. They took their orders directly from the president himself. The invitation only squad was so exclusive, sometimes they went years without finding a soldier good enough to join them. There was no getting out once accepted. You were Omni for life. Roman's mental and physical strengths, intelligence, exceptional vision, focus and fearlessness made him the youngest recruit ever invited to join Omni.

He cross-trained with every division of the military: Delta Force, Army Rangers, Navy Seals, Green Berets...The Omni Squadron's black uniforms had no markings or insignia of any kind. Only other members of the squad knew of the secret signals they shared to identify themselves to each other. The group had been established thirty some odd years ago by Lincoln Mallard.

~~~~~~

Busier than a cat carrying kittens. Jeanette had heard the saying a million times, but never fully understood it until now. Roman put that busy cat to shame as he walked the grounds, searching for what she didn't know. He kept roaming in and out, making it hard for her to concentrate. When she asked him what he was up to, he'd said securing the perimeter.

What perimeter? There were no houses for miles. The road to their location was a private one off and off road from a two-lane highway. No one knew Roman was on his trail. Hell, they didn't even know who they were searching for. And Papa might be a butthole to the Nth degree, but what motive would he have to spy on them? He'd called them for help, not the other way around.

Why God wasted so much sexy-fine on a nut, I'll never know.

Professor Meany. A smile tipped her lips. She liked the moniker and Roman—even though he was a tad bit odd. Unfortunately, when she was nice to a man, he thought that meant she wanted his advances. Being a "meany" was the best way to keep an interested man from pursuing. And Roman was definitely interested—at least in her body. *Men. All they think about is sex.* She had to give it to Roman. He had actually liked Rissi, so he couldn't be too bad.

I'm not a meany. She laughed at herself. Who was she kidding? She was mean, just like her daddy. It wasn't like she tried to be mean. It just slipped out naturally from time to time.

She returned to the printout of the documents Papa had sent her. One of her brothers was in the upper echelons of NSA, which made her anti-Internet. It was too easy for Big Brother to snoop in her business. No, she'd rather have a fax any day of the week than an attachment in an e-mail.

Reading through the documents, she could hardly wait to hit the lab, but first she had more information to absorb. Come morning, she'd be prepared to tackle the toxin. Her stomach growled. Roman was so busy searching under rocks for terrorists, she knew he wasn't thinking about preparing dinner. She organized the documentation neatly, then headed for the kitchen with death on her mind. She had requested photos of the victims, but Papa had refused. Reading the effects of the agent was not the same as seeing it. If she couldn't examine actual victims, the least Papa could do was supply her with pictures. What was he trying to protect her from and why? He wouldn't even tell her the number of casualties, only the symptoms. All he'd said was they knew the contaminant had been ingested over a period of time. The food and water supply had been tested with no luck.

He's always acting like my damn daddy, yet he's the reason I can't see my real father. All too familiar resentment and pain resurfaced as she entered the kitchen. The love-hate relationship she had with Papa drove her mad half the time—no, make that most of the time. Their bond was so odd she couldn't even begin to describe it.

Then there was her father...Years ago she hadn't understood why she was angry with him. She'd been the one who ran away. Then it hit her. Rejection. Subconsciously, she'd wanted him to come for her, to save her, but he never did. The part that really hurt was the truth—Papa hadn't kept her from her father; her father didn't want her. Same went for her brothers.

Last Thanksgiving, she had been back home and watched her father and brothers from afar. She'd wanted to join in the festivities so badly, but wouldn't. The "why" behind their turning their backs on her was a complete mystery, but the result was an unbearable pain she had no choice but to bear.

She spied Roman through the kitchen window stalking across the grounds. *If my own father would turn his back on me...* She didn't finish the thought.

Enough of Papa, Daddy and Roman. My life is a lonely life. Get used to it. She had to re-energize, then solve the riddle before the nutcase who created the toxin released it on the world.

~~~~~~

Fort Lauderdale, Florida...

Lincoln watched Jeanette enter the kitchen on a computer monitor. The cameras and bugs he had hidden throughout the house were so small and inconspicuous that no one would find them—no one except Roman. He wondered just how long it would take. The longer the better. Spying on his two bad-tailed kids was the only way he could stay apprised of their activities, but once they discovered the bugs...A shiver traveled along his spine. Maybe he should have just placed his trust in them.

He smirked. Trust wasn't the issue. He'd been plain old nosy.

Black Widow and the Sandman sharing a home—this was better than anything reality TV could offer. How could he not watch?

Jeanette was upset with him, and he knew he was impeding her progress, but he couldn't show her the bodies or pictures of the deceased. Yes, she had killed, but she killed in nice neat packages. She had never seen anything like this...and the children. The images were too disturbing. He had already done more than enough damage to her. He had to protect her from this. There had to be another way.

He picked up his cell phone and called Dominic, then switched the view on his monitor to the rear outside camera—one of the four tiny, hidden cameras mounted on each side of the house—and watched Roman enter the garage.

"*Hola.*"

"Hey Dominic, it's Lincoln," he said in Spanish. "I need close-up photos of the victims' lesions. Have the adult males been buried yet? Are their bodies too decomposed to—"

"There were more deaths confirmed from the mystery illness today," Dominic cut in. "I was just about to call you. This plague, it's..."

"Shit, shit, shit." Cell phone pressed against his ear, he pushed away from the desk and paced about his makeshift office. "How many, who, where?"

"Three children and two adults, all in Las Tunas. The children died earlier in the week, but the adults died yesterday."

"Why the fuck didn't you tell me there were people who were still symptomatic! I could have had my scientist—"

"Don't you think I would have fucking told you had I known? This has the possibility of becoming an unstoppable plague. I'm supposedly in charge of the investigation, yet am being fed tiny bits of information like an infant. I need the bureaucrats to get out of my fucking way and let me do my job of saving lives."

Asking himself if he'd done the same thing to Jeanette, Lincoln stopped pacing in front of the large map of Cuba he'd had mounted on the wall. Simple answer, yes. His protection had kept her from doing her job. "I'm sorry. I spoke out of turn.

Of course you are doing everything you possibly can." He stuck five red tacks onto the map to join the seventeen already there. The location for this set of tacks: Las Tunas, Cuba.

Damn. Jeanette had to find the cure before the map turned completely red. "I'll need those photos as soon as you can get them to me." He wondered if Dominic's granddaughter, Vanessa, could actually have the mysterious illness.

"It's a done deal. Are you sure...?"

"Sure what?" He returned to his seat.

"There are grumblings here...that the United States is testing a biological weapon on our citizens. Soon, word will get out to the public about the deaths. Our government will call it a plague. We'll have to blame someone."

"It's not fucking us!"

"I know. I know, good friend. I just wanted to give you a heads-up. As you see, I'm not privy to all of the information, but what I do know, I report to you. You have connections over there—government connections you can trust. I don't want a war."

"I know who I need to speak with." He sighed. "I know the exact person." He ended the conversation, disconnected, then picked up his glass of gin and downed it.

Colin. He had known he would need to bring him in on this eventually. He'd just wanted "eventually" to come at a much later date or never.

He clicked on his laptop's desktop and opened a picture of him taken with the president awarding him a medal of valor years ago. He was about Roman's age in the picture. He and Colin had just killed the five most important and elusive members of a dangerous Iranian terrorist organization the previous week. He poured himself another shot of gin. Twenty innocent victims had been eliminated in the process. All those years ago, his mindset had been in a different place. In any mission, collateral casualties were to be expected. He hadn't thought he would ever actually care that innocent victims were dying.

Chapter Seven

Miami, Florida...

Marta reached from her bed and cried out in pain, "Please, Mama, please."

Sarafina choked back tears. "I know, baby, I know. But I can't give you more." She held her daughter's trembling hand. "When the doctor comes tomorrow, I'll ask him to increase the dose." The on-duty nurse, Pablo, had refused to contact the doctor, saying increasing Marta's dose would cause her to overdose. She knew the nurse was most likely correct, but the agony her baby was in...

A child shouldn't die before her parents, but Sarafina closed her eyes and prayed harder than she ever had in her life for God to take her child. Marta hadn't been perfect, but she was perfect for Sarafina and didn't deserve this...this whatever it was that was slowly eating away at her baby. In Marta's short thirty years, she had grown into a fine young woman with three beautiful children and a promising life ahead of her.

When the fever first broke out, they'd thought Marta was just battling the flu. Her primary care physician had prescribed antibiotics and sent her on her way. Over the next few weeks, the fever had left, but she complained of feeling like something was crawling under her skin. She had returned to her doctor, but after a host of tests, he basically said she was imagining things.

Then the pains began. Not on the outside, but on the inside. For a short time, Sarafina feared Marta was some sort of drug addict. Then odd open sores that began as tiny pricks, but grew as if dissolving her skin appeared. Her boyfriend, who just happened to be her boss, was very understanding and had hired a team of doctors to figure out what was wrong. He had even hired Pablo as her live-in nurse.

Sarafina was truly impressed. She'd never liked that British, pompous jerk of a boyfriend, but when he was needed, he had stepped up to the plate. Thanks to him, Marta had round-the-clock care.

She wiped the tears from her eyes, thinking all hope was gone now. She didn't know how much more pain her baby could bear. The nurse kept the narcotics locked away, so that wasn't an option.

God, why couldn't this be me? I've lived my life. I'd gladly give my life for her. Please, please don't keep her suffering. Take her now. Please take her now.

Knowing what she must do, but not the how, she stroked stray hairs from her daughter's face. *If you don't take her, I'll have to give her to you.* She wiped the tears from her own face. *Her suffering has to end.*

~~~~~~

After e-mailing Hillbilly and telling him Heath would have someone stop by his Oregon compound and pick up the goods, Roman went into the living room and joined Jeanette. The aroma of baking pizza punched him in the nostrils. A timer sounded in the kitchen. He watched her get up and head for the kitchen. He followed her. "Thanks for making dinner. I'm as hungry as a hostage."

She eased a large knife out of the block of knives on the counter, tossed her hair back and looked at him over her shoulder. "Don't get used to it, Mr. Hostage."

While she sliced the pizza he removed two plates from the cabinet, picked a piece of pepperoni off a slice and ate it. "I thought you genius-types knew better than to eat this garbage."

"Cute." After cutting the pizza into eight perfect slices, she placed the knife in the dishwasher and went to the fridge. "Did you learn that at rent-a-cop school?"

Crumbs dropped from the slice of pizza he picked. "I don't believe it. Professor Meany has a sense of humor."

After opening a bottle of white zinfandel, she set it on the counter and wiped up his crumbs. "Would you like some wine, wise guy?"

"Are you kidding? Do you *really* drink wine with pizza?"

"Doesn't everyone?" She pulled down two wine glasses from the cabinet over the sink, filled one glass and turned to him. "Do you want some or not?"

He forced his eyes off hers, ripped a couple of paper towels off the rack mounted to the bottom of the cabinet and handed her one. "Yeah, I think I will. I've had worse food combinations."

She poured a second glass of wine, then grabbed the spatula, scooped up two pieces of pizza and arranged them neatly on one plate, then repeated the process. "So what's your deal? Are you a bodyguard or something?"

He closed the blinds on the kitchen window and glanced around the darkening yard before closing the blinds on the back door. "Something like that." He set their plates of pizza on the counter extending from the sink. "At least that's what I'm supposed to do for you."

Handing him a glass of wine, she took a seat across from him on one of the wooden barstools. "What if I told you I don't need your help?"

He adjusted his wife-beater T-shirt to cover some of the long scar going across his chest. "I'd say I've never quit on a job I've been paid to do."

"How about if I double your pay to leave?" She bit the tip off a slice.

*Damn, her lips are sexy as a...*He caught himself watching her chew and took a sip of wine. "That's a union violation. No can do."

A smirk fixed her lips. She picked up her glass and held it to her desirable mouth. "Ah, do I sense a hint of integrity?"

He picked up a slice of his pizza. "Do I see the hint of a smile from Professor Meany?"

They talked, drank and ate and became more comfortable in each other's company. After a good amount of chatter, she placed the dishes into the dishwasher, threw away the empty wine bottle and stretched. "Well, Mr. Hostage, I'm going to shower and read some more about this contaminant. I'm putting in some serious lab time come morning."

Seating himself on the sofa, he flipped through the satellite TV news channels. "Leave your bedroom door open."

She stopped in her tracks on the way to her room, turned and looked at him. "You're joking, right?"

He turned up the volume on *Agencia Cubana de Noticia*, the news station owned by the Cuban government. "Not at all. No closed doors. I need to be sure I can reach you in case of an emergency."

"You're out of your damned mind if you think I'm leaving my door open. You're taking this little security guard job a bit *too* seriously. Good night."

She slammed the door and locked it to reinforce her feelings about his wanting her to keep the door open. As a news anchor teased about an upcoming story on possible toxic water in Cuba, he stood. "Some people don't believe water's wet until you throw some in their face."

He went to her door, put his ear against it and heard water running in the shower. *Guess we do this the hard way.* He entered his room, got his lock picking tool kit and easily opened her door. The sight of a set of fine gold underwear from Victoria's Secret on her bed made him long to change places with it. *Concentrate on what you're doin', fool.* He pulled the throwing knife out of the sheath on his leg, used it to pop the pins out of the hinges on her bedroom door, took it to his room and slid it under his bed.

A short time later, while checking the pictures he'd taken earlier with his digital 35mm camera, he heard her bellow, "Where the hell is my damn door?"

He looked up from his camera bag and saw a very mad and wet woman striding to his room. He could barely take his eyes off the wet, long legs protruding from the bottom of her damp robe. "May I help you?"

She pointed through his open door to the place where her door once hung. "I'm not here to play games with you! Put my fucking door back!"

He set his camera on the bed. "Look, my job is to keep you safe—period. And that means you'll have to follow the rules."

She took a step toward him. A lock of her hair fell from underneath the lavender towel wrapped around her head. She grimaced. "You and your rules can go to hell! Put my door back or I swear to God you'll rue the day you were born." She walked out and slammed his door behind her.

His heart began to race. He hurried and opened the door, and then his blooming anxiety attack subsided. *Much better.* "Crazy broad." He shrugged, went to his laptop and fired it up. *Let me get to work before I have to strangle her ass.*

A short while later, Jeanette gave him a sinister look when she exited her room and passed his, brushing her hair. "I'm still waiting for my door."

She didn't wait for his rebuttal. He watched her walk away wearing red, two-piece, footed pajamas. It was apparent she hadn't bothered to put on her bra.

Ignoring Jeanette, he took out his phone and called one of the few connections in the region who wouldn't bother with trying to collect the bounty on his head, a scum bucket named Jorge "The Terror" Olcina. Jorge, a five-foot-small madman, ran the most ruthless group of black market bandits in Cuba. His network of criminality stretched well into the United States, with a heavy concentration in Florida.

Legend was, he had killed so many men, Castro, instead of hunting him down, often used him to take care of some of his dirty work. He and Roman had met in a mercenary chat room disguised as a Dungeons and Dragons chat. Jorge had become Roman's most reliable source for purchasing C4 explosives—any quantity. Nothing went down in his world without his knowledge. Roman knew he could trust Jorge; the FBI wanted Jorge as bad as the CC gang wanted him. Also, Jorge was worth a small fortune and genuinely liked Roman.

After an hour of trying to locate the madman, he gave up and surfed the net. The main topic of his interest: the toxic water story in Cuba he had missed on *Agencia Cubana de Noticias*. He took a toothpick off the nightstand and nibbled on it.

If there's anything to the contaminated water story in Cuba, the news outlets have it buried deeper than Jimmy Hoffa. He peeked out the blinds on his window into the darkness. He really needed to catch up with Jorge, or be forced to contact the next best thing. *Damn, don't feel like dealing with her ass.*

Daphne.

Although she was now a multimillionaire casino owner, she had been raised in the roughest parts of Cuba and still had serious connections to the Cuban underworld. Her father had worked his way up the ladder of the Cuban black market and amassed enough money to buy a trip to America for his family. From there, he'd connected with a wealthy group of visionary criminals like himself. After a five-year battle, they'd managed to bribe, muscle and terrorize a Native American business group into starting a Las Vegas-style casino for him.

Daphne, for practical purposes, was her father's only child—he didn't claim her half-sister, Nina, who he said was the daughter of a whore he had a one-nighter with—was raised to run the business. By the time she was twenty, she ran eighty percent of the business herself. When her father died six years later, her late father's former partner was killed in a robbery attempt set up by Daphne, leaving her sole owner of Miami's first Las Vegas style casino, the Diamond Dust Casino.

Hell no. He had no intentions on contacting her unless there was no other way. He put the phone on the charger, then returned to his laptop and hacked into the City of Miami's servers. He found grid maps of the area and made note of alleys, traffic light patterns, road construction, police shift schedules and freeway entrances and exits. He also mapped out the places the CC gang frequented and the number of current members operating in the Miami area.

~~~~~~

Glad she'd had the foresight to bring groceries and a few extra supplies, Jeanette took the time to make her favorite treat—homemade chocolate chip cookies. Roman had been pretending to ignore her, but she felt him watching, undressing her with his eyes. What red-blooded man could resist a well-built woman in Christmas red-footed PJs, in the kitchen preparing a little dessert?

When she bent over and pulled the cookie sheet from the oven, she heard him approach. Ignoring him, she used the spatula to place the cookies on a platter.

Over her shoulder, so close she could feel his warm breath on her neck, he said, "Those smell delicious."

Having him so close sent her heart racing. *Damn he's fine.* With a sweet, calm voice, she said, "Thank you. They are payment for my door. Would you please replace my door, Roman?"

He held her by the hips, gently brushed his nose along her earlobe, and whispered, "That crap you learned about the way to a man's heart being through his stomach is complete bull."

When she turned her head to reply, their lips were paper-thin close, and his eyes filled with passion. "I'm not interested in your heart. I just want my door hung." To keep from indulging in the most kissable lips she'd ever seen, she tasted a cookie. "Delicious."

She took a glass down, then went to the refrigerator and

leaned over to grab the milk carton, knowing his eyes were glued to her butt. Yes, he should have gotten a fantastic view of the hourglass tattoo she had on the small of her back.

"Damn," he chuckled, "you must really be mad at me. I can't hang the door, but I can think of another way to channel your anger."

She poured herself a tall glass of cold milk. "Can't or won't hang the door?" Head leaned back slightly, she drank the entire glass of milk while he stood frozen in place watching. Finished, she slowly licked her lips, and poured another glass.

Breaking out of his trance, he said, "I won't re-hang the door. We're two consenting adults. I'm sure we can think of some other arrangements." He wrapped his arms around her waist and drew her close.

Though she wanted to back away from the heat, she stood her ground. She'd never had this much difficulty leading a man on. This time it felt different, as if she were being led as much as he. Distraction needed, she nibbled along a cookie's edge.

A grin tipped his lips. Then he leaned in and took a bite of her cookie. "Umm, sharing can be fun." Holding her close with one hand and feeding them both a cookie with the other, he said, "I think we'll get along just fine. See, following the rules won't kill you."

The beat of her heart had become so strong, she was sure he could feel it. Body all out of whack in the most carnal way, she knew she had to distance herself.

Before she could calmly escape, he began suckling her neck. A moan escaped her.

"The cookies aren't half as delicious as you."

She backed away. "Will you please hang my door?"

"Sorry, but no can do."

"Okay." Regrouping, she took the platter of cookies and glass of milk into the living room and sat on the couch. Oh how she hated leather furniture.

He settled close to her. "Are you planning on eating the entire platter alone?"

"Nope. I'm eating one more, then throwing the rest away."

"You shouldn't waste food. Don't you know there are starving children in Africa?" He flashed a million-watt smile and laid his hand on her thigh.

His touch started discombobulating her again. Laughing lightly, she said, "How your eating cookies will keep African children from starving is beyond me." She handed over the platter. "But far be it from me not to do my part to end starvation."

She moved to the plush armchair across from the sofa and waited for the poison she'd laced the cookies with to take effect. The milk, of which she'd already drunk a good amount, was the antidote, so she wasn't worried for herself.

While Roman ate, she skimmed over some of the scientists' notes.

Roman rubbed his stomach.

"You shouldn't eat so many sweets," she said calmly. "They aren't good for you. Especially those cookies, being as I poisoned them."

The cookie he'd been eating dropped from his fingers onto the floor, and his eyes were wild with disbelief.

"Sweat is already beading on your brow. Can you stand?" She held her hands out. "You'd better not try. Once the poison starts taking effect, the symptoms usually come pretty quickly."

"Bitch." He jumped for her.

She easily moved to the side. He crashed to the floor and clutched his stomach.

"I told you the poison works fast." She knelt beside him and gently stroked his brow with her fingers. "I'm re-hanging my door, and you'd better not take it down again." She set the glass of milk before him. "This is the antidote."

She walked toward his room. "Milk does the body good."

Chapter Eight

Fifteen miles off the coast of Las Tunas, Cuba

Casino owner Daphne Peres; Oasis Resorts owner Enrique Morales; British banker Walter Bagley; and American real estate mogul J. Michael Lipton stood on the deck of Lipton's 228-foot mega yacht, *My FantaSea*. Transforming a ten-mile stretch of Las Tunas beach into a modern, ultra-luxurious resort would return billions on the millions they were pouring into the project.

Lipton held out his glass of mimosa. "To a very profitable venture." They all clinked glasses, downed their drinks, then tossed the empty glasses overboard.

Enrique lifted the binoculars to his eyes and smiled as he scanned the once private beach they planned to occupy. "Very profitable." Thanks to the crooked government official who had accepted his bribes, he would be able to make the beach open to those rich enough to pay for the privilege of staying at the most exclusive resort ever created.

"Brunch is ready," a server said.

The four moguls walked past the yacht's heliport and to the main deck's dining area. Conversations on how best to transform beachfront property into a resort ensued. They were interrupted by Bagley's cell.

He checked his caller ID. "I'm sorry, but I must take this call."

"Unless it's going to cost you a few billion, I believe this is a little more important," snapped Daphne.

If he didn't want to bed Daphne so badly, he would have slapped the shit out of her. They had already used her Cuban gaming connections in order to build a casino into their resort, so in his opinion she was useless now. He excused himself and returned to the deck to take his call. "This had better be good."

"I'm sorry to have disturbed you," the man said slowly, but in a Spanish accent so thick Bagley could barely understand him. "Five dead here in Las Tunas over the last few days and some health officials are snooping around."

"Shit!" Bagley said under his breath and punched at the railing. He had been uncomfortable using Las Tunas as a testing ground, but his sponsor for this project had insisted.

After a full report, the contact asked, "What should I do?"

"Don't worry about it. Just keep your ears open." Testing was finished in Las Tunas. He didn't care what his sponsor said. He couldn't risk losing billions on this craziness.

He disconnected and continued to chastise himself. Using Las Tunas citizens for testing had been stupid. The only reason he'd relented to his sponsor was because he hadn't realized the assbackwards Cuban government would be able to connect the cases. He'd always heard such horror stories about Cuba—turned out they were just that, STORIES, not the truth.

~~~~~~

At two in the morning, Roman entered Jeanette's room, sat in a chair to the side of her bed and watched her sleep. After she poisoned him, he had considered shooting her in the foot, but instead decided to pay her back later. He moved and his chair squeaked.

"Are you out of your damned mind?" She stood in what looked like a kung fu fighting stance. "What the hell are you doing in here?"

Impressed at how quickly she woke up and leapt out the bed ready to fight, he said, "I'm doing what I was paid to do—guarding you." Gold underwear had never looked so good. "If you insist on having your door closed, then I will sit here and watch you every night."

"The hell you will!" Outrage lived in her face. "If you don't get the hell—"

Standing, he said, "Hey! Enough! Let me remind you this is *only* a job to me—nothing more. And I always get the job done. Now, we can either get-a-long or get-it-on, your choice. In the meantime, there will be no more screaming, no more bitching and *definitely* no more poisoning. In return, you can close your goddamned door, but not lock it. That's the best I can offer under the circumstances." He traded defiant glares with her before walking out.

Crazy broad.

After she slammed the door behind him, he didn't hear her lock it.

He smiled. *Compromise is a good thing.*

Unable to sleep and used to roaming the world at night, he left his room and went into the living room. Her laptop sat on the coffee table. He resisted the urge to fire that bad baby up to see what she was working on that was so top secret. Instead, he checked the windows in the living room to see what the landscape looked like at night. The surrounding darkness bothered him.

He selected one of his pistols and went out the back door. Once he stepped outside, the entire house, garage, front yard and the surrounding cinder-block walls were instantly illuminated. Motion sensor perimeter lights. "Okay, that's better."

The way the house was set up bothered him. *It's as though I designed this place myself.*

After he tucked the gun in his waistband, he walked the perimeter. Jeanette's beautiful eyes opened in his mind. That sexy, sexy hourglass tattoo on the small of her back made parts of him move.

Just like a Black Widow's mark. Humph, Black Widow. I like it. He chuckled. *That's what her mama should have named her. She's not your everyday egghead. The way she jumped out of the bed tonight...no normal person wakes up ready to battle. She was fully conscious of what she was doing. You can only get that kind of prep from training—lots of it. Reminds me of some of the training I did with the Navy Seals and Delta Force. She couldn't be military...could she?*

The grass whispered beneath his feet as he crossed the vast lawn, en route to check out the front of the property. He stared out at the empty road through the wrought iron bars at the driveway gate and thought about the thousands of people in Miami looking to collect the million-dollar bounty on his head. After a moment's reflection, he found himself more worried about keeping Jeanette safe from the assholes looking for him than their catching him. He spoke to the three-quarter moon. "Soldier, you have too much Jeanette on the brain."

One of the reasons he had become such a successful mercenary was because of his ability to focus one hundred percent on the task at hand. Distractions led to coffins. His mother came to mind. He missed her.

She had vehemently objected to him joining the military, but after seeing many of his friends die in the street, he didn't see an alternative. He also wanted to honor the old Jewish pawnshop owner, Mr. Kramer, who had saved his life when Roman was only seven. Mr. Kramer spent twenty-five years in the marines and taught Roman almost everything he knew about guns—how to use them as well as to respect them.

The exterior lights suddenly shut off, shaking him out of his trip down memory lane, yet the light in Jeanette's room remained on. She was probably elbow-deep in scientific journals.

After he moved from the gate, the lights once again blazed on. He returned to the house and quietly looked in on

Jeanette—who *was* literally elbow-deep in documents. She was so immersed, she didn't even spare him a glance.

Back in his room he forced himself to sleep. A few hours later, he immediately woke up at the sound of Jeanette's door opening. His years of training had taught him to be alert—even while asleep. He relaxed a while, then grabbed the pistol from under his pillow and got up.

The smell of bacon and eggs filled his nose when he entered the kitchen wearing camouflage green boxers and T-shirt. Jeanette closed her red satin robe and tied the belt, then walked across the kitchen floor, barefoot. *Does this woman ever wear shoes?*

Neither one wanted to be the first to speak. Finally, while scrambling eggs, she looked over her shoulder at him. "Sorry, I only made enough for one." His pistol got her attention. "Do you always have to carry that thing with you?"

The calmness of her demeanor surprised him after the night they'd had. "That's okay about the food. I have no intention of eating anything you cook anyway. And yes, I do carry a weapon at all times."

Ignoring his verbal jab, she picked up a piece of hot bacon, bit off half and held the other piece to his lips. "What? You don't trust me?" Her smile was awesomely appealing.

"Like a fly trusts a spider, Black Widow."

"I'm wounded. And by the way, I'm actually called Black Widow."

"It suits you perfectly. Too perfectly."

The aroma of the bacon and the desire to touch her won out. He gripped her wrist lightly and stared into her eyes. *Where have I seen you before, Black Widow?*

Fifteen seconds into their staring contest, he ate the piece of bacon she offered.

"If you like, I'll split what I cooked with you...*if* you feel you can trust me."

A quick glance told him she *had* made enough for two. "I'll take my chances." After the grits, eggs and bacon breakfast, he stood behind her and gently massaged her neck and shoulders. When her eyes closed with pleasure, he put his lips close to her ear and said, "If you *ever* poison me again, you'll find something ticking in your spider web." He then left her in mid-massage and went back to his room.

~~~~~~

Now that was flat-out rude. How could he get her all relaxed and ready for a much-needed massage, then walk out? She cleared their dishes and placed them in the dishwasher, then returned to her room to dress for the long day ahead in the lab.

With his door wide open, she caught a glimpse of him readying for his shower when she passed. Tempted to stay and enjoy the show, she continued to her room. She had too much to do to play voyeur.

A giggle tickled her. At least she had let him enjoy the cookies before she lowered the boom. She liked the way he pushed back when pushed and the way he watched her. The usual lust she received from admirers was there, but there was also a protectiveness, which she found oddly comforting.

She selected black jeans and a long-sleeved T-shirt to wear, no socks or shoes, then went into the bathroom to change. That she'd been able to fall into such a deep sleep with him in the house unnerved her. And that she'd felt warmed when he checked in on her after making his rounds of the yard scared her out of her mind. The only one who had ever cared about her safety was her father. She could remember many a night when he'd peek into her room, thinking she was sound asleep. He would leave as quietly as he'd entered, just as Roman had.

Another Thanksgiving without her family had just passed. She'd always been a loner, but never lonely. At least, never lonely until she'd given up her family. Looking back, she had been young and stupid for allowing Papa to manipulate her. She had panicked. Then again, a small part of her always knew her father would come for her. Then he didn't.

An all too familiar feeling of abandonment flowed through

her. Hell, Colin was in the upper echelons of the CIA. If he'd wanted to find her, he would have. The fact that he hadn't tried hurt her more than she was willing to admit. That pain had come to the surface and was impossible to ignore or push away any longer.

Fully dressed, she headed for the lab. It just didn't add up. Why would he basically allow her to walk out of his life? Was he keeping an eye on her, as she had been on him and her brothers over the years? Did he know of Papa? No, she couldn't see him knowing about Papa, but then again, she couldn't have imagined him abandoning his baby girl all of these years.

There was no time to dwell on her family issues. This was the last time she'd do Papa's bidding, and the only reason she was pulling off this mission was because she couldn't let the monsters who created this toxin complete their mission—whatever that mission was.

I need answers. After this she'd be free of Papa and return home for confessions and answers.

The bi-directional lighting scheme distributed light both upward and downward. The light fixtures hung a foot below the ceiling, in continuous rows above the lab bench. The energy efficient and expensive setup impressed her. A humongous exhaust fan, mounted in the ceiling, waited to suck out any vile odors or toxic gases.

She laid notes across one of the granite counters and set out pencils, then washed her hands in the stainless steel sink. After Roman left her room, she had stayed up the rest of the night, poring over her binder full of documentation about the toxin. The kill potential of this toxin was a perfect illustration of why she chose to live a secluded life. There was too much evil out there for her. Anyone who would do this didn't deserve to live.

She took the goggles off the shelf above the sink and set them on the counter. Chemical compound and anatomy charts decorated the bright, white walls. A small incinerator, the size of a nightstand, was mounted to the wall across the room. Her green vinyl, ergonomic lab chair rolled easily across the black and white checkered tile floor as she wheeled over to the computer console.

She could tell the lab was a recent addition to the house. The faint smell of the glue from the freshly installed tile floor lingered in the air. *Papa spared no expense.* She smiled. *He's still an asshole.* A black coffee mug with the slogan, *I Be Da Genius*, emblazoned in white letters sat full of ink pens and pencils. She grabbed a pen, leaned back in her chair and tapped it on the palm of her hand, deep in thought.

The who, what, how, and why needed to be determined quickly before this monster struck again. Dismayed Papa hadn't given her full details on the death statistics, she concentrated on the task at hand. She knew the toxin had been ingested over a period of time, but by what mode? Was it a product in the store that only a few purchased? Free samples? What?

Her satellite phone rang with the ringtone she'd assigned Papa. With too much work ahead of her, she grumbled and looked around for Roman, whose shower was no longer running. *He's probably out searching for terrorists or something.*

She'd never seen anyone so uptight in her life, yet he showered with the doors open. That whole open door thing of his was odd to her. Yes, their mission was important and time was short, but he'd give himself a heart attack. Shoot, they were the ones looking, not being looked for.

"How have you and Roman been getting along?"

"As long as he doesn't take my door off the hinges, it's all good." She propped the phone between her ear and shoulder, then grabbed the spray bottle of bleach and a few hand towels.

"He's the best, is well-connected, can find out anything and is deadly as hell. This is not the type of case you're used to. While you work on stopping the toxin, Roman will discover who is responsible. Plus..." he trailed off.

"What?" She layered the counters with a light mist of bleach.

"You need protection."

She slammed the bottle onto the shelving unit above the

sink. "I'm not some baby! I can take care of myself. And why do you suddenly care about my safety."

"You were never in danger."

"Excuse you?"

"Not this much danger," he amended.

"You're sounding as nutty as Roman acts." She rubbed the counters down with a clean cloth. "I don't need his or anyone else's protection." She sprayed down her examination table with the bleach solution.

"This is not up for debate. What's your status on the toxin?"

"I'd be doing a hell of a lot better if I had photos and statistics. I have no idea how long it takes for the toxin to work, how many have been infected or anything. How is it ingested? Was it a liquid, solid, cold storage food, room temp...Had it been heated in something? How?"

"Just find the cure."

"What about future outbreaks? We have to cover all of our bases with this." She tossed the soiled towels into a bucket under the sink, to be incinerated later.

"I agree, but finding the cure is the most important."

"I can do both simultaneously. As I learn exactly what this is, I'll learn more of the hows."

"Keep Roman in the loop. He'll be able to find out exactly how it's ingested."

She laughed. "What is he, Super Bio Detective? There are thousands of possibilities. Your boy wonder won't be able to identify the source."

"I know it's a long shot, but Roman has the best shot around. Neither of you are used to working with others, but there is no choice. You know how the saying goes: Desperate times call for desperate actions. From what you've read, you know what this toxin has the potential to do. Can you set aside that lone wolf streak of yours and do what needs to be done and work with Roman?"

"I didn't say I wouldn't work with him. I said I don't need his protection." She pulled a package of Petri dishes and a box of slides out of the cabinet. "What's his connection to all of this? To you? Is he really as good as you say?"

"He's better. Keep me updated." He disconnected.

As she set the phone to the side, Roman entered. She'd lay odds he was about to look for spies under the microscope. She didn't like it, but she'd have to ask for Roman's assistance. Just about anything outside of the lab was foreign to her. Papa was correct. This toxin was larger than her ego.

"I need your help."

The briefest moment of shock flickered in his eyes before he approached her.

"Don't worry. This doesn't involve poison." She winked and got a slight smile out of him.

"Did Papa tell you about the toxin?"

"Papa...? Yeah, he told me you're some big scientific muckety-muck who can find an antidote."

"Muckety-muck. I think I liked Professor Meany better. Well, my skills are in the lab, but we need someone to find the individuals behind the toxin. Papa says you're the best."

Roman shrugged and popped a toothpick into his mouth. "I do okay for myself. What do you have for me?"

"So we're partners on this one?"

He folded his arms over his chest. "Will you be leaving this lab door open?"

"I can't. I need to keep contaminants to a minimum. But I've learned to compromise. I'll leave the door unlocked."

He picked up her binder of information and flipped through a few pages. "What do you need, partner?"

After explaining her needs and the area of Cuba where Papa had said the last toxin exposure occurred, she gave him her preliminary list of the types of items the toxin would most likely be in.

She had narrowed it down to items that would be stored at room temperature or in the refrigerator, not the freezer. For verification, she'd have to run her own tests, but from everything she'd researched, she was certain. "I could really,

really use more of the infected blood and tissue samples."

An odd look quickly skimmed over his face, a mix of gratitude and pride. "I have a few people in mind who might be able to help with that. I'll check around. You find the cure, and I'll find those responsible."

"Great." Awkward silence filled the room. "Well, I have a lot of work to do." She walked over to the control panel next to the door and turned on the speaker system in the lab. A few seconds later, the sound of fiddles filled the room as her favorite song, "Devil Went Down to Georgia," played.

"Show time!" She clapped her hands together once and slipped into work mode.

Chapter Nine

After being dropped off on the heliport atop her casino's roof, Daphne waved good-bye to the pilot of Lipton's helicopter. She smiled as the heads of her security staff walked over to greet her. "How was your trip, Ms. Peres?" her gigantic Dominican chief of security asked.

She removed her dark shades and tucked them into her expensive clutch bag. "It was fabulous! Just what I needed to recharge my batteries."

The security second in command, a huge Irishman, stooped over and picked up her bags. "Sure is good to have you back, boss."

She walked ahead of the men as they gave her security reports for the past two days when she had been out at sea with the rest of the Soulless Four. At her penthouse suite, one floor below the heliport, she dismissed the men and stepped inside. She set her purse down and walked over to her fifty-gallon fish tank. "Hi, babies! Did you miss me?"

The pair of red piranha fish, given to her by her good friend Hector as a birthday present last year, fascinated her. He was a periodic visitor to her casino as well as a high roller.

She opened the small refrigerator mounted below the tank, removed half a dozen raw shrimp and tossed them to her babies. "Lunch time!"

She kneeled down, watched the fish jet out of their hiding places in the chunks of coral in the tank and attack the shrimp. In seconds, the shrimp were history. The fish still looked hungry. "Don't worry, Mommy has a treat for you." From the small tank next to the piranha tank, she scooped out two fat, live goldfish and tossed them to the piranhas.

She marveled at how efficiently and swiftly the fish killed and devoured their live food. *Would love to be reincarnated as a piranha.* Moments later, at her desk, she booted up her computer and clicked on an icon named Happy.

A picture of her and Roman together three years ago at the Miami Seaquarium opened up. *Mmmmmm, I remember how he fucked me that day behind the dolphin stage while the event was going on.* Her crotch tingled. *Roman can be sooo erotic, not like Ju—*

The sound of the sliding glass door, leading to the pool, stole her attention. Her boyfriend, Juan walked in, toweling himself off, fresh out the pool. "Ahhhh, *mi Chiquita*! Welcome home!"

She quickly closed Happy and logged into the casino's mainframe to check on her profits for the past couple of days. Shrugging off his hug, she said, "Stop, you're wet. I don't need you dripping onto my computer." In reality, she would much rather be in Roman's embrace.

He smiled, dropped his swimming trunks and showed her his excitement. "Okay, but when you are done, *Chiquita*, I have something I have been waiting to give you for the past couple of days." Juan, the son of one of the Cuban Army's most powerful and respected generals, served as a semi-fill-in for Roman from time to time. He enjoyed the lifestyle she afforded him and had no problem being her "man-toy."

"Not now." She turned back to her computer. "I have much to do. Why don't you go shopping or something?"

He grinned and picked up his trunks. "Can I take the Porsche?"

With a dismissive flip of her wrist, she said, "Yes…go."

With Juan out of her hair, she picked up her phone and

called her baby sister, Nina. Her mood immediately changed from okay to pissed off as soon as Nina's no-account husband, Arturo, answered the phone. "Where's my sister?"

"What the fuck? You can't say hello like normal people?"

"Just give the pho—"

Before she could continue cussing him out, he yelled, "Nina, phone! Your stuck-up sister."

The sound of him dropping the phone onto a table infuriated her. Seconds later, Nina answered. "Hey, Daphne, what's good?"

"How many times am I going to have to tell you to leave that sorry, no-account bum you call a husband? He hasn't done shit for you, but fuck up your life."

"Look, just because you have no idea what true love is, is no reason for you to disrespect my relationship. You need to get a *real* man in your life and quit being such a bitch."

Daphne held the phone in one hand and rubbed her eyes with the other. *Calm down. You don't need to get her upset in her condition.* "Whatever. How is your pregnancy coming along?"

"I'm due in a couple of weeks. I think I'm gonna have a girl. I wanted to ask the doctor to tell me, but Arturo said we should let God surprise us."

Daphne rubbed her barren belly. When she was twenty-four, her doctor had informed her the probability of her surviving a pregnancy was slim and recommended she have her tubes tied and adopt if she wanted children. Stunned, she had left his office, refusing to accept her inability to become a mom. A small part of her envied her sister for her pregnancy. Actually, a *large* part of her did. "Make sure you keep all your doctor appointments. They are very important. Let me know if there's anything you need."

Just like clockwork, Nina hinted that she needed a few bucks. Although Daphne had all the money she would ever need, and then some, she refused to give Nina more than a few dollars at a time because of Arturo. "I will electronically deposit five hundred dollars into your bank account in a few minutes."

"Uhhh...you can't do that."

Daphne paused and accessed her online banking website. "Why not?"

Nina cleared her throat. "My account has been closed because of too many bounced checks."

That goddamned Arturo. I know he did it. He never lets her write any checks. She struggled, but managed to bite her tongue. "Fine. I'll bring the money to you later."

~~~~~~

Back in his room, after his interesting breakfast with Jeanette, Roman found himself in an unfamiliar mood—a baffled mood. *Still can't believe she actually asked for my help. Figured she was way too bullheaded for that.* Although his chemistry knowledge was limited, after going over a few of her notes, he could tell she was working on some heavy-duty shit. *Gonna need Jorge's help.*

He picked up the brown slacks he'd worn when he arrived and checked the pockets. *Almost forgot about this.* He made sure the door to the lab was still closed, then searched through his suitcases for the empty aspirin bottle he'd brought. After finding and opening the bottle, he dumped the sand on a piece of paper and funneled it into the bottle. He tossed the bottle of sand in his duffle bag, wishing he were sprinkling the sand over Shadow.

The photos of the dead Cubans spilled out of the envelope as he unpacked his bag. The agony on their faces was inexplicable. He could look at the pictures of the dead children for only a second before stuffing them back into the envelope. "What kind of a devil could do that to a *child*?"

Normally for the Sandman, a job was a job and a life was a life, but when it came to children that changed the game. His dormant love of kids resurfaced briefly. Out of nowhere, a thought popped into his head. *Wonder how Jeanette would look pregnant?* Pissed at himself, he shook his head. "Get her the hell out of your head, soldier."

Fully dressed in loose-fitting blue jeans and a gray, Property of Alcatraz T-shirt, he e-mailed Heath and found out the Navy courier jet with his goods would be landing in Fort Lauderdale in an hour. "I had better go round up Professor Meany."

Inside the lab, for a nanosecond, he lost his breath. When she didn't try to be sexy, her sexiness was amplified even more. He rushed to his room, returned with his camera and began snapping shots of her at work. And those feet. Damn, she seemed to never wear shoes. He found that hot as Hades. Seeing her with her head bent over her keyboard, hair dangling, made his manhood rigid. "Yo, Professor Meany, time to take a break. I need you to come with me. I have a few errands to run, and I can't leave you here alone."

"No way." She glanced from the calculations on the screen to him. "I'm in the middle of something very complicated. I can't afford to leave and lose my train of thought. You'll have to go without me."

Not the attitude again. He ran his hand over his face. *Time for plan B.* "I'll be right back."

Back in his room, he put away his camera, strapped his lucky knife to his leg and tucked one of his pistols behind his back. He went to the garage and opened the door of the Yukon. Inside the center console, he grabbed the Glock and four loaded magazines. *Why do women have to be so damn stubborn?*

The garage door closed quietly behind him as he went back inside the house. He walked over to Jeanette's desk, ejected the magazine, popped the bullet out the chamber and set the magazines and Glock down in front of her.

Her eyebrows furrowed. "What the hell is that for?"

"It's for your protection since you wanna be hardheaded and not come with me. Do you know how to use a gun?"

She snatched the gun off the table, grabbed one of the magazines, slammed it into the pistol, cocked a round into the chamber and pointed it between his eyes. "No, why don't you show me?"

Unmoved, he said, "Good. Don't leave this house or let anyone in." On his way out, for a second, he expected her to put a bullet in his ass. He chuckled and closed the lab door.

Outside, he walked toward the rental car, but stopped at her goat. He knocked on the windows, door panels and fenders. *Need to pimp your ride, Black Widow.*

Inside his rental, he called Gator. Gator was a toothless, moral-less, baldheaded redneck whom Roman had met through Hillbilly. Gator hated everything black, except Roman. Roman had gained his respect after kicking his ass years ago. Hillbilly had taken Roman along on a trip to the Everglades to do some hunting and introduced Roman to his cousin, Gator.

While they were hunting Osceola turkeys, Gator had used his time to size up Roman. It was hard for him to accept that Roman was this bad ass Hillbilly had told him about. Roman's refusal to react to his heckles had forced Gator to take drastic measures. He'd grabbed Roman by the shoulder and said, "How tough are you, nigger?"

He figured since he was taller and bigger than Roman he could handle him. Before Hillbilly could intervene, Roman broke Gator's nose, split his lips and had his foot pressed against Gator's throat. Finally, Hillbilly was able to talk Roman out of killing his ignorant cousin.

Once released, Gator got up, gave Roman a bloody smile and shook his hand, saying, "You *are* one tough sum bitch!" From that moment on, Roman became his favorite "Colored."

Gator operated a combination gas station, tow truck company and body shop. He also specialized in hard to find parts and metal fabrication. Roman gave Gator all the info on the GTO and told him what he needed. Gator was more than happy to oblige. He told Roman to bring the car by tonight and he would have it ready before sunrise.

Roman got out of the rental, tried the door on the GTO and found it open. "Why am I not surprised?" Thinking she'd unlocked the car and left the keys in the ignition to irritate him, he shook his head. It didn't matter that the property was gated.

There was no excuse for her being so sloppy with security. He took the keys and put them in his pocket. "If she does try and leave, she'll have to take the Yukon. I feel a hell of a lot better about her driving that."

The sixty-five mile trip to the naval airbase took him a little over an hour. At the gate, he showed his fake CIA badge and was given directions to the hangar where the jet was located. He drove over, got out the car and met the pilot, his buddy, Jeff Tolbert from the Navy Seals.

"How the hell you been, Roman?"

Roman broke their handshake. "I've been fair for a square. You have some goods for me?"

"I sure do." He pointed at a bundle of bags near the rear of the jet. "How long are you going to be in Florida? I have another stop in Puerto Rico this weekend. You want to come? I can pick you up, no problem."

Roman flashed back to the crazy time they'd had there years ago. He had gotten so drunk playing "quarters"—using rum instead of beer—with Jeff and a few other Seals, he put three Puerto Rican police officers in the hospital when they tried to arrest him. Two of them were still collecting money from Uncle Sam for their injuries. *That's why I gave up hard liquor. I make a real bad drunk.* "No thanks, I don't think I can hang with the way you party."

Jeff laughed at his old friend. "Well, if you change your mind, you have my number."

Jeff helped Roman carry the two large duffle bags and black, three-foot-long drag bag containing his magic wand back to the Altima. "Thanks, Jeff. I appreciate your help."

"No problem, I just made a slight detour from delivering some crap to Admiral Coolidge on an aircraft carrier near Bermuda." He offered Roman his hand. "Anything for a brother Seal."

Roman watched as the jet taxied out of the hangar. Jeff smiled at him from the cockpit window and saluted.

Roman reluctantly saluted Jeff back.

Roman turned back toward his car and saw the blackest, sleekest jet he'd ever seen in the next hanger. He walked over and examined the plane.

The deadly Black Falcons were smaller and faster hybrids of the now obsolete SR-71 Blackbirds, a luxury Gulfstream jet and the Nighthawk stealth fighters. They had the capability of flying at nearly 80,000 feet at speeds up to Mach 5. They also were designed with the most sophisticated stealth technology on the planet. If need be, they could be fitted with an array of weapons. Their propulsion system had been inspired by that of the hypersonic cruise missiles. They could deliver a nuclear bomb to any place on the planet in a matter of hours.

Gotta get me one of these. After checking the time, he went back to his car.

~~~~~~

Lincoln was amazed at his bad kids. Jeanette's chemistry skills made his head spin. It had taken a lab full of top-notch geeks two months to determine half the info Jeanette had in a couple of days. Her ability to formulate on the fly, calculate at lightning speed and her amazing memory were like that of no other. That, coupled with her attitude, murderous abilities and natural charm made her one deadly spider. And Roman. Watching those two at breakfast made him queasy. Their body language told him more than he needed to know.

The beeping alarm on the portable monitoring device almost gave him a coronary. He ran over to his desk and stared at it. "What the fuck is he doing *here*?"

He ran to the security gate monitor and saw that unmistakable face talking to the security guard. He grabbed his binoculars and kept them on Roman as he drove across the airfield. His grenade launcher equipped assault rifle was in arm's reach. He couldn't recall the last time he was that close to death. "That soldier is too damn resourceful..." His heart rate returned to normal as he watched Roman leave the hangar, and the red dot headed back toward Miami. Finding out what

Roman was doing on the base without giving away his own location would be tricky.

~~~~~~

Irate, Bagley pushed away from his desk. "You seem to have forgotten who signs your paycheck, Professor Wyatt."

Obviously unmoved, Wyatt calmly said, "And you seem to have forgotten I don't need your paycheck. If I had known you were this morally bankrupt, I would have never signed on for this project. But I did, so here I am and it is what it is. You may have no integrity, but I do."

As usual, Bagley tuned the professor out as he ranted about yet another regulation he refused to ignore. Bagley had paid through the nose to bring Wyatt onto his team. The man was brilliant but impossible! All he was asking the jerk to do was reproduce tissue for transplants, but this asshole of a doctor was dragging his feet and blaming it on regulatory red tape.

Fuck that. Bagley was paying him to cut any obstacle that might come his way. But noooooo. Wyatt was actually following the rules. The reasoning behind the doctor's stance: Once they were able to duplicate organs, every aspect of their research would be scrutinized, so they had to go by the books. *Why can't he be more like Snow?*

Okay, so maybe the asshole is right, but damn, does he have to be so arrogant?

Hell, he's as bad as that fucking Hector Vazquez, he thought of one of the best known transplant surgeons in the world. Bagley had flown Vazquez in to consult with Wyatt about transplants. The two had hit it off instantly. Bagley couldn't stand either one and together they gave him the creeps.

"I think it's time for you to return to work," Bagley cut into the professor's tirade. His bodyguards, two large blonde-haired, blue-eyed Germans—and the twin sister of the larger man—rose to escort Wyatt to the door.

Wyatt smirked and walked out.

It pissed Bagley off to no end that Wyatt wasn't intimidated by him in the least. And to make things worse, Wyatt wouldn't allow anyone access to the findings in his research. Instead he gave results and explained things as if Bagley were a two-year-old.

Knowing just how smart the good doctor was, Bagley chuckled. If he had the findings, he'd give it to other scientists to finish up the job. Scientists he could control—like Snow. *He isn't quite as good as Wyatt, but he's a suitable backup.*

His cell phone rang. The name displayed on caller ID made him grumble. Two months ago he had received a call from the "sponsor" of his most secret endeavor. The sponsor was ecstatic with the progress to date, but wanted additional testing.

"That's a no go," Bagley had said. "Those fucking Cubans are more resourceful than I expected."

"What the hell? You're testing on a bunch of kids and malnourished adults."

"Malnourished my ass—"

"We need to know if this will work on your average, overindulgent minority Americans. We want death, not a bunch of open sores."

These Americans were a bunch of ignorant, fat slobs in Bagley's opinion. He could barely wait to return to England. Reluctantly, he had agreed to run additional testing. He wished he could make Wyatt the guinea pig, but he still needed him.

And his client. The man actually had the audacity to suggest using the African-American mayor of Miami as the test subject. The challenge of lacing the mayor's food with the toxin was intriguing, but not that intriguing. They needed a nobody.

"Fine, but I'll select your 'nobody,'" his client had said.

"That'll cost you an additional ten million."

"*Ten million!*"

"Yes, and you can't pick an elected official or anyone else with a high profile."

"Three million, and this bastard had better be dead within three months or your ass is dead."

The client had hung up on him, then called with the name of

the nobody a few hours later. Unfortunately, Bagley hadn't realized his crazy ass would select his stateside assistant Marta, a Brazilian single woman with three children. Bagley didn't worry about leaving them without their mother. He worried about how close she was to him. He didn't want to be connected to anyone who suffered from this illness. His project sponsor had reminded him of the one-hundred-million-dollar payday he'd receive if this toxin brought all that was promised.

Hell, since he was screwed either way, he might as well be screwed with money. His client agreed to give him five million up front to deal with any complications Bagley might encounter since Marta was so close to him.

Unwilling to speak with his sponsor at that moment, he clicked the ignore button on his phone. He had already given Marta several doses of laced Crystal Light powder, and it was working. Marta was getting sicker and sicker by the day. He didn't think she'd survive another month. With her death would come his financial freedom.

God, how he hated dealing with those crazy assed terrorist bastards—especially American born and bred terrorists—but their money would save his ass. Over the years, a few bad business decisions had made him have to "borrow" a few million from his company's coffers from time to time. Now he owed close to sixty million and wasn't sure how much longer he could keep his secret loans secret. If he could just find a fall guy, someone to pin his embezzlement on…

Chapter Ten

After returning his rental car, an hour into his cab ride and five miles from the house, Roman knocked on the Plexiglas divider and told the cabbie, "You can drop me off here." Once the cabbie was out of sight, he shouldered the drag bag, grabbed the two duffle bags and hoofed it.

Should call Professor Meany to pick me up...nah, she probably has her face stuck in one of her Petri dishes.

Chuckling, he traversed the sleepy suburb. The sight of Christmas trees and decorations in the neighboring houses seemed out of place in the seventy-four degree sunshine. The homes thinned down to none a few miles from his current lodging. He spotted the six-foot high cinderblock wall surrounding the house several hundred yards ahead. The property stuck out like a medieval stronghold. No other homes or structures were within a mile on either side.

Jeanette stood in front of the house with an irritated look on her face. "Now, if I shot your ass for taking my car keys, you would say I was wrong. What is your damn problem?"

Damn, if looks could kill... "Sorry, ma'am. Security first." He dropped his bags, pulled the keys out and dangled them in front of her. "I figured if you needed to go someplace—even though I told your ass to stay in the house—you'd have sense enough to take the Yukon."

She snatched the keys out of his hand. "You really make me think you have a death wish, asshole. I didn't want to drive no big-assed truck. I wanted to drive *my* car."

"Just doing my job, lady."

"Anyway. Did you talk to any of your contacts about the things I need?"

"Not yet." He picked up the bags. "But I will pretty soon."

A skeptical look crossed her face as she turned and went back in the house. "If you say so, Boy Wonder."

Boy Wonder? He scowled at her behind her back. *Crazy broad.*

The smell of butter-flavored, microwave popcorn greeted him inside. Another Rissi Palmer song drifted down the hall. He poked his head in the lab and enjoyed the sight of her bent over the autoclave. "Did you save me some popcorn?"

"Sure didn't." She turned toward him, messing up his view of her booty. "I called myself going to get some food, but some smart ass had run off with my car keys."

The lock of hair covering her right eye was so sexy, she could have put Venus to shame. *She does need to get outta here and get some air.* "I tell you what, I'll take you to the store in a few minutes, okay?"

A genuine smile bloomed. "Wow, I get to actually leave the house? I guess you do have a soul in there somewhere."

"So I've heard. Let me go put this stuff away."

Back in his room, he put the bags on the bed. "Let me see if Hillbilly was able to get everything on my shopping list." A set of experimental, woman's size eight body armor sat on top of the other items. It was available only to the most elite military branches—or to those with the connections of the Sandman. It was half the weight of the best Kevlar on the market, but twice as strong. "This should mold to her jugs nicely."

"What is all that junk?"

His head whipped around at the sound of her voice. *She just snuck up on me. Damn, she's as quiet as a mouse pissing on cotton.* "A few gifts for you." He tossed her the lightweight armor. "Size eight, I presume?"

She held the graphite-colored gear up to her body. "Does it come in red?"

Ignoring her, he removed another set of body armor in his size, a pair of night vision goggles, a bug sniffer designed to locate even the most sophisticated bugs, and an electronic lock code finder. He gave her one of the two earpieces designed to look like wireless cell phone earpieces. They were actually two-way communication devices with a five-mile range. There was also a tube of lipstick that was actually a tracking device and five hundred rounds of .45 caliber armor-piercing bullets. As a bonus, Hillbilly had also included one hundred rounds of .50 caliber, *Raufoss* explosive tipped ammo for his magic wand. *Good lookin' out, Hillbilly.*

"Damn, are you supplying the troops?" She reached for his drag bag. "What's in here?"

A prideful smile curled his lips as he unzipped the bag. "This here is my magic wand." He unzipped the drag bag and displayed the most advanced sniper rifle on the planet—the Wahlberg LongThrow 500. A handheld weather station, laser, infrared and scope attachments, and three seven-round capacity magazines were also in the bag. The rifle was no joke. He had unofficially broken all world long distance records with a similar model. "This is my favorite toy."

The sight of the powerful rifle earned her respect. "Nice, but it would be better if it came in red."

He shook his head and closed the bag. "I'll make note of that."

"Well, have fun with your toys. Come get me when you're ready to go. I'm changing out of these work clothes."

The thought of helping her change made him chuckle. He picked up the "bug sniffer" and turned it on. This particular sniffer wasn't on the market, but a specialty item he'd had commissioned a few years back. Nothing could get past this sniffer, no matter how small. There were only three in the world, and he had all three in safekeeping, along with the schematics of the design. The "bug sniffer" beeped loudly when he walked past the TV. He held it next to the speaker grill and it beeped even louder.

Son-of-a-bitch.

Using his lucky knife, he punched a hole in the speaker grill and found a high quality micro camera. A scan of the rest of the room turned up a listening device behind his headboard.

His face burned with anger. *Spying on me is not part of the deal, muthafucka.* He ripped out the bugs and sprinted to Jeanette's room. "Hey! I foun—" He averted his eyes just as Jeanette pulled her black bra over her luscious breasts. "Bugs."

"What? Can't you see I'm getting dressed?"

The stern, serious look on his face must have silenced her because she stopped her tirade.

A scan of her room turned up another camera and listening device. "I don't know about you," he snatched the camera out of her TV grill, "but I don't like being watched."

She quickly put on her red and white stripped tank top. "Shit! Did you find any more of them?"

"I'm about to check the rest of the house now." Between the house and garage, he found ten more cameras and microphones. Before ripping the last camera out of the wall-mounted thermostat in the living room, he looked into the tiny lens and said, "Fuck you, asshole."

They sat on the couch and looked at the handful of bugs Roman had tossed on the coffee table. She picked up one of the cameras and scowled at it. "I can't believe Papa would have the nerve to spy on me like this."

"I don't know why you're so surprised. Shadow's your father."

"Shadow? Who the hell is Shadow?"

"Your father...don't you call him 'Papa'?"

A confounded look filled her face. "Wait, wait, wait. Are we talking about the same person?"

Fifteen minutes later, they connected all of the dots and found out they shared a common foe. Roman went to his room, got a pack of cinnamon toothpicks and returned to the living room. Leaning against the wall that divided the living room from the kitchen, he popped a toothpick in his mouth.

"It's time for complete honesty. Knowing Shadow and the way he uses me, I know for damn sure he has to have his hooks deep in you as well. Deep enough for you to come way the hell out here, in the middle of nowhere, and put up with an ass like me. There has to be more to you and your relationship with him. No way am I gonna buy he just likes the way you look in a smock."

Her calmness impressed him. None of the fidgeting or other telltale signs of a liar he had been trained to look for surfaced. She rose from the couch, walked over to the picture window and stared out at the sprinklers soaking the lawn. Gigantic fluffy clouds rolled lazily across the sky. "I'm here because Papa thinks I have to be here."

"What the hell does that mean?"

"Just say your Shadow knows more about me than he should and threatens to tell my secrets. But I don't give a damn anymore. I'm here because I choose to be."

The underlying anguish in her words was undeniable. For a second, he thought he saw her bottom lip quiver the tiniest bit. A pregnant pause sat between them before he responded.

The toothpick jumped up and down on his lip as he walked over and gazed out the window with her. "It sounds like we have a lot more in common than I thought. And I'm done taking orders from his ass also, but this project...I couldn't let it pass."

Another long pause. "What exactly do you do?" she asked. "You have too much...I don't know, *something*, to be just a bodyguard. If I didn't know better, I'd say you are a military man. No average Joe has access to the kind of hardware you showed me in your room. Who are you?"

That question was one he'd asked himself countless times. After changing identities so many times over the years, he sometimes woke up and literally had to think about who he was supposed to be. *Deception is everything.* He spun the toothpick around in his mouth and a fresh burst of cinnamon flavor coated his tongue. "I guess you could say I'm the guy people call once the hero fails."

A cloud passed in front of the sun, temporarily dimming the sunshine. "Do you want to find Papa...er...Shadow, as badly as I do?" she asked.

"Even more."

"Good. Once we finish this, we find him and put an end to his game."

"Works for me." Her dedication to duty pushed her three rungs up his ladder of respect. It no longer mattered what or who she really was, as long as she was as committed as he was to making Shadow pay. The sun reemerged. "Did you try on the armor I gave you?"

"Yes, fits me well, thanks. I can't believe how light it is. It feels like I'm wearing a T-shirt."

"I have a few other things to give you, too. Oh, and keep the Glock for yourself." They turned toward each other at the same time and tried to read the secrets in each other's eyes. Something too intense for them to handle made them break eye contact.

He nibbled his toothpick and checked his watch. "Let's, uhhh, let's go to the store."

"Yes...let's do that."

On the way out to the garage, he grabbed the "bug sniffer."

"I thought you already scanned the garage?" Jeanette slipped into her red-and-white flip-flops.

"I forgot to check the cars." He found GPS tracking bugs mounted under the front fenders of both the Yukon and GTO. After ripping them out, he tossed them on the floor of the garage and crushed them with his foot. "Fuck you deep, Shadow." The sound of the Yukon starting up startled him. "What are you doing?"

While adjusting the driver's seat, she said, "I'll drive. I know a few shortcuts to the store."

"I planned on going to a store in Miami, give you a chance to stretch your legs."

"Even better. I know a few shortcuts there, also."

She looks good as hell when she's not givin' me the evil eye. "Okay, but if you wreck, I'm suing."

"Just get in."

Inside the Miami city limits, Roman was thankful for the tinted glass on the Yukon. It allowed him to spy on his enemies undetected. *Looks like the number of Haitian gang bangers has at least doubled since last time I was here.*

~~~~~~

Damn you, Roman. Finishing her second shower of the day, Daphne fought to keep her hand from massaging her hot valley. *Just when I was getting over you, I find I want you more than ever.*

She slipped into her off-white peasant dress and a pair of white sandals. The image of her, Roman and her sister's baby clouded her thoughts. *We'll make the perfect ready-made family.*

"Where are you going, *mi belleza*?" Juan asked.

She tied her hair back into a ponytail as he hugged her from behind. "I'm going to visit Nina...she hasn't been feeling well."

He reached around and rubbed her firm breasts. "My 'little Juan' hasn't been feeling well, either. He needs you to comfort him."

She gently removed his hands. "I'm really not in the mood for this, Juan. It's too hot."

He took a long swallow of his beer. "Is it the heat or are you saving it for *Roman*?"

She faced him and sighed. "I told you I was *dreaming* when I called out that name last night...it was a fucking *dream*!"

He took another swallow of beer. A few drops landed on his hairy chest. "I've been living with you for over a year now, and I've *never* heard you call *my* name out while you were sleeping!"

You probably would if you were as creative in bed as

Roman is. She picked up her sunglasses and put them on. "Juan, please...not now. I don't have time to argue with you."

He ran his fingers through his shoulder-length hair. "Who the hell is this *Roman* anyway?"

She picked up her car keys off the dresser. "I don't know! It was a *dream*! Maybe someone named Roman was trying to kill me or something in my dream..."

He followed her as she walked out of the bedroom toward the front door. "How the fuck do you explain you grinding your hips in your sleep as you moaned his name? What the hell was that all about, Daphne? Huh?"

"Please don't tell me you're jealous over a dream." She stepped out into the near ninety- degree heat. "We'll finish this later. I'm going to Nina's."

~~~~~~

Close to Nina's house, she dodged groups of children as they played in the streets of their ghetto neighborhood. In that impoverished section of town, her year-old Mercedes SUV stuck out like a cat in a dog pound. No matter how poor the neighborhood was, the spirit of Christmas was still prevalent. Several of the trees and bushes outside of many of the homes were decorated with cheap or homemade Christmas decorations.

Nina's place looks smaller every time I see it. She parked under a virtual black spider web of power and phone lines.

She set her alarm, then walked up to Nina's front door and knocked. The blistered and peeling white paint was as old as most of the cars in the area. The door opened and the hinges squealed.

"Hey, Nina...your sister's here." Arturo walked away and left Daphne at the open door.

I see you're still an ill-mannered asshole. Daphne stepped inside the hot, one-bedroom apartment and perched her sunglasses on top of her head. A big fan in the corner of the tiny living room blew the hot air from one side to the other. A white-flocked Christmas tree with red lights stood beside the TV. A few neatly wrapped gifts sat under the tree. "Where are you, Nina?"

"I'm coming."

Daphne took a seat on the stained and uncomfortable brown sofa and waited. She watched a pair of roaches race up the wall and disappear behind a framed picture of Bert Campaneris, the famous Cuban-born American baseball player. She sighed. *This is no place to raise a baby.*

"Hey, big sis." Nina waddled out of the bedroom. "I've seen you more since I've been pregnant than I have my whole life. Maybe I need to have more babies if it'll get you to hang out with me."

Just the one child will do just fine. Daphne approached Nina. "You know my business world keeps me tied up. But I am working on making more free time for things like this."

Arturo emerged from the kitchen with a beer bottle in hand. "Don't waste any of your free time comin' to see us. We don't wanna be responsible for you hurtin' yourself climbin' down from your ivory tower."

Nina glared at Arturo. "Arturo! Don't start. I'm not in the mood to listen to you two get into it."

Daphne stared Arturo down. "Don't worry, Nina. There's not going to be any drama today." She dropped her eyes from Arturo, turned and rubbed Nina's swollen belly. "You're enormous! And you still have another two weeks to go?"

Nina eased onto the sofa. "Yes...another couple of weeks left. I was hoping to have a Christmas baby, but it looks more like a New Year's baby."

Daphne heard the faucet running in the kitchen as she placed the back of her hand on Nina's extremely dry forehead. "You're burning up! When's the last time you went to see your doctor?"

Nina weaved her fingers through her tangled hair and scratched her scalp. "A few weeks ago."

Daphne placed her hands on her hips. "Why so long ago? You're at the point where you should be seeing your doctor at *least* once a week!"

From behind them, Arturo said, "Because we ain't got transportation."

Daphne snapped her head toward him. "What happened to the Jetta I bought for Nina?"

Arturo handed Nina a glass of water and wiped his nose with the back of his hand. "I sold it to pay for food...we needed food more than a goddamn car."

Daphne glared into his red eyes. "Are you out of your fucking mind? Who told you, *you* could sell a car I bought for *my* sister?"

"Daphne, calm down!" Nina attempted to get up and get between Arturo and her sister.

"Look, Miss High and Mighty. Nina is my wife. What's hers is mine."

It took every ounce of her willpower not to pull the switchblade out of her purse and cut a second mouth in his throat. "You lazy piece of shit! If you ever—"

Nina stepped in front of the grinning Arturo. "Stop it! Stop it, both of you, I'm getting a headache."

Daphne dropped her glare from Arturo, looked at Nina and took her hand. "Come in the kitchen with me. I need to talk to you in private."

Nina reluctantly followed as Arturo sat on the couch and turned on the TV. "What is it?"

After pulling ten, one-hundred-dollar bills out of her purse and slapping them on the kitchen table, she cupped Nina's face in her hands. "I want you out of this shithole. I'll buy you a home anywhere you like if you just leave Arturo. He has done nothing but put a baby in your belly he can't and won't take care of. Look, Nina, I'll even take the baby and raise it."

Nina brushed her sister's hands off her face. "What are you saying, Daphne?"

Daphne stood straight and looked Nina in the eye. "What if I gave you a million in cash in exchange for your child? We both know you'll never get a better chance than this to get out of this shitty life you're living right now."

Nina scowled and rubbed her belly. "You're crazy!"

Daphne read the look of confusion beneath the layer of shock on Nina's face. "Let's get real for a minute, sister. Don't act like I don't know about Arturo's fucking cocaine habit. And I hope like hell you weren't stupid enough to let him brainwash you into trying it—especially with you being pregnant. Take the money and leave that fucking loser."

A tear rolled down Nina's cheek. "I don't want to hear any more! Stop it!"

Arturo ran into the kitchen. "Get out! Get out of our house! How dare you upset my wife at a time like this! Go back to your fancy house and leave us alone...we don't need you!"

The mention of the million dollars had changed the look in Nina's eyes. The way she licked her lips told Daphne all she needed to know. Daphne knew that look well—the look of greed. "Think about what I said." Daphne pushed past Arturo and headed for the door.

Arturo followed Daphne as she stormed out to her SUV. "You're not welcome in my house. From now on, when you have money for Nina, I will come out to your car and get it. Besides that, you're useless."

The burning rampage inside her was unwilling to be quieted. Pointing her finger in his face, she let it go. "Motherfucker! If I hear of you touching one single dime or *anything* else I give my sister, I swear on all that is holy, I'll kill your ass."

He wiped his nose and backed toward the door. "Just get the hell out of here."

On the way home, images of Nina's belly burned into her mind, and her intense desire to become a mother hit a new level. Disappointed Nina had turned out to be a whore just like her mother, she knew at least something good would come out of the situation. Nina was poor, not stupid. With a little time to think, Daphne knew she'd take the money. *Hope like hell she isn't stupid enough to pass up my offer, but she's showing me more and more she's just an ignorant whore-baby like my dad told me she was.*

~~~~~~

"This is un-fucking-believable." Colin ran his large, dark hands over his short-cropped hair, then looked dead into the camera mounted on his computer monitor. "Why didn't you tell me sooner?"

Though the images being streamed in were a bit shaky, Lincoln could clearly see the agitation on his friend's face. Similar agitation had been brewing within Lincoln since Dominic had contacted him about the mysterious illness that was taking hold in Cuba.

"I've known all of four days," Lincoln said, sarcasm clear, "and have my two best operatives working on this. You know I work on a need-to-know basis. Before now, there was no need for you to know. But now that Cuban officials have decided America is the cause behind this 'attack…'"

"You have always been full of shit. Cuba is only a hop away from U.S. soil. What affects them affects us! What if this agent is contagious? How does it spread?" He ground his teeth. "I had a fucking right to know four damn days ago."

"And what would you have done—" He stopped himself. "Do you believe this is a productive use of the little time we have?" He grabbed his glass of gin.

"You're right…you're right." Colin leaned back in his executive chair. "I'll do a little digging around and head on to Cuba. In the meantime, we need more than your mercenaries." He drew in and blew out a long breath. "I'll be asking Jeanette to help find a cure for this." He hunched his shoulders. "Whatever the hell it is."

The gin stung Lincoln's nose as it made a reappearance. He hacked and coughed, spilling the majority of his drink.

"Damn, I told you that sauce would be the death of you. Raise your hands above your head."

Eyes watering, Lincoln raised his hands above his head to help clear his air passage. Between hacks, he quickly calculated how to keep this reunion from happening. Yes, it would be yet another nail in his coffin, but saving the lives of the countless many had become more important than his own life.

In his heart he knew that when Jeanette told Colin why she left, it wouldn't take any time for Colin to know it was Lincoln who had kept him separated from his daughter all of these years. Lincoln who had made her become a mercenary.

"I'm about ready to choke, too," Colin said slowly. "Choke on my own stupidity. How could I have allowed this to go on so long? I miss her so much. We all do. It's time for my baby to come home. God, how I want her to spend Christmas with me."

Still reeling from Colin's intentions, Lincoln looked at the large picture of Ambrosia on the wall behind Colin. *Can't believe how much Jeanette resembles her mother.* "So what's the plan? You drop by her home after all this time and say, 'Hey, I know I could have come for you years ago, but I didn't need you until now. Will you find the cure for this illness for me'?"

"Son-of-a-bitch," Colin spit out. "Why the hell did I wait so long? What was I thinking?" He touched Jeanette's Vassar graduation picture he kept beside his monitor screen. "You're right. I can't go to her wanting something, but as soon as this Cuba mess is straightened out, I'm going for my baby."

Crisis averted, Lincoln relaxed. "I know how hard it's been for you. Initially, I agreed with you. I thought you should stay away, that she'd return home when she was ready, but I think it's time."

"Past time." Colin tapped the picture. "Look, Jeanette can run circles around any scientist out there, so we don't have a choice but to bring her in on this. She doesn't know who you are, so you contact her and pay her whatever is needed to convince her to find an antidote."

The ultimate opportunist, Lincoln couldn't allow this opportunity to save his ass pass by. "I'll bring Jeanette in."

"Good...good." Colin held his baby's picture. Lincoln could feel Colin's pride in Jeanette through the screen. "She'll find a cure."

"That she will." He poured himself another gin. "I'm keeping my identity secret though."

"None of your operatives know who you are. I expect the same with Jeanette. Keep her safe, Lincoln. If whoever is behind this agent discovers she's working on the antidote, they'll go after her."

"You didn't even have to ask."

"I know, good friend, I know."

~~~~~~

Jeanette pulled into a gated condominium community.

"This doesn't look like the grocery store to me," Roman said.

"I know." She punched in her gate code. "I need to pick up a few things from my place while we're out this way."

"I'd appreciate it if you'd let me know ahead of time about any unplanned stops. I'm still on the job, you know."

She surprised the shit out of him by gently stroking his cheek. "I promise I won't report you to your boss, honey."

"Very funny." After she pulled into stall 607, he hopped out the truck. "Let's make this quick."

Looking at him over the hood, she asked, "Where are you going?"

"Where you go, I go."

A chuckle escaped her lips. "Kind of like *my* Shadow."

This light-hearted side of her was refreshing. Lord knows with all the pressure they were under, they needed it. He shared a small smile with her. "Just when I was starting to like you…"

"Oooh, lucky me."

"I'll go in first," he insisted after she unlocked the door.

"By all means."

"Just stay put." He pulled the pistol from his waistband and glanced around the elegantly decorated living room. Nothing seemed out of place.

I'd love to break this bed down havin' butt-naked fun with the Black Widow. He poked his head into her bedroom.

Satisfied the place was secure, he went into the living room and waved to her as she watched him from the open front door. "All clear, lady."

"And I thought *I* was anal." She went into the spare bedroom. "I'll be right out."

Scanning the walls, he noticed there wasn't a single picture of herself or her family. *This spot is cool, but it's missin' that homey feeling.*

A surprisingly short time later, she emerged from the room with a pair of cat-eye sunglasses hanging on the front of her tank top and carrying a black Vassar University volleyball bag. "I'm ready."

"Ha! Who did you borrow that bag from?"

"I'll have you know," she slipped her shades on, "I not only attended the great Vassar University, I was also a kick-ass volleyball player. Brewer pride, baby!"

"Yeah, right." He held the front door open for her. "What the hell is 'Brewer pride'?"

"It refers to our mascot."

"A brewer?"

"Google it, dear."

"I'm gonna Google you if you don't bring your butt on."

~~~~~~

Although Roman was still on red alert while in Miami, the trip did both of them a lot of good. Away from test tubes, notebooks, bullets and perimeter searches, they managed to turn the trip to the grocery store into a semi-date.

"Would you mind shopping in Coral Gables instead of here in Miami?" Jeanette asked. "It's closer to the house, and I love the Publix Market there. They have a great selection."

"Okay." He held his hands out for the keys. "But I drive."

Two hours later, they loaded the Yukon with at least two weeks' worth of groceries and returned to Homestead. After packing the food away as a team, he pulled out some pots and pans.

She closed the cupboard containing the seasonings and stared at him. "What are you doing?"

"Since you've been such a good girl, I'm going to cook dinner."

"Wow, Mr. Roman!" Genuine surprise filled her face. "I didn't think you had it in you."

"That's what you get for thinking." He winked at her, laid his pistol on the counter and got busy.

Two hours later, in the midst of their baked salmon, rice pilaf and shrimp salad dinner, his ears perked up at the sound of a phone ringing. He put down his glass of wine. "That sounds like it's coming out of the den."

Across the octagon-shaped kitchen table, she swallowed down a spoonful of rice. "Let it ring. You know who it is."

"I had better go check." He wiped his mouth with a napkin and went to the den. The fax machine spat out a single page fax.

> *Sorry about the security devices you found. But I'm sure a person like yourself can appreciate surveillance. Things are heating up internationally. This needs to be resolved. Quickly. When I call the house phone, answer it. That goes for both of you.*

The urge to heave the fax machine across the unfurnished den surged through him. Taking orders was not on his list of things he loved. He read the last line of the fax again before wadding it up. *You can talk to your kids like that, muthafucka, but not me. I'm not havin' it.* His thoughts seemed to bounce off the bare walls as he walked over and peeked out the blinds. His mind went back to the fax. *Things are heating up internationally...*

"What's going on?" Jeanette said from the doorway, holding her glass of wine.

"Nothing...just another fine day in your Papa's paradise." Turning away from the twilight outside, he walked toward the doorway and handed her the balled-up fax. "Here's his apology for spying on us."

She set her glass on the only piece of furniture in the room, the small walnut desk the combination printer and fax machine sat on. "Him apologizing? I have got to see that for myself." After she unballed the fax and read it, she laid it on the desk, then picked up her glass. "What a dickhead."

"Well said."

"Anyway, come finish your dinner before it gets cold."

Little green flecks in her hazel eyes grabbed his attention. Her eyes seemed to change color with her mood. *Damn, you're beautiful.* "I—" Back in his room, his satellite phone rang. He ran to get it.

"Hey! What about your food?"

On the third ring, he answered. "Hello?"

"*Hola, mi amigo!*"

A grin touched the Sandman's lips. "*¿Cómo está, Jorge?*"

"*Muy bien, gracias.*"

Roman continued the conversation in Spanish, saying, "Good to finally hear from you, my friend. I need your services."

"Sorry for the delay, but there's a rumor going on about tainted water here in Cuba. I have moved more bottled water than pistols in the past week. What can I do for you, amigo? Need some more fireworks?"

Roman looked over his shoulder and saw Jeanette seated at the dining table, eating and reading through her notes.

"Is your line secure, Jorge?"

"Yes. Always. Just like I'm sure yours is."

"Tell me, what have you heard about the tainted water situation?"

"Very bad, my friend. Very bad. Every day a few more of my people turn up sick."

"But the news said there were just a few isolated cases."

Jorge laughed in his ear. "Come on. You know better than to believe that propaganda bullshit! I personally know of five people who died from it in Las Tunas alone over the last week. The Cuban government is too prideful to admit they don't have a handle on the situation. But there are strong rumors going around blaming America for the plague."

Roman closed his eyes and massaged the bridge of his nose with his thumb and forefinger. "Las Tunas...that seems like a high number for that small area."

"It is."

"Has anything unusual been going on there lately? Any new factories or businesses open up?"

"Funny you should ask. I was talking with another good customer, such as yourself, and he told me over a bottle of Bacardi that he and his friends are going to turn Las Tunas into a gold mine."

Roman stopped pacing the room and paid full attention. "What? Who is this guy? Who are his friends? What are they gonna do?"

"Ahhh, you ask a lot of Jorge...I sometimes don't remember so good."

After dealing with Jorge for almost a decade, he had learned how to cure his selective amnesia. "Okay, Jorge, how much is it gonna cost me to help you remember?"

"Well, my daughter has been asking me to send her to Rome for a college graduation present..."

"Fine. I'll get her round-trip airfare."

"And she needs a place to stay, rental car, meal money..."

"Fine, fine, fine. Will ten grand cover it?"

"I think fifteen grand would really help her have a good time."

Goddamned bloodsucker doesn't even have a daughter—at least not one he claims. "Done. I'll wire it to you using our usual method. Now, what can you tell me about your friend?"

"It must be a miracle!" He chuckled. "My memory is coming back. His name is Enrique Morales, owner of Oasis Resorts. He, along with a hot Cuban woman and two gringos, have been buying up miles of beachfront property in Las Tunas for the past eighteen months. I even heard Enrique has thrown around thousands of dollars in bribes to Cuban officials, to secure use of the private beaches."

Roman grabbed his notepad and pen. "Names, give me names, Jorge."

"Enrique Morales, J. Michael Lipton, Walter Bagley and Daphne Peres. A bunch of rich fucks. Ahhhh, and that sexy Daphne. I would pay American money to sample that pussy."

Daphne! What the fuck?

The beginnings of a headache throbbed in his temples as he wrote down the information. "Are you *sure* of the names on this list?"

"You insult me! Have I ever given you bad information? My word is my life. You *know* me, Roman."

After underlining Daphne's name, he sat on the bed. "Sorry, my friend. My mistake. Thanks for your help."

"No problem, amigo. When you get a chance, come visit me. I have some new inventory you might be interested in."

"I'll do that. Later, amigo." He disconnected and took a deep breath. *What in the hell is that money-hungry Daphne and her crew up to?* He fired up his laptop and did a background check on her partners. *Hmmm, they've formed an investment group called Heavenly Associates.* Before he could dig deeper, he saw Jeanette enter her room. A check of the time on his MTM Special Ops military watch revealed it was nearly eight o'clock.

"Shit, I have to get down to Gator's place pretty soon." He looked at the list of names and rewrote it, leaving off Daphne's name. *I'll deal with her myself.* At the last minute, he scribbled down the number to his satellite phone on the list for Jeanette.

"Knock, knock." He rapped on the bedroom door. "Are you decent?" After no answer, he twisted the knob and eased the door open. Behind the bathroom door, he heard the sound of the shower running. A black leather pantsuit with entirely too many studs on it lay neatly on the armchair. He hadn't seen it previously, so he figured she must have brought it back from her condo.

He placed the note containing the names J. Michael Lipton, Walter Bagley and Enrique Morales on her bed, next to her robe. The sight of her car keys on the nightstand made him grin. *Thank God for small favors.* He put the keys in his pocket. *Now I won't have to hot wire her precious car.*

Back in his room, he grabbed his black leather jacket, two spare clips and satellite phone before hurrying out of the house. After he started the engine of the goat, he saw the porch light come on.

"Time to go before she tries to shoot my ass." Once the gate opened wide enough for the car to squeeze by, he stomped on the accelerator and burned rubber out the driveway, onto the street. He smiled. "Yeah, I kinda like this Spider ride!"

Before he made it to the end of the property line, his phone rang. "Hello?"

"Don't hello me! Where the *fuck* are you going in my car? What the hell are you doing?"

Before disconnecting the call, he sped onto the freeway onramp. "Sorry, bad connection, can't hear you. I'll try you back once I get to a better location. Night, night."

Chapter Eleven

Jeanette tossed the phone onto the sofa. The salmon Roman had prepared for dinner was literally the best she'd ever had, but it wasn't so good she'd let him steal her damn car—her baby! Hell naw. First Papa was spying on her, now Roman had stolen her car to chase imaginary spies, terrorists or some other craziness.

"If he gets even one scratch on my baby, I'll kill him," she bit out between clinched teeth. She hoped Roman's lame ass didn't think she fell for that weak reception crap he had shoveled her way.

While she was in the kitchen taking her anger out on the pots and pans, her phone rang a familiar ring tone. Grumbling, she shook the dish suds off her hands and marched into the living room to release her wrath on Papa.

The buttons just about popped off the phone because she snatched it up so quickly. "How the hell you gonna spy on us, you fucking pervert? First, I have Roman's crazy ass taking off my damn door, and now I find out your ass has been playing new school peeping Tom. What kind of sick game are you playing?"

"I'm sorry."

Did he just apologize? "Well...you should be. You have no right to—"

"You're a hundred percent correct," he cut in. "There's no excuse for my actions. I swear I didn't have the video on in your room. Only audio."

"Why even that?" She went into the kitchen to finish the dishes, so she could return to the lab. On her way, she picked up a few of Roman's discarded toothpicks off the coffee table. He was worse than her bother Greg was when he went through his sunflower-seed stage. You always knew where he'd been because he left a sunflower-seed-shell trail.

"Let's be honest here. By now you and Roman know neither of you works for me willingly. I needed to know what is going on in the case. How was I to know if you'd tell me everything I need to know?"

Lips pursed, she propped the phone between her ear and shoulder. "I think you just wanted to find out if we were coming after your ass, but that's neither here or there. Like it or not, you must *trust* us to do what needs to be done."

He chuckled. "It's hard to trust someone who wants you dead."

A genuine laugh bubbled from her. "Well, it is what it is."

In her mind, she had clear distinctions between those who deserved the death sentence and those who didn't. As hard as it was, when she backed away from her current situation and looked objectively, Papa's manipulating her was worth an ass whipping, but not the death penalty. Now the bastard who created the toxin was the type of person who deserved the death penalty.

"I am sorry about spying on you two, but there's a psycho planning mass genocide. I just don't have time to filter through your and Roman's anger for the information I need to find these bastards and stop them. We have to be a team."

"A team, huh?" She placed the last dish on the drain board. "You won't even allow me to see the victims' wounds or tell me how many victims there are. You need to stop wasting your time spying on me and Roman and give me what I need to develop an antidote quickly."

"I know, it's just..."

"There is no just. Do you want me to create an antidote or not? You're the only one hindering the progress of this project." She leaned against the kitchen counter. "What's going on, Papa? This isn't like you." Apologies or sounding iffy was not his way.

"You and Roman aren't the only ones tired of this life. If you can call it a life. After this job, I'm giving you and Roman your freedom."

"Giving? Humph, we're done working for you. The only reason we're on this project is because we believe in it. So please stop trippin'. We don't have time for it. Are you a member of the team or not?"

So much time passed without a word, Jeanette thought he wasn't going to answer. Then he said, "I'm in. What's the status report?"

Now he sounded more like the Papa she knew. "Roman stole my damn car! Asshole."

He laughed. "I wondered how long it would be before he took it for a spin."

"Spin my ass. And he left a list of names." She headed for her bedroom to change into her lab clothes and hang up her leather suit. She'd made it herself for a very special occasion. As she recited the list for Papa, she felt the special occasion for her suit would come soon. "I don't recognize any of the names."

"Roman will track them down."

"I need pictures. Actually, I need to see a symptomatic victim. And additional blood and tissue samples."

"I'll try to get the additional samples, but I'm 'not' involved in this project."

"Who called you in 'not' to help?"

"I can't tell you, but samples are hard to come by. I'll do my best."

"Thanks." She knew either Papa or Roman would be able to obtain the additional samples she needed.

"I'll send pictures, but I need to warn you. Most of the

victims are children."

"What!" The phone dropped from her ear. She caught it in midair. "This bastard is targeting children? How many so far? Are there any victims in the throes of symptoms presently?"

After giving her complete statistics on the victims, Papa told her to check the printer in the den. She walked out to the den where she saw the printer spitting out photos. *He has a wireless connection to our equipment. I wonder if Roman can find him using it?* She pushed the thought out of her mind. They were supposed to be working as a team.

"Thanks, Papa. I'll get back with you when I know more." She disconnected and gathered up the photos. The top one was a close-up of the open sores described in the information Papa had given her. The color images were a thousand times better than the sketches she'd been given. They reminded her of lesions she'd seen before. She sorted through the pictures and returned to her room.

The sight of three small children, no older than five, covered with huge lesions, with what was left of their tiny faces contorted in agony, stopped her in her tracks. Body trembling, the pictures fell from her hands.

"Babies...They're only babies..." Tears fell from her eyes and the salmon she'd had for dinner returned with a vengeance. Breathe, she couldn't breathe. Picture after picture of lesion-covered babies littered the floor. Dry heaves took over where the salmon left off. Breathe, she couldn't breathe.

"Stop!" Eyes closed tight, she began reciting the formula for photosynthesis. "$12H_2O + 6CO_2$ + sunlight," tears continued to fall and her body continued to tremble, "produces...?" She drew in a deep breath. "What the hell does it produce? Focus dammit, focus! What does it produce?" She wiped the tears away.

"You have to save the babies. Snap the fuck out of it." She picked up the photos that weren't covered with vomit. "$12H_2O + 6CO_2$ + sunlight produces $C_6H_{12}O_6 + 6O_2$."

She placed the photos on her bed, then went into the kitchen for cleaning supplies. "No more babies die. This bastard must be stopped."

After cleaning up her mess, she took the photos into the lab with her and got to work. She didn't care if she had to work twenty-four/seven, she wouldn't stop until she found the antidote.

Hours into her lab work, emotional and physical exhaustion overtook her. Holding one of the pictures of the children close to her, she dozed off.

"Hide-and-seek has to be the bestest game ever!"

Five-year-old Jeanette ran for the tool shed in the backyard. No way would her brother be able to find her this time.

The door creaked softly when she closed it. "Be quiet, you stupid door." Tiny bits of fear crept into her. Though it was bright and sunny outside, she hadn't thought about how dark it would be in the shed.

"Man, who left the shed unlocked?" her thirteen-year-old brother said with a laugh. Click-ump. "I sure hope no one is in that dark, stinky shed."

She pushed on the wood door, but it wouldn't open. "You'd better let me out of here, Greg!"

"What's wrong with you, big baby, afraid of the dark?"

"No," she lied, refusing to be outdone. "I love the dark." The only light in the shed came from a softball-sized hole in the wall of the shed near the floor. She shuffle-stepped close to the light for comfort.

"Good, because you'll be there for a while. I'm sick of you following me around. I already have a shadow. Me and my shadow are going swimming!"

A soft meowing caught her attention. Kittens! Fear of the dark almost forgotten and eyes quickly adjusting to the lack of light, she followed the sound around the lawnmower and stumbled over the weed whacker on her way to the opposite corner.

She bent down, saying, "Hello, little baby kitties." She felt their soft fur and no longer cared that she was trapped in the dark until she sensed something lurking in the shed with them. Scared the Boogie Man was after her and the kittens, she quickly picked one up. "Don't be scared." She shakily reached for another. "I'll protect you."

Some ferocious sounding animal hissed. Jeanette screamed, "Greg!" as she turned toward the sound to see what was after her and the kittens. Huge green eyes and claws went straight for her face.

"No!" Heart pounding, Jeanette woke from the nightmare. The attack had actually happened, and whenever she worried too much it recurred in nightmares.

She traced the thin scar that ran along her hairline, then touched the nick beside her eye. *I hate cats.*

A quick check of her watch told her she'd been asleep only twenty minutes, tops. She shook off the Z Monster and returned to work.

~~~~~~

Just before 10 P.M., Roman entered Chokoloskee, Florida, and made his way to Gator's garage. "This looks more like the place where young, horny teenagers wind up hacked to pieces by a nut in a hockey mask than the way to a hick's garage," he mumbled and drove off the main road.

On the right side of the narrow dirt road, an old vegetation-obscured sign from decades past welcomed customers to Chad's Gas and Go! Clusters of trees and high grass lined both sides, and potholes deep enough to bury a small animal tested the suspension of the goat. *Damn, have they ever heard of asphalt?*

The sound of a thousand different bugs and other critters serenaded him when he let down his window and spat out a chewed up toothpick. The dense tree cover blocked out the stars and crescent moon, making it black as a raven outside. A quarter mile into his bumpy ride, he spotted a light in the distance. *You really need to look into a better location, Gator.* Gratefully, he found the road gradually smoothed out when he neared the source of the light.

The faint sound of country music filtered through the forest. The dirt gave way to a smooth, gravel composition and about a hundred yards in front of him, Gator's junkyard/garage materialized. *Welcome to redneck central.* He pulled his gun out of the inside pocket of his leather jacket and put it on the passenger seat.

A small mountain of vehicle carcasses surrounded the rundown repair shop. Light bulbs of various wattages dangled here and there, obviously Gator's attempt at perimeter lighting. Surprisingly, they lit the four-acre property. Two new-ish flatbed tow trucks and one ancient, refurbished rear-hook model were parked willy-nilly in front. A pair of refurbished gas pumps, circa 1950, stood like space aliens on the oil-stained concrete fuel island. He rolled up to the dented and dinged rollup door and parked.

Blinking lights on the roof caught his eye. "You have *got* to be kidding." He stared at a large lighted Santa and a half-naked woman in a sleigh pulled by eight Harley Davidson motorcycles. In one hand, Santa held a bottle of Jack Daniels, in the other, a large toy bag with the word "Beer" stenciled across it.

"Sounds like the boys are having a serious hoedown." He stepped out of the goat.

Lynyrd Skynyrd music punched its way out of the wood and corrugated metal building. Dilapidation had a firm grip on the aging structure. After tucking his pistol in the waistband behind his back, he pounded on the metal fire door.

"Who the fuck's there?" a man's voice said in a thick southern accent as the volume of the music dropped. A second later, a pair of tooth-challenged rednecks yanked the door open and glared at the black stranger. The taller of the two corn-fed fellas, who was wearing a confederate flag bandana, took a step toward Roman. "Who you, boy?'

Really was hopin' not to have to beat any ass tonight but...Roman moved his head side-to-side, stretching his neck. "I'm lookin' for Gator."

The shorter, porkier redneck advanced on Roman. "He didn't ask you who you was lookin' fer, boy, he as—"

Just as Roman squared his feet to commence some anus kicking, Gator pushed the two hillbillies aside, stepped between them and bear-hugged Roman. "Goddamn good to see you, bubba! How the hell you been?"

Roman turned his head in hope of avoiding the stench of Gator's beer, chewing tobacco and garbage-scented breath. "I'm good."

"I'm glad you could make it." He released Roman and looked at his friends. "Don't just stand there catchin' flies in ya mouths. Back the fuck off and let my colored friend in! This here is my cousin Abe's ol' marine buddy, the shooter."

The confederate bandana-wearer hesitated, scowling at Roman. "That ain't shit in my book. Any fool wit' a gun can shoot it."

Gator grimaced and elbowed him out the way. "Shut the fuck up and get outta the way before I let him kick your fool ass 'til you shit footprints." He turned to Roman. "Come on. Let me show you around."

"I'm gonna have to take a rain check. I'm really kind of pressed for time."

Gator reached into the front pocket of his grimy overalls and pulled out a small can of chewing tobacco. He then whistled loudly before adding a pinch of tobacco between his cheek and gums. "All right, let's go see your car."

Four other men emerged from the building in response to Gator's whistle. They followed the rest of the crew over to the now-dusty GTO. Roman checked his watch as Gator opened the door and sat behind the wheel. "Can you do the job?"

Gator popped the hood, got out and shared a laugh with his crew of men surrounding the car. "Can I do the job?" He spit a puddle of tobacco juice close to the toe of Roman's shoe. "Shit, me and my boys will have the job done before the sun shines on your black ass in the mornin'."

"I'm from Missouri; show me." He tossed Gator the ignition key. "And you say you can duplicate that key? You know it's microchip-encoded."

Gator shot a snot-rocket out his nose, then pulled a blank microchip key out of his pocket. "Never doubt a good ol' boy. All I need to do is work my magic, and it's done."

He's one smart son-of-a-bitch to look so dumb. "Cool."

Gator glanced at confederate-flag-bandana man. "Go on inside and open up."

"Oh shit!" Roman said as the roll-up door opened. Inside, the shabby-looking garage was fitted with all the latest equipment on the market. Racks of tools, car parts, tires, engine blocks, and other items filled the room. The garage had been expanded to five times its original length. Looking at the building head-on, you couldn't tell how large the garage really was. All the interior walls were solid; the deteriorated exterior was obviously a façade. Four top-notch Harley Davidson motorcycles and three customized four-wheel drive trucks were parked on the west side of the huge garage.

A Peterbilt semi-tractor sat in the air on one of the four hydraulic hoists. The entire interior was as clean and well lit as an operating room. Hooters' posters featuring the famous well-endowed women decorated much of the available wall space. Neon beer signs and a collection of cowboy hats filled the rest. On the far side of the building, next to the restrooms, was a fully operational bar with six black leather barstools sitting in front of it.

Gator walked over and draped his arm around Roman's shoulder. "Not bad for a bunch of country boys, huh?"

"Man, you must be kidding. This looks like it came right out of NASCAR."

"Check this out." Gator led Roman to a stack of wooden crates and boxes. He opened one of the crates and showed Roman a pair of new, armored replacement doors for the goat.

"Already painted to match the car. All we gotta do is put 'em on and you're good to go."

"Nice...real nice." Roman inspected the armor plating. *Made from the same stuff as the body armor Hillbilly sent me.*

Gator pointed at another stack of big boxes. "There's the new armored truck lid, hood, grill and armored skins for the quarter panels. The bulletproof glass is over there, too."

Roman smiled. "I gotta admit, Gator, you're the fuckin' man!"

Gator gave him a snaggle-toothed smile. "Hey, there's more." He walked over to the racks of tires and pointed to a new set of GTO tires and rims, identical to the ones on Jeanette's car. "Here's your set of run flat tires. These babies are way better than standard. You damn near have to shoot 'em with a howitzer before they go down. They self-seal just as fast as a hole is punched in 'em."

Roman nodded with satisfaction. "I was *really* hoping you could find those. Good job, Gator."

Gator grinned. "Right on!" He then whistled. "Hey, let's get 'er done!"

A moment later, the crew fired up impact wrenches and torches, then started dismantling the goat. Roman reached into the inside pocket of his leather jacket, pulled out the envelope of cash he'd taken out of the Yukon and tossed it to Gator. "You'll find a few extra bucks in there to buy your boys some pizza."

Gator beamed after peeping at the thick wad of hundred-dollar bills inside the envelope. "I likes your style, bubba!" He pointed toward the bar. "You can go hang out in the break room over there 'til we get done. But don't wander off too far from the garage unless you want your ass eaten by a real gator—or worse."

"I'll keep that in mind." Roman walked over to the goat and took out his laptop. In the break room, he was impressed all over again. The room featured a gargantuan plasma TV, coffeemaker, satellite TV, a DVD player, currently showing a black porn movie, a large refrigerator, two microwaves, a pair of black leather sofa beds, three vending machines, a pay phone and two of the largest stuffed alligators he had ever seen.

These hillbillies are a trip. He shook his head at the image on-screen of three black porn stars doing their thing as he put his laptop bag on one of the sofas. *I need some air.*

Outside, he turned on his phone and listened to a nasty, nasty message from the Black Widow. He chuckled. "I'm *damn* sure not gonna eat any of her food now." In the clearing around the garage, he looked up just in time to see a shooting star. *I wish...*The face of his mother popped into his head. He wished he could spend Christmas visiting her like a normal son, but with Shadow threatening to reveal what he'd been up to, that wasn't an option.

He sighed, let that wish go and returned to the business at hand—Daphne and her crew. This poisoning business didn't seem her style, but if money was involved, her style was subject to change.

He kicked a few pieces of gravel as he walked toward the road leading out. *She's always been interested in a quick fuck or a quick buck...*

A rustling in the trees a few feet in front of him made him draw his gun. "What the hell?" He looked up in a tree close to him and spotted a swamp owl silhouetted by the perimeter lights. It had what looked like a mouse in its mouth. "Let me get my ass inside before I shoot something." Back in the break room, he shut off the porno. *That's the last thing I need to be watching right now with my overdue ass.*

He turned on the news, sat on the sofa and fired up his laptop. "Now I can finish checking out these Heavenly Associates."

His search on J. Michael Lipton showed he was a multi-millionaire. His father had been old fashioned and expected J. Michael to become head of the family after his death. Therefore, he left the bulk of his money to him. Lipton hadn't given either of his siblings a dime of the nearly five-hundred million he had received for selling his father's oil holdings and had placed his mother in an elderly care facility.

What a cold piece of work. He reminds me of Daphne, cold as a witch's tit.

Although a search showed Enrique Morales to be a spoiled rich boy and basic scumbag, he was far less scummy than Lipton and Daphne. The most that came up on Enrique after Roman searched the databases of Interpol, the CIA, FBI, NSA, DGI and local authorities was his conviction for being a slumlord in Brooklyn, New York fifteen years earlier. Five of the eight tenements he owned were in such bad shape, he had been fined half-a-million dollars and forced to sell the condemned properties. After being humiliated in the press, he had sold all his remaining property, changed his name from Fredrico Cepeda to Enrique Morales and fled to Cuba.

After he lined the pockets of the right people in Cuba, he had been able to open a string of resorts that made him super wealthy. All he had for America was his middle finger, which he waved at every opportunity. *But is that motivation enough for him to start this poisoning and have America blamed? Doesn't add up.* Roman chewed his toothpick down to splinters.

The sound of a loud crash and Gator cussing somebody out, cut through the blaring country music. Hoping they'd hurry, he checked the time. He hated leaving Jeanette so long. Subconsciously, though, he had a gut feeling she could take care of herself. Besides, no one he was aware of was after her and the CC gang had no turf in the Homestead area and no idea the Sandman was in town. He took the worn toothpick out his mouth and put it on top of one of the *Hustler* magazines adorning the coffee table.

All right, your turn, Walter Bagley. He popped a fresh toothpick in his mouth and ran Bagley's info. A full page popped up. "Lookie here." He was repulsed by Bagley's fetish for humiliation sex and his bank's record for turning down more minority loans than any other bank in the UK.

Interesting, a freaky, racist asshole.

He also had three ex-wives and four children he had bought off and was estranged from. Amazingly, he had found a way to write off the money he spent on his mistresses and various hookers around the globe.

"I see Bagley is one of those pricks who thinks he can fix all his problems by throwing money at them." An hour into investigating Bagley's connections, financial statements and hacking into his bank's network, he discovered Bagley owned a new fifteen-story high-rise in Miami.

Hmmph. He sat back and stroked his chin. *Let me check out this building.* He re-hacked into the city of Miami servers and looked up the blueprints for the Royal Investments' building. He saw nothing unusual about the recently completed building until he scanned the layout of the fourteenth floor. "Why is your security system so much more elaborate for this floor, Mr. Bagley?"

Further investigation showed the floor had not only more security, it also had much more plumbing, gas lines, ventilation, electrical wiring, networking cable and no occupied office space. "What kind of shit is going on there?" He dug deeper and found mention of several items that could only belong to a laboratory. "Stainless steel sinks, cryogenic tanks, Bunsen burners, microscopes, biohazard disposal containers?"

Rising from the sofa, he paced the floor, blocking out the music in the background. Something wasn't right. The building had been put up in record time using the cheapest materials available—except for the fourteenth floor. Not even a quarter of the offices were leased out. He sat back in front of his laptop. *Gonna take another look at the security system.* Even though the security system was over the top, he was not overwhelmed by it. "I'm damned glad I had the foresight to have my electronic code detector shipped to me."

Just before sunrise, the sounds of air chisels, hammers, swearing, laughing, clanking, wrenches falling to the floor ceased, replaced by the sound of the GTO starting up. He checked the time on his laptop before shutting it down. *That quick? No more doubting your word, Gator.*

While he was packing up his laptop, one of Gator's goons opened the break-room door. "Hey, boy, you good to go."

Roman walked over and stood face-to-face with him. "You did say 'Hey, *Roy*,' right?"

Fear wafted off the blue-eyed country boy's body like steam. He managed a nervous smile. "Ahh, shit, I ain't mean nothin' by it."

Roman continued to stare into those frightened eyes until his message was clear. "Good. I would hate to have to teach you how to pronounce my name right."

Blue eyes held the door open and stepped aside. "No problem, Roy, I got you. Ya car's ready."

Gator wiped a set of greasy fingerprints off the windshield as Roman approached. "Well, what you think?"

Roman nodded his head and grinned as he circled the goat. It looked as if it had just rolled off the assembly line. "Outstanding job, fellas!"

Gator picked up a fruit jar and spit a mouthful of tobacco juice into it before offering Roman his greasy hand. "Good doin' business wit' you! Come on back, ya hear?"

Roman declined his greasy hand and patted him on the back instead. "I'm sure I will."

Chapter Twelve

The orange-pink color of dawn winked at Roman when he pulled up to the driveway gate just after six in the morning. *What are the odds of Jeanette being asleep and not noticing me getting back?* After he pulled into the driveway, he saw his odds were slim and none—and slim had just left town.

Blocking his path, wearing a black bandana, black sweat suit and tennis shoes, she looked mad as a hornet in a pickle jar.

Well, here we go. He got out the car. "Good morning. What's for breakfast?" Her glare was a little less harsh than he expected.

"Why do you insist on fucking with me? I told you not to take my damn car! I swear, you are the most disrespectful asshole I have ever met!" She angrily swiped her finger over the dusty hood. "Where did you take my car? Four-freakin'-wheel driving? What do I—"

That was the first time he'd seen her wear a ponytail or noticed the little scar by her right eye and another that followed along her hairline. He continued to let her vent without saying a word, thinking the imperfection perfected her.

"—have to do to get you to understand? Hello? Are you lis—" She tensed up when he reached into his inside jacket pocket and pulled his pistol. Her glare intensified. "What a pussy...pulling a gun on a woman."

While staring in her eyes, he pointed the gun at the windshield and fired two rounds. Outrage filled her face. "Are you out of your damn mind?"

"No." He fired another round into the front tire. It hissed for a second, then hushed as it self-sealed. "I just gave it a tune up."

Jaw dropped, she pushed him aside and rubbed the windshield. Not a mark on it. She bent over and inspected the tire, good as new. He read the conflicted look in her face. *Doesn't know whether to kill or kiss me.* Putting the pistol back in his waistband, he said, "I needed to make sure you'd be safe. That included fortifying your car." He saw her face relax a little, but she still didn't seem like her normal self. *Has she been crying?* "No charge."

"You should be careful firing that gun in the open." She looked away from him, then left him. "You could hurt somebody."

Watching her walk away, he shrugged, opened the door and got his laptop. "I'll take that as a 'thank you,' Black Widow."

~~~~~~

Of the three men Roman had just given her the rundown on, the only one who interested her in the least was the Bagley fellow, the one who owned a high rise in Miami—the one with a mysterious fourteenth floor loaded with what seemed to be labs.

"I need to snoop around his labs. It's a long shot, but..." Jeanette hunched her shoulders.

"I'm already on it." He settled in the dining room, yawned and booted his laptop.

Glad he had anticipated her need and was on the job, she had to admit that having Roman around had definite perks. With all the snooping he'd done on the triple threat, as she called the enemy, and the arming of her car to the hilt, he couldn't have slept a wink, and it was showing. She was sure he thought she couldn't tell.

Standing behind him, she laid her hands on his shoulders

and gently massaged. Knots, large knots, were gathered in the juncture between his neck and shoulder. A few minutes of kneading left her fingers sore, but the knots were gone. He was so relaxed he'd forgotten about what was on his computer screen and was dozing off.

She knew exactly how he felt. She was so tired she could barely make the simplest calculation, but she couldn't stop until she found the antidote.

He jerked awake. "Whew." He rested his hands atop hers. "That was nice, thanks." He locked his computer. "I'm catching a nap before we leave." He pushed away from the table. "Don't leave."

Arms folded over her chest, she said, "I'll leave if and when I want, and you'd best not take my car again without my permission."

His lips curled into a sly grin.

"What's so funny?"

"So we've moved from me not being able to touch your car to I can use it 'with permission.' I guess that's a step in the right direction."

"You stink. The right direction for you would be the shower."

Laughing, he pulled off his shirt and headed for his shower.

Exhausted, yet refusing to rest, Jeanette returned to her bedroom to review the results of testing she'd conducted and to write additional notes. The shower running brought a smile to her face. She'd take off Roman's door, but he never closed it and he'd probably like it.

Leaning against the headboard of her bed, she continued to read through logs of various scientists and compared her notes on the contaminant. A few of the pictures fell from between the pages of her journal.

"I'll find the antidote and make whoever did this to you pay, I swear."

She continued pouring through others' notes and making her own until she slipped into dreamland.

The heat and humidity in the schoolyard made it hard to breathe, but hospitals refused to take the lesion-covered children into their facility for fear of infecting the other patients. The sounds of the children crying out in agony as the toxin ate away at their skin sent chills down her spine and renewed her hatred for whoever was responsible.

The inoculation she had created would work; she just knew it would. She stooped beside a child who couldn't have been more than eight years old. The lesions had eaten away at the poor child so badly that Jeanette couldn't tell the child's sex.

She reached into her bag for a syringe and prepared the needle, then turned to give the child a dose. Suddenly, a tabby cat appeared out of nowhere and clawed at her face.

"Roman!"

"Roman!" She fought the cat.

Shaken from her nightmare, she couldn't catch her breath. The children were gone, the schoolyard was gone, the cat was gone, but Roman was there, holding and rocking her. The look in his eyes didn't show lust, but concern.

He pressed her head against his bare shoulder. "It's okay," he said softly and set his .45 caliber HKS on the nightstand. "I'm here."

Tears fell from her eyes. "I have to save them." She nodded toward the pictures scattered about the bed.

"You will, but first you must sleep." Holding her with one arm, he cleared the bed of pictures, journals and other documentation with his free hand, stacking it all on the nightstand.

"I can't stop. There's no time." She wiped her eyes.

He ran his hand over her soft hair, down to her ponytail and removed her black bandana. "How much sleep did you get last night?"

"About twenty awful minutes," she answered reluctantly, but truthfully.

"And the night before?"

Shoulders hunched, she guessed, "Around two hours, but this is different—"

Combing her hair with his fingers, he spread it over her shoulders. "You're so tired, you can't think straight. That's why you're having bad dreams." He pushed her off the bed and finished clearing the area of books, pencils. "You're no good to anyone like this, and you have to be at the top of your game tonight."

"Roman, thank you, but I can't stop, not now."

"Strip to your underclothes." He held the comforter open for her.

Brow raised, she would have argued with him, but saw it was a losing battle. Plus, he was correct. She *was* too exhausted to think straight. If she weren't so tired, she would have been able to remember where she'd seen lesions similar to the ones on the children. She stripped and slipped under the comforter and sheet. "I can't stand you."

"And?" He tucked her in, then sat in the chair close to her bed. Another yawn escaped him. Instead of going to bed, he inspected his pistol.

She could tell he was as exhausted as she was, but knew he'd stay up and watch over her. Though she didn't like it, she found comfort in knowing someone genuinely cared. Somehow, she had become more than a job to him and him more to her. Too drained to examine whatever was happening to them, she said, "You've slept even less than I have. We both have a long night ahead of us." She lifted the covers.

"I'm fine."

"Don't worry, I promise not to sting you."

He chuckled and joined her in bed. Since he'd come into her room wearing only his briefs, there was no need for him to strip.

Hoping the dream wouldn't return, she rolled away from him and closed her eyes. As silly as it was, she somehow felt with Roman near, the nightmares would stay away, and she'd be given the time she needed to recharge.

"Now don't sting me," Roman said softly, then wrapped a protective arm around her and pulled her into his body. "Sleep, Black Widow. We both need a good three, four hours."

Relaxed in his arms with the heat of his body against her back, she felt something she had never felt—loved as a man loves a woman.

~~~~~~

Still doubting whether he should have sent Jeanette the pictures of the deceased children, Lincoln poured a splash of Grey Goose into his black coffee.

Commander Vickers shook his head and watched Lincoln attempt homicide on his liver. "How are you able to drink so much without killing yourself?"

Lincoln took a sip. "It's a holistic diet I learned from a very special woman in Japan many years ago."

"Yeah, right." Vickers chuckled and placed the manifesto of the plane Roman's shipment had come in on, on Lincoln's desk, then left.

Lincoln quickly scanned the manifesto, doubting he'd find anything out of the ordinary or what was actually being carried on the plane. He tossed the manifesto to the side, wondering how he'd keep tabs on his rogue kids and Colin. Keeping Colin and Jeanette apart could easily become a full-time job.

Pissed at himself for not making the time to Roman-proof the bugs, he opened his e-mail account. Then again, even if he had made the time, Roman would eventually have found the bugs. Tired of crying over spilled milk, he read an encrypted e-mail from Dominic. Somehow, word had leaked to the Cuban press about a "mysterious, killer disease," which might have been planted by Americans.

The leather office chair creaked as Lincoln leaned forward and grabbed his phone to call Dominic.

"I knew you'd call," Dominic said in Spanish.

"You've got to squash the talk of America being behind the illness."

"Don't you think I've tried? A plague! One of the papers called it a plague. I told you this would happen. This is out of control. I didn't think you should bring Mason in on this yet, but now...now he needs to stop this war before it starts. Where is he?"

"Looking into terrorist organizations that have the capability and inclination for this type of biological attack."

"So he's looking to place the blame somewhere else?"

The fury and anxiety in Dominic's voice was clear. Lincoln knew his old friend was releasing his frustration, so he remained calm. "He's looking to place the blame where it belongs—on the responsible party."

"I'm...I'm sorry, it's just..." Dominic trailed off.

"I have my best people on this project. They'll find the antidote and bring the responsible party to justice. I know there is no time, but time is what this will take."

"I know." He released a deep sigh.

"What's going on, Dominic? What aren't you telling me?"

"It's Vanessa. She has this sore developing on her leg and she's been feverish for days," he said of his granddaughter. "The doctors don't know what it is."

"Shit!" Lincoln pushed away from the desk and paced the room. He'd hoped beyond hope that Vanessa wasn't infected. "Shit, shit, shit!"

"Lincoln, please, please, tell your people to hurry."

Lincoln wiped his free hand over his face. "We can't remain in denial. I'm smuggling Vanessa out of Cuba tonight. I want her stateside with my scientists." He didn't feel the need to say Vanessa would be a guinea pig of sorts. In the end, she'd be cured, that's all that mattered. "She'll be the first to receive the antidote."

"I can't leave, not now, but I'll send my wife with her. Thank you, Lincoln."

After giving Dominic the necessary instructions, Lincoln then logged onto his computer to access the only camera Roman hadn't found—yet. The small camera was mounted on the spotlight next to the driveway entrance. It recorded each time the driveway gate opened or closed. The best he could do was monitor when his bad kids came and went.

He skimmed through the footage and saw they were both presently at the house. From the last Jeanette-and-Roman conversation he had heard, he knew chemistry between them was at work. They reminded him of the only woman he had ever loved, and how he had fucked up their relationship. Many days he'd wished he could turn his rifle into a time machine, go back and do the right thing.

He took a bigger swig of his spiked coffee as the bitter pain of his past crawled over his heart. That pain served him well; it always made him focus. He couldn't allow Jeanette to know the details of the samples he would get from Vanessa. He began to dial Roman's number, then changed his mind. He didn't have the time or patience to listen to him bitch about the bugs. Instead, he sent him an encrypted e-mail.

> *Roman,*
> *I'm smuggling a young child out of Cuba tonight who has early signs of this mysterious illness. Jeanette needs samples. Obtain the needed samples from this child, but do not allow Jeanette to have contact with the child or even let her know the child is within her reach. I can't afford for Jeanette to lose focus right now.*
> *I'll send full details later.*

Worried about Jeanette's reaction to the pictures he had sent, he strummed his fingers on the desktop.

> *I know you don't owe me anything, but...*

After deleting his last line, he sipped more of his "coffee."

> *I know you don't owe me any favors, but keep a*

close eye on Jeanette. Yesterday I sent her photos of the victims.

Regretting sending all of the photos, he ran his hand over his face.

She's not as tough as she acts. She has a soft spot for children. I should have kept the more explicit photos to myself. We need her to stay focused. Do whatever is needed to keep her mind off those children and on finding the antidote.

Quickly, he hit the send button before he could change his mind, then called Colin and gave him an update about the Cuban media and the rumor that this was an American biological weapon.

"This is fucked the hell up!" Colin bit out. "Do you know how many terrorist psychos are out there itching to commit genocide? And those are the organizations we know about. Hell, I'll just have to head on over to Cuba empty-handed."

"I think that would be best. You need to sit the Cubans down and make them see they're doing more harm than good." He realized he'd sent the e-mail to Roman without blocking the sent-from address. *Shit! Hope like hell I can get that e-mail back.* He reopened his e-mail program and tried to retrieve the e-mail he'd just sent to Roman. If Roman hadn't opened it, the program would snag the e-mail back as if it hadn't been sent.

"Have you heard from Jeanette yet?"

Shit! Roman had a program on his computer that prevented Lincoln from retrieving the e-mail.

"Lincoln, did you hear from Jeanette?"

"Oh, yes, yes, she's onboard."

"Excellent. I knew my baby would come through for us. I'm headed on to Cuba. I need to speak directly with your contact first."

Times like this, Lincoln longed to be back behind the scope

of his sniper rifle instead of all this bureaucracy bullshit.

"I'm sneaking his granddaughter and wife out of Cuba tonight. I'll let him know to expect to hear from you soon."

"What the...? You're not bringing her on American soil."

"Yes, I am. His grandbaby is showing symptoms of the plague. I'm taking her to Jeanette. Don't worry. The illness is not contagious."

"So you think."

Chapter Thirteen

A ray of late afternoon sunlight crept between the blinds and landed on Roman's closed eyes. He blinked, disoriented. *What time is it? Am I in bed with—* He opened his eyes and saw the back of Jeanette's head. The aroma of her Kiwi-scented shampoo rode into his nose. The immensely good feeling of her soft hindquarters against his now-throbbing member embarrassed him. *This is no good!*

He gently eased away from her and checked his watch. *Shit! Damn near three o'clock! We've been sleep eight hours!* The last time he'd slept that long was eight years ago after staying awake for four straight days, tracking a pedophile and child murderer through the Canadian wilderness. It was one of the rare instances where he had taken on a job on his own accord in order to dish out some vigilante justice. The authorities had given up trying to find the expert mountain climber after a week of searching. Roman refused to let him get away. On the fourth morning of his quest, groggy and running on adrenaline, he spotted the creep standing knee-deep in a creek, masturbating to a *Boys' Life* magazine. The pleasure Roman felt after watching the perv's head explode through the scope of his rifle was euphoric. He then made a bed of leaves in a shallow cave and slept for eighteen hours.

Haven't slept more than four consecutive hours since. He

tried to slip out of the bed without waking her. *Sure hope she didn't feel my wood!* He managed to get one foot on the floor. *In a different world, and a different situation, I wouldn't be getting outta this bed for shit.*

His other leg got halfway out the bed. *She's mean as rabid dog, but she cooks for me—when she's not poisoning my food.* A grin surfaced. *And the way she keeps this place spic-and-span! Better than having room service.*

After a much-needed cold shower, he put on a conservative gray suit, planning to get to Bagley's building before it closed at six. He glanced at his watch. *Just under three hours.* He took the "blood hound" out of the duffle bag, put it in his briefcase and left his room.

His heart twitched at the sight of her cooking in an oversized T-shirt. Even though he didn't have much of an appetite, whatever it was she was cooking smelled great. Not even the baggy shirt could hide the sexiness of her body. He put on his fake eyeglasses and walked toward the kitchen. *This keeps up, I'm gonna start sleeping in the garage.*

While he was adjusting his teal tie, she turned from the stove and whistled at him like a flirting construction worker. "I see you clean up nice."

"Thanks," he mumbled after opening the fridge and taking out the orange juice. "And I see you are in full 'Julia Child' mode." He pulled a small 35mm digital camera out of his pocket and snapped a few shots of her.

"Are you ever without a camera?"

"No."

She removed a basket of yam fries from the deep fryer and let them drain. "Oh, and I only made enough for one."

"Good thing you did." He put the camera back in his pocket and poured a glass of orange juice. "Because I have to head over to Bagley's building before they close."

A glimmer of disappointment was quickly replaced with apathy. "Okay...good."

His eyes moved from the four juicy turkey patties on the

plate on the counter to her face. "I should only be gone a few hours. I'm scouting out the building to see what I need to get you a peek at that laboratory."

She chewed on one of the yam fries. "Have fun. I slept so good, I came up with a few new ideas I need to work on."

"Good." He pulled his pistol out of the holster under his jacket and checked the safety. "You keep that Glock I gave you, near you, and stay inside until I get back."

"Now you should know," she added condiments to her turkey burger, "I am the last person you need to be babysitting. Go do whatever it is you do."

Outside at the garage, he looked at the house and shook his head as he got into the Yukon. Before starting the truck, he called Jeanette. "Hey!"

"Argh! What is it, man?"

"What did I tell you about keeping the blinds closed?"

"Good *grief!*"

He watched her stick her tongue out at him before she closed the blinds.

"Thank you, ma'am."

"Good-bye, Roman."

Forty minutes later, a little past four, Roman arrived in front of the Royal Investments building. He cruised past the front double doors and looked for a place to park. *Pretty generic layout.* The granite building took up half the block. Smoked glass windows dotted the light gray edifice like square freckles.

Around the corner, he pulled into an alley behind the building. *Cheap ass. Only has one camera monitoring the alley.* After parking behind the deli two doors down, he removed his gun and lucky throwing knife. Even though the blueprints showed no indication of walk-through metal detectors, he couldn't take a chance they used hand-held detectors. He put the weapons in the center console and walked out the alley to the sidewalk. Being without a weapon was almost like not having air to breathe. Especially in the hostile territory he now walked.

The air reeked of crime. CC gang graffiti decorated many of the walls, mailboxes, bus benches and newspaper racks. When he rounded the corner in front of Look-Good Cleaners, a convertible Mercedes carrying two older gang members pulled to the curb.

Ah, shit. Roman looked straight ahead and walked toward the car. *They look like some high-ranking members.*

Both men had blond-tipped, salt-and-pepper dreadlocks down to the middle of their backs. As Roman got closer, the passenger got out and spent a few seconds studying Roman's face. It looked as though he wanted to say something to Roman, but the driver took the cell phone off his ear and told him, "Yo! Marquis, Randall wants to holla at you!"

Thankful for the intervention, Roman un-balled his fist as he passed. *Good, I hate fighting in a suit.*

At the entrance to Bagley's building, he followed a UPS driver, who was wearing a Santa hat, into the lobby, and waited until he spoke to security before approaching them. *Cool. No kind of metal detection. Won't have to try and explain the bloodhound in my briefcase.* He then noticed the UPS driver and most of the previous employees had signed their time in *and* out at the same time.

Large photos and paintings of London scenery decorated the walls. A picture of a little boy saluting one of the Buckingham Palace Guards hung behind the security guard desk. He walked over to the building directory across from the security desk. *Funny, nothing for the fourteenth floor.*

The directory also showed the building manager's hours were from seven to four. "Silent Night" played at a low level throughout the lobby speaker system. *That song sucks like a black hole.* He made mental note of some of the few companies in the building, then went to speak with the pair of guards.

"Good afternoon, sir."

The bored-looking Spanish guard looked up from his sci-fi novel. "What can I do for you?"

Roman adjusted his glasses. "I was hoping to speak to the

building manager about leasing some office space."

"Too late. He's already gone for the day. You can try back tomorrow." He went back to his reading.

"Awww, crap. I really like this building. Do you mind if I take a quick look around?"

The gray-haired, white security guard slid him a clipboard with an ink pen chained to it. "Sure, just let me see your ID and sign in."

"Sure thing."

Roman went into his jacket pocket and showed the guard his Glenn Noble driver's license. The guard looked up at Roman. "California? You quite a ways from home, ain't ya?"

Putting the ID back in his pocket, he said, "Yes, I'm here to open our southeast regional office."

The guard showed the mildest of interest. "Good deal. We have plenty of space available."

Roman entered the elevator and saw a cardkey was needed to access the fourteenth floor. *A way inside from the thirteenth floor? Elevator plus camera equals no "bloodhound,"* he joked internally. On the thirteenth floor, just as the blueprints had showed him, all the doors used electronic card keys for entrance. "Time for my 'bloodhound' to sniff out the codes."

At the end of the long corridor, which veered off to the right, he found the stairway. Up the stairs, he ran into a locked door with an AUTHORIZED PERSONNEL ONLY sign. *Bingo! This must be the lab.*

You really should have spent a few more dollars on your security, Bagley. Cheap ass doesn't even have stairwell cameras. Using the electronic code detector in his briefcase, affectionately called a "bloodhound," he successfully jimmied the lock. *If I remember right, this corridor leads to the lab area, where the security gets real thick.* The short hallway contained only a janitor's closet, supply room and maintenance room.

Interesting. He stopped at the maintenance room door. *Let's see if my hunch pays off.* He picked the lock and entered the room.

Thick bundles of electrical wiring and conduits covered the ceiling. Relays, switches electronic meters and junction boxes decorated the walls. A smile grew on his face after seeing an electric panel with a decal of an eye inside a triangle and the words "Third Eye Security" above it on the cover. *That's a big help.* He'd hacked into the high-tech alarm company's systems many times before.

He left the room, went to the end of the hall and peered through the small, glass window in the electronically locked door. Overhead, behind the door, he saw a clear plastic bubble that housed a rotating security camera. He checked his watch and timed the rotation of the camera—seventeen seconds. He made a mental note of the rotation times before leaving.

Back at the guard station, Roman gushed to the Spanish guard about how nice and secure the building was. "I'm sure my boss will like it."

The white guard put on his cap. "I'm about to make my rounds before the next shift comes on."

Roman pretended to be in awe when he spoke to the Cuban-American guard. "Wow! You have twenty-four-hour security?"

The bored guard yawned. "Yeah, but the graveyard is so dead and the building so secure we don't really need a guard."

Roman laughed. "This will be a great place to operate out of."

The guard leaned over and turned up the volume of the Miami Heat/Golden State Warriors basketball game on his portable radio. "Sounds good."

Roman glanced at the log sheet next to the radio. *Only one guard on the graveyard shift. That'll work.* He smiled. "Sorry for talking your head off. I'm sure you have work to do. Thanks for your help."

~~~~~~

Outside the building, Roman was relieved to see the gang members' Mercedes was gone. "What now?" he wondered as his phone vibrated. The screen showed he had received an e-mail on his private, encrypted server. The smell of cooking pastrami from the Allstar Deli steered him to the entrance.

"Sit anywhere you like," the smiling waitress said as her eyes roamed his body. "The specials are on the insert inside the menu. Let me know when you're ready, hon."

"Thank you." He took a seat at a table near the rear of the deli. Christmas decorations and a painted-on depiction of Santa Claus riding his sleigh through the snow obscured most of the window next to him. Before checking the menu, he pulled out his phone. He grimaced once he saw who the e-mail was from. *How in the hell did you get my personal number, Shadow? Gotta have some serious connections.* Roman's signal was routed through several different government agency satellites, making it impossible to track. So he thought.

After ordering a pastrami sandwich on sourdough, he read the first line of the encrypted e-mail.

> Roman,
> I'm smuggling a young child out of Cuba tonight who has early signs of this mysterious illness—

By the time he finished the e-mail, he was in an emotional hurricane.

I don't get Shadow. At first, he is just some dictating, threatening asshole, and now he's trying to save lives?

He took a small bite of his sandwich. *And Jeanette...what exactly is his connection to her? From the sound of this e-mail, it's not sexual...almost sounds like he really is her father. But what father would torture his daughter by showing her pictures of infected children knowin' it would upset her?* He grimaced at the image of how distraught Jeanette had been after seeing the pictures. *I swear, Shadow, if you did that just to fuck with her, I'll make sure you suffer a slow, painful death.*

His appetite waned as his mind sorted through this new information. *Need a place to house a kid and her* *grandmother. Great...*Before closing the e-mail, he checked the address of the sender. "Ah ha! What do we have here?" Next to the anonymous address was a blinking red exclamation point. "I need my laptop." He laid a twenty-dollar bill on the table next to his half-eaten sandwich and left.

Inside the Yukon, Roman pulled out his laptop and logged into his private mail server. To keep track of hacking attempts and other breaches of his system, he had installed a powerful e-mail security software program called Cyclops. Roman, with the help of an Interpol software genius from West Africa, had created the server-monitoring software. Cyclops could track down the originating IP address of any worm or virus that tried to "attack" his system. Shadow had apparently used an e-mail snag program that Cyclops thought was an attack. Cyclops had stopped the invasion and tracked the IP address.

You fucked up this time, Shadow. In a minute, I'll see where you sent this from.

The program scanned web and e-mail addresses at lightning speed. Three minutes later, it stopped at the generic IP address the snag program had originated from. Next to the address, the message:

Decode address? Y/N?

"Hell yes!" Roman hit the Y key. Cyclops ran millions of attacks in a matter of two minutes. It stopped at an IP address in Fort Lauderdale, Florida.

"Son-of-a-bitch!" Stunned, he sat back in his seat. "That muthafucka is right here under my damned nose!"

A whirlwind of new information swirled in his mind. He set the laptop in the passenger seat and stared down the long alleyway. There was still a link missing from this chain.

What's Shadow's connection to Jeanette? One minute he's fuckin' with her mind, the next he's an overprotective daddy... and this military IP address...Is he someone I know?

Breaking the endless loop of questions in his mind, he went into his jacket pocket, removed a toothpick, stuck it in his mouth and started the Yukon. "I need to get back to Jeanette and work out a plan. Mission first. I have to find a safe house for the infected kid and her grandmother, work out a strategy for getting into the lab, then deal with Shadow's ass."

Chapter Fourteen

A layer of tension washed off Roman when he entered the Homestead area and then arrived at the gated driveway to the house. The house looked very inviting. *Because of Jeanette?* "Quit trippin'," he told his subconscious and parked in the circular driveway. His stomach growled like a mountain lion.

Pushing aside thoughts of how to get into Bagley's lab, he entered the house. Walking directly to Jeanette's lab, he spotted Jeanette busy inside, typing away with a pencil in her mouth. *Damn, she's a serious workaholic. It's time for a little R&R.*

She removed the pencil from her mouth. "How did it go?"

"Good...I think I have a way to get us into Bagley's lab."

She graced him with a smile. "That's fantastic! I can't wait to see what kind of operation he's running there."

A barely touched turkey burger sat on a plate beside her keyboard, along with half a bottle of cranberry juice. He pointed at the remnants of her meal. "Is that dinner?"

She looked at the leftovers. "The other burgers are in the kitchen. I can warm one up for you."

The unfamiliar feel of butterflies tickled his stomach. "We're going out for dinner."

A smirk crossed her face. "Are you asking me to go on a date with you, Mr. Sandman?"

His necktie was suddenly too tight. He ran his finger under

his collar. "I'm just saying you have to step away to see things clearly. I'm kind of hungry and was just wondering if…"

"Yes, Roman. I would love to go to dinner with you. That little 'nap' we had worked wonders for me. I know where I've seen similar lesions and am running a series of tests to see if a salve I created a while back is the key."

So caught up in her excitement, he almost missed that she was closer to finding a cure.

"In five maybe six hours," she continued, "I'll know more. So until then, let's celebrate."

"Cool…let me change from this monkey suit, and we can get out of here."

"No, I like that suit on you." She smiled and rose from her seat. "Let me change and we can go."

Man, sweet as ghetto Kool-Aid when she wants to be. His smile matched hers. "That works for me. Now, you don't have to get too fancy, ma'am."

"Let me worry about that. Oh, and I want to drive my car, so I can see what kind of shape you left it in."

"Whatever, woman. Go get dressed."

Twenty minutes later, she emerged from her bedroom in very form-fitting black slacks, equally snug red v-neck sweater and black, sexy high heels. Her French roll hairdo was immaculate. Never had she looked so beautiful to him. "You, ah…hmmm…look real nice, Black Widow."

"Thanks. Now, where are we going?"

Struck by her loveliness, he ran to his room. "Don't move!"

Arms akimbo, she asked, "What are you up to?"

He sprinted back and stopped a few feet short of her, camera in hand. "Smile!"

"Roman, you are touched in the head!" she said, all the while posing for him like a pro model.

Once he finished the photo shoot, he helped her slip on her black sweater. "I was online while you were getting dressed and found this steakhouse called High Note Jazz Club in downtown Miami. Have you heard of it?"

"Oh yes! That place has a reputation for having the best porterhouse steaks in Florida. I hear the jazz band is also excellent. Good call, partner."

Outside, the mild temperature was perfect. No moon, but the stars seemed to shine just a little brighter. The fact that she held his hand on the way to the car put his mind on red alert. *Easy, soldier this is—* "Shut up," he said to himself. *I'm gonna enjoy this...*

On the way to the restaurant, her driving skills impressed him. They managed to steer away from "shop talk" and just enjoy the moment. Just inside the Miami city limits, she pulled into a convenience store/gas station. "You owe me a tank of gas, sir. You ran all mine out 'pimpin' my ride,' as you described it."

Shaking his head, he opened the door. "Women. Never grateful. Stay in the car."

~~~~~~

"That is one fine-assed bitch." Rashad leaned on the convenience store counter and watched as the jerk-off with her, tried to get her to stay in the car. "That's right, try to keep her to yourself, stingy bastard." He chuckled, thinking if he had something half as fine, he sure wouldn't let her ass out of his sight.

Nails tapping on the counter called his attention from the couple to his impatient customer. "What?" he snapped. "Can't you see I'm busy?" He watched the woman get out of the car anyway and approach the entrance.

"Stop drooling and ring up my chips. And get me a pack of Winston's."

He quickly rang up the old bat's order and sent her on her way, then approached Jeanette.

"Hey, baby, is that guy giving you trouble? I have connections, ya know?" So he wasn't exactly a member of the Caribbean Connection, but his cousin was and that was close enough.

When her big beautiful hazel eyes looked over those cat-eyed sunglasses, the hardness in his pants demanded attention.

"I'm fine, thank you." She returned to perusing the candy section.

"I'm Rashad. What's your name?"

"Taken!" snapped a deep voice.

Rashad spun around toward the harsh voice of the tall, muscular man. "My bad." He ran his hands over his short locs and returned to his post behind the counter where he continued to watch the couple.

There was something vaguely familiar about the jolly bald giant.

The sex-pot handed the ass-wipe a handful of Snickers.

Ass-wipe chuckled lightly and pulled her into his body, teasing, "I'm taking you to the High Note Jazz Club, and you want to ruin your appetite with candy."

"There's always room for a few sweets."

"Well, we need to hit the road to be on time for our reservation." He picked up a *Miami Herald* and placed it on the counter with their other items.

The way the giant stared down on Rashad made him nervous. There was something familiar about his face. As he rang up their order, he tried to place the man's face.

"Thanks." Ass-wipe dropped a few bucks on the counter, then took too-sexy-for-television by the hand and led her out of the convenience store.

Rashad hit himself in the forehead with the palm of his hand. "That's it. I know who that bastard is." Members of the Caribbean Connection came by at least once a month with flyers with that asshole's mug on it.

He quickly sorted through the stacks of paper in the shelving unit under the counter until he found the flyer.

"I knew it." He flicked the flyer, then phoned his cousin who was a member of the Caribbean Connection. "A nigga 'bout to get paid!"

~~~~~~

Twenty minutes later, Roman and Jeanette entered The High Note Jazz Club. The three-story club was as well known for its live jazz band as it was for its tender steak dinners. Each floor had its own jazz band and full bar. The top floor featured a renowned steak restaurant as well as a band. All four walls of the top floor were gigantic windows, providing a great view of the Miami skyline.

After finishing off their steak dinners, and a slice of strawberry cheesecake, Roman watched Jeanette sway in her seat to the band's cover version of Sade's "Smooth Operator." He stood and took her hand. "C'mon...dance with me."

"No...uh-uh! No, Roman, I don't want—"

He smiled at her as she protested with her voice, but followed with her body. "Shhhh..." He placed his arm around her waist and pulled her close. "We're supposed to be relaxing, right?"

She wrapped her arms around his neck and smiled. "Okay, Mr. Sandman."

The band seamlessly transitioned from "Smooth Operator" into Sade's "No Ordinary Love." Roman and Jeanette left all thoughts of child victims, genocide and running out of time behind. For the first time since they'd partnered up, they both let their emotional guards completely down.

While dancing next to the gigantic Christmas tree beside the stage, Roman rubbed his hand between her shoulder blades down to the small of her back. In return, she lightly thumbed the back of his neck. You couldn't have slipped a sheet of paper between the two as they danced. For a brief moment, they locked eyes and forgot they were on a mission. The tiny scar beside her eye continually drew his attention, not in a negative way, in a baiting way. He traced the scar with his finger, glad she didn't pull away.

After dancing her over to the wall-sized window, he looked into her eyes and saw the same desire he felt flowing through his body. He placed his hand behind her head and drew close to her desirable lips. For that moment, they remembered they were a man and a woman.

Fuck! Roman saw a red dot appear on her cheek. They each instantly pulled the other down to the floor, alerting Roman to the fact that Jeanette must have seen a similar target dot on him. Glass shattered from two high-powered rifle shots that came in simultaneously.

He gave her a quick inspection. "Are you okay?"

She sat up and shook glass off her arm. "Yes...you?"

Shaking glass off himself, he jumped to his feet, knowing the snipers would be on the run instead of chancing another shot. He instinctively looked for the natural place a sniper would use for such a shot as the crowd scattered in panic. He helped Jeanette to her feet and pointed to the roof of the four-story office building across the street. "I bet the shots came from over there!"

Running through the screaming crowd to their table, she shoved her short-strapped purse up on her arm and followed him out. As Roman ran through the stairwell door, she kicked off her heels in order to keep up with him. They rushed to the office building across the street and found the doors locked.

"Around back!" he yelled and sprinted down the alley toward the rear of the building.

They saw two men with rifles strapped to their backs frantically climbing down the fire escape. A man standing next to a white van yelled, "Hurry up! We gotta get the hell out of here!"

Fuck! I left my gun at the house. Pissed he'd lost complete focus, Roman removed his lucky knife out of his shin sheath.

Jeanette pulled the Glock out of her purse. After tossing the purse to the ground, she signaled with her fingers for him to cover the driver, then she nodded toward the men on the fire escape.

The sharp shooter closest to the ground on the fire escape spotted them. "Ricky! Behind you!"

The dreadlocked man on the driver's side of the van spun around as Roman ran toward him. Before the man could pull the gun out of his waistband, Roman stopped, planted his feet and threw the knife. It buried itself four inches deep in the side of the man's neck. A geyser of blood jetted out of his severed jugular vein. He hit the ground hard, dead.

Jeanette fired and hit one of the shooters in the right thigh when he jumped from the fire escape. He attempted to get his rifle off his shoulder. "Put your hands up before I blow your fucking head off!"

He bared his teeth at her and tried to hop behind the garbage dumpster. A dark patch grew on the thigh of his right pant leg. "Fuck you, bitch!"

She took aim at his left shoulder and fired. The chocolate-colored man fell against the front of the dumpster and slid to the ground.

Standing over the wounded man, she pointed the gun in his face. "What was that you called me?"

Roman heard a sickening, wet *snap* as the other shooter snapped his shinbone after falling fifteen feet to the ground off the fire escape in his haste to get away.

Roman ran over to the bloody, dead man and wrenched the knife out of his neck. He then walked over to the howling man on the ground with the compound shin fracture. His eyes grew wide as Roman kneeled next to him with the bloody knife in his hand. "Who the fuck sent you?"

He spat in Roman's face. "Ya momma!"

Roman wiped the saliva off his cheek. "Okay, I see we have to do this the hard way." He grabbed a fistful of the man's long dreads and used it to wipe the blood off his knife. "Give me that damn rifle!" After disarming the injured man and searching him for other weapons, Roman stood and stomped on his broken leg. His screams nearly drowned out the sound of police sirens in the area.

"I bet you wish you had kept that spit in your mouth, huh?" He hovered over the howling man and looked at Jeanette. "We need to move this party away from here."

"I concur, but let me get my purse first."

"Make it quick." While she ran to retrieve her purse, Roman dragged the dead man by his feet to the back of the van and opened the doors. Inside, he found a roll of duct tape, two black hoods, three shovels, two body bags and an eighty-pound bag of lime, which helps a body decompose quickly—in other words, murder equipment. *Oh, these muthafuckas were gonna do us for real!*

He slammed the dead man inside and went for the broken-legged shooter. Pissed off about the murder gear in the van, he grabbed the man by his hair and arm and dragged him to the back of the van. "So, you planned on putting us in body bags, huh?"

The man nearly blacked out in agony as Roman stood him up on his shattered leg and slammed him on the floor of the van. He picked up the roll of duct tape and taped his hands together. The shooter glared at him. "Fuck you, punk-ass nigga!"

Jeanette returned with her purse and climbed into the back of the van. "Oh, Mr. Potty-mouth, shame on you."

Roman taped his mouth closed. "He just volunteered to be questioned first." The sound of the police helicopter in the air got his attention. He looked at Jeanette. "It's gettin' hot around here. I'm gonna move us. If any of these fools act up, shoot'em."

Jeanette cocked her pistol. "No problem."

After taping the bleeding shooter's hands and feet together, Roman dragged him into the van. He then closed the rear doors, ran to the driver's door, hopped in the driver's seat, found the keys in the ignition, started the van and drove out of the alley. Ten minutes later, he pulled into the Westchester Truck Stop and parked between a pair of 48-foot trailers. He then went around back, opened the rear doors and joined in the interrogation. "What's up with this asshole?" Roman looked down at Jeanette's bleeding prisoner. "He have anything useful to say?"

"Not yet." She dug in her purse and handed Roman a small penlight. "I think he will once I give him a dose of my 'medicine'."

Roman shined the light and watched her remove a small vial of milky fluid from her purse.

Jeanette shook up the vial. "Open up their shirts for me." She slipped her gun into her purse and came out with a syringe. "I have a way to make them talk...if they're smart, that is."

Roman looked through the front windshield and watched a fire truck speed past the truck stop. "Good, 'cause time is running real short."

She took off the plastic cap and held the syringe over the bleeding shooter's face. He tried to yell through the tape covering his mouth, while thrashing about the van. "Be still before I skewer your fucking eye!" She placed the point of the needle a centimeter from his pupil. He calmed down.

She carefully opened the small vial as the wail of sirens continued to sound in the distance. "I get really pissed off when people shoot at me." She pricked the bleeder in his wounded shoulder with the needle and drew a drop of blood. "Let's see what this one knows." She held the vial above his face and dipped the bloody tip of the syringe into the milky fluid. They all watched as a wisp of horrid smelling smoke rose from the vial. "This is a poison I created that I call 'Mother's Milk.' It creates a chain reaction with human blood, causing it to literally boil. If you're lucky, you'll pass out before it cooks your heart."

Roman leaned back from the sulfur-scented vial as the bleeder's eyes followed Jeanette's every move. Roman ripped the tape off the shooter's mouth. "If I were you, I'd seriously let go of the macho shit and speak up."

After filling the syringe with "Mother's Milk," Jeanette ran the needle across the man's chest. "Who sent you after us?"

He glared at her. "Santa Claus."

Jeanette smiled at him. "You're real hardcore, aren't you?"

"You damn right, bitch! You can kill me if you want, but you'll *never* stop the Caribbean Connection...*never*!"

She continued to smile. "Too bad you won't be around to see me kill your boss." She pointed at his arm. "Could I get a little light here, Roman?"

Roman complied. "Talking shit until the end, I see."

Jeanette shoved the sniper's sleeve up, then thumped his bicep. "Oh such lovely veins. This is your last chance. Who sent you?"

"Fuck you, bitch."

"Not quite," she said.

Roman restrained the bleeder. She eased the needle into his vein and emptied the syringe. "Fuck *you*."

Within seconds, the bleeder's body began to shake violently as the poison scalded his bloodstream. The other shooter forgot about the pain in his snapped-shin and tried to scoot away from his convulsing friend.

Roman grimaced as a mix of saliva and bloody vomit erupted from the bleeder's mouth. The capillaries in his eyes burst as the poison made its way to his brain. Seconds later, the convulsing stopped; he was as dead as a box of rocks. Roman looked into the horrified eyes of broken shin. "Now, are you gonna put us through this drama again?"

He shook his head vigorously as Jeanette refilled the syringe. Roman pulled the tape off his mouth, and words flew out. He gave every name he had. Unfortunately, he didn't know who gave the order for the hit. He was assigned the mission because he was in the area. Minutes later, the spotlight beams from the police helicopter shined on the surrounding buildings.

Jeanette looked at Roman. "What are we going to do with him?"

Roman reached into her purse, removed her pistol, stuck it against the shooter's heart and pulled the trigger. "Problem solved."

They took no chances and quickly wiped their prints off the van and weapons with the black hoods, then caught a cab back to the GTO. Inside the cab, Roman looked down at her cute feet. "What happened to your shoes?"

She grinned. "I run faster in my bare feet."

Chapter Fifteen

Damn, she stayed in here all night. Roman set the coffeemaker to brew. He then quietly walked to the sofa where Jeanette slept. He secretly wished she had joined him in his bed instead of insisting on working on the cure. After finding her at two in the morning, sitting on the sofa buried in books and mumbling to herself about brown recluse spiders, he'd given up and gone to sleep.

Spotting the biochemistry book on her chest, he decided to leave it there rather than risk waking her. He just watched her for a moment, longing to rub his hand across her red silk pajama top and relish the feel of her soft breasts.

She really gave her all when she decided to do something, he realized. He smiled as she took a deep breath and turned toward the back of the sofa. He wondered if that would include lovemaking.

His smile ebbed as he quietly walked across the kitchen and out onto to the redwood deck. He couldn't believe he hadn't paid more attention to the cashier at the gas station. *I'd bet all the tea in China he's the one who snitched me out last night. Have to pay him a visit later.* The morning sun had yet to reach the deck. The crisp, winter air was refreshing.

After stretching to loosen up, he removed his T-shirt and stood in his loose-fitting, navy- blue, Golden State Warriors' basketball shorts. Last night, Jeanette had shown him she could handle herself. He bent his knees and stood in an aikido defensive stance. He wouldn't ask her to have his back against a city full of murderous gang members, yet he knew she'd be there when needed, whether he wanted her there or not.

He reached forward and disarmed his imaginary opponent, then switched to kung fu and did three rapid, shoulder-high sidekicks on a second invisible opponent. *Even for me it's a big challenge.* He did a few of his hand-to-hand blocking moves.

His smile returned. *Funny how a woman as sexy and innocent as she looks helped me kill three men last night.* A sigh of admiration escaped him. He'd never seen a more beautiful killer. *Never thought I'd want a partner, but Jeanette...glad she has my back.*

Two jump kicks. The way the wannabe CC gang member practically raped her with his eyes came to his mind. *For the rest of the mission, she doesn't leave my sight.* He briefly stopped his workout. The image of her tied in duct tape with a black hood over her face and stuffed in a body bag made his heart triple beat. *Roman, you sure are worried about that woman...Are you fallin' for the Black Widow?* He shadow-boxed the first ray of sunlight as it entered the patio. "Hell no!"

~~~~~~

The front-page news article about the shooting at the High Note Jazz Club didn't raise a red flag. Even the three bodies found in a van at the truck stop weren't cause for alarm to Lincoln. But the fact that one of the victims had died from a highly toxic "unknown" poison sounded every alarm within Lincoln. The Black Widow had crept out of her web.

The thought of someone trying to kill her puzzled him. She didn't have those types of enemies. In an attempt to make sense of the issue, he logged onto his computer and checked what the camera at the gate—the only camera Roman didn't find—had recorded for the past twenty-four hours. Halfway through the replay, he saw Jeanette and Roman leaving and returning together in her car. He checked their time of departure and return and was not surprised to see the times coincided with the killings.

His focus shifted from someone trying to kill Jeanette, to someone trying to kill Roman, which would make a lot more sense in his book. Roman had too many deadly enemies to count.

"I can't leave your bad asses alone for one night. Damn."

The Black Widow and the Sandman could take care of themselves. Preventing genocide was his main concern. He looked at the list of names Jeanette had given him and called Dominic.

"How is my granddaughter?" Dominic asked.

"Still asleep. I can't leave them on the base. I'm handing them over to my people later today." Using Vanessa as a guinea pig was the only chance they had of saving her life, if she had the illness. And Lord help him, no matter how wrong it was, he wanted her to have the illness, so Jeanette could find the cure. Sacrificing one for many was so much more difficult when that one was a part of his heart.

It reminded him of a problem one of his professors had posed to him many years ago: A train is racing down the tracks and the conductor sees a child in the way. There is no time to stop the train, but there is a second set of tracks the conductor can switch to. Unfortunately, the second set of tracks is not finished, so if the conductor switches tracks to save the child, hundreds of passengers on the train will die when the train goes over the cliff. You are the conductor. Who do you save, the child or the passengers and yourself? Now imagine the child is yours. *And people wonder why I drink.*

"I want them under your care."

"My people are the best. They'll be safe here," he said, referring to Vanessa and her grandmother. "We may have a lead." He went on to tell Dominic the three names Jeanette had given him. Dominic knew of Enrique, who had defected *from* America after selling off a fortune in real estate in order to open up his own resort almost twenty years ago. Since that time, he'd managed to turn his modest resort into a chain of the most glamorous and profitable resorts in Cuba. Overall, Enrique was scum, but no one had been able to pin anything serious on him.

After their call was complete, Lincoln hung up and dug a little deeper into Enrique's past and saw Enrique had never officially joined any gangs, but as a side enterprise, he supplied them with weapons and other hard-to-find items. His influence reached over into America as well—especially the Southeast. He dug into the government gang database and saw Enrique allegedly worked heavily with the Caribbean gangs.

One of the men killed last night was in the Caribbean Connection. He read through everything he could find on the Caribbean Connection and discovered the three sons of the leader had been killed several years earlier and a hit had been put out on their murderer.

After he opened the image file, he laughed. "I'll be damned." He chuckled, looking at the unmistakable drawing of Roman. *I take a little vacation, and look what your bad ass got yourself into.* A few years ago, Lincoln had taken a much-needed vacation. It coincided with the time Roman had conducted the hit on the CC gang leader's sons.

Lincoln left instructions with Lolita, Vanessa's grandmother, then headed into Miami to do a little recon. He didn't want the police going after his two bad-assed kids. As he cruised down the highway, he decided to call Jeanette.

~~~~~~

Without his knowledge, Jeanette quietly watched the shirtless Roman go through his exercise ritual. What looked like a scar from a gunshot wound was near the right shoulder blade of his muscular back. Her mind wandered to last night when he'd fingered the scar by her eye—how she wished she could trace his scars. No doubt about it, Roman was an incredibly handsome and intelligent man. A tad bit arrogant, but she actually liked his confidence. And that he'd actually rid the world of that slime last night in front of her showed he trusted her. Last night, they'd truly become partners. Partners—she'd also like to become partners with him in another way, a much more carnal way, but they couldn't. They had bonded in a way most wouldn't understand, in a way she didn't quite understand. In a way that had her worried about their time together and what it could lead to.

And the events of last night...They were just about to share a kiss when a red dot of reality homed in on his lovely golden-honey cheek. At the same time she pulled him to the ground, she'd felt him pulling her to the ground. Thus, she knew he'd seen something similar on her. The "who" who had ordered the hit was a given—the Caribbean Connection. The "why" was still a question. Though she'd wanted to know why, she wouldn't ask. *He'll let me know when he's ready.*

In a mood to get her own blood to pumping, she adjusted her favorite black bandana, moved the coffee table out of the way and began mirroring Roman. His back was turned to her as he jump kicked twice. Set aside him being the most handsome man she'd ever seen, and he was—*still perfect,* she grumbled internally. She also admired his intelligence and skill, but the real killer was how he made her feel free: free to laugh, free to cry, free to be Jeanette instead of just the Black Widow or Professor Meany.

He began a kung fu form she was familiar with. She dropped her robe onto the couch and began performing the same movements.

He turned and their eyes locked. Neither moved for a few seconds, then he slowly began a combination where he mixed different types of martial arts. As she mirrored his movements, she noticed what appeared to be the other side of the scar near his shoulder blade on the front of his upper right shoulder and some sort of long scar from his left clavicle to the bottom of his breastbone. Just as he'd traced the scar beside her eye, she wanted to trace his scars, but not with a finger. She'd like to kiss them and make them better.

Roman opened the patio doors, picked up his T-shirt and wiped his face as he entered the living room. The blue shorts he wore didn't cover enough. No, she needed him to wear something that covered him from head to toe in several thick layers.

He stood before her: hot, sweaty and entirely too sexy. She gazed into his deep, penetrating brown eyes and saw a drive that matched hers, a desire that matched hers, and a determination that matched hers. They had so much in common, it was scary. She subconsciously licked her lips and slowly ran her index finger over the ridge of the scar from his clavicle to the bottom of his breastbone.

He inhaled slightly, but allowed her to continue exploring.

"How did this happen?"

"A North Korean drug lord." He tossed his T-shirt to the floor, then weaved his fingers through her hair. "We had a small dispute he tried to settle with a machete."

The guards of a North Korean drug lord, who had a fetish for kidnapping, raping, and killing young South Korean girls, had chased him through a dense portion of jungle near the border to South Korea as Roman tried to reach the helicopter waiting to fly him out. Jeanette could tell he was reliving the experience as he repeated it. He was so vivid; it was as if she were with him, experiencing it.

Bleeding from the deep machete slash across his chest and suffering from fatigue, Roman saw what looked like the helicopter on the ground between the trees. He staggered forward only to find the wreckage of a plane that appeared to have been there for at least a year. He crawled inside the damaged fuselage and listened as footsteps in the brush got closer. Inside the wreckage, he saw three skeletons wearing tattered and disintegrating clothing. Judging from their clothes and the plane's proximity to the China border, he assumed they had been opium smugglers.

He'd had no time to pack his rifle after killing the drug lord.

To make matters worse, he'd lost his pistol while running from his pursuers. Desperate to find something to defend himself with, he patted down the nearest skeleton but found nothing. Then he felt the eyes of the angry pursuer on him and heard him yell at him in Korean. As Roman rolled over to confront him, the guard smiled when he saw Roman was unarmed. He lowered his assault rifle and removed the machete strapped to his back, fully intending to carve him up.

Roman's hand landed on the leg of another of the skeletons and brushed against bone and steel. As the guard turned to yell for the others, Roman looked to his right and saw the handle of a throwing knife hanging out of its sheath, dangling from the skeleton's shinbone. Without a second thought, he grabbed the knife and threw it into the left eye of the guard. He then pounced on him, pulled the bloody knife out of the screaming man's eye and slit his throat. He then took the guard's AK-47 rifle and easily dispatched the other three guards.

Returning to the present, Roman positioned Jeanette's head to look up at him, then lowered his lips to hers. The sex pheromones in the aroma of his sweat tickled her G-spot.

Eyes closed in anticipation, her satellite phone rang and shattered her chance as easily as the snipers' bullets had shattered the windows in the club last night. This had to be a sign they weren't meant to be.

Familiar with the ring tone, she snatched the phone off the coffee table. "What, Papa?" She hit the speaker button, then set the phone on the coffee table.

Roman grasped her free hand and sat on the sofa, then pulled her to sit on the floor between his legs with her back toward him. Glad their contact hadn't stopped, she relaxed and allowed him to massage the stress knots from her neck and shoulders.

"Jeanette, are you okay?" Papa asked.

"Of course I am. Why wouldn't I be?"

"Come off it. I saw the reports of the shooting at the High Note Jazz Club and know about the three dead men. The death of one of the men had Black Widow written all over it."

"Oh, so because I'm in town at the time of a shooting, I must be involved, right?"

"In this instance, yes."

"Whatever." To give Roman's magic hands better access, she leaned her head to the left. Sleeping on the couch and in chairs had caused a serious kink in her neck—but not half as bad as the pain in the neck Papa could be. A bolt of pleasure went from her neck to her toes as Roman's hands eradicated a ball of tension behind her neck.

"Where's Roman?"

"I don't know. Being shot at played into his paranoid tendencies." Roman pulled her hair.

"When someone is actually after you, you're not paranoid. I know you're used to working alone, but you have a partner now. Keep an eye out for him."

Roman stopped massaging and stared at the phone.

"He can take care of himself."

"Without a doubt he can, but you're a distraction."

"I'm not a distraction," she said with more confidence than she felt. The fact that Roman had forgotten his gun at home proved without a doubt that he was distracted. His gun was like his knife, camera and heart. He never left home without them.

"I'm just saying to keep your eyes open."

"Don't worry, I've got his back." She faced Roman, who looked completely perplexed. "I've got his back," she repeated.

"Good. Give me an update."

She reported that preliminary testing indicated the salve she'd created would stop necrosis—death of the tissue—caused by the bite of a brown recluse spider. The lesions on the victims resembled those caused by the brown recluse spider. Her intention was to adjust the salve for the M.I., mysterious illness, but to do that she needed additional samples. It would be difficult without additional samples from the victims, or better yet, a symptomatic victim or two. Creating a version of the salve that could be injected into the bloodstream had its own complications—if it could be done.

"Oh Lord, don't get me started on the possible side effects."

"Well, the side effect of this illness is an agonizing death."

"I know. I know. I still have to be careful. I don't want to prolong a death in an attempt to 'save' a life."

"I'm sure you'll work it out. Colin's in Cuba."

"What!" A million and one conflicting thoughts went through her mind. If her father had been called in, then her brothers wouldn't be far behind. "Why is Daddy in Cuba?"

"They're blaming America for the 'plague,' as their media is deeming it. He's heading off a war."

"Yeah, that makes sense. If anyone can talk sense into the Cubans, he can. What about Tweetle-Dee and Tweetle-Dum?"

Papa chuckled. "He hasn't called your brothers in on this, yet. I just wanted to give you the heads-up."

Bitter her family would move the world to help strangers, but hadn't lifted a finger to find her, she said, "Look, I need to get back to work."

"Sounds like you're making good progress. Keep it up." He disconnected.

"So who the hell is your daddy that he can make the Cubans get in step?"

"The one and only Colin Mason," she bit out. "His daughter has been missing for years, yet this head official of the CIA can't find her. Even though she stayed in the same field as her majors in college *and* she only changed her name from Mason to Stone."

Roman laughed, breaking the tension that had filled the room.

"What?" she asked. His laugh was contagious, but she refused to give in. "What?"

"That mean-assed bastard is your daddy?" He shook his head. "Now I fully understand your disposition, Professor Meany."

Gut-wrenching laughter erupted from her. "You are soooooo wrong for that."

~~~~~~

Roman slipped on his pants after yet another cold shower. *Damn, she's got old man Mason's eyes.* He shook his head and chuckled. *They look a hell of a lot sexier on her.* Tired of thinking of Jeanette, he forced his mind back to work. He needed a safe house for the child and her grandmother. He picked up the phone.

Jorge answered on the second ring. "*Hola!*"

In Spanish, Roman said, "Jorge, I need a big favor."

"Big favors are my business."

"I need a safe house in the Miami area to house a little girl and her grandmother for a few days, maybe a week or so. And I need it yesterday."

"Hmmmmmm...strange request, *amigo.* Is this your kid?"

"Hell no!" He tied his red-and-blue-striped power tie. "The last thing I want in this world is a kid. Just say these two people are very important to the job I'm working on."

"How old is the kid? Boy or girl?"

"Girl, five years old. Why do you ask?"

"Jorge wants to make sure the accommodations will suit his tenants."

"I'm touched. Can you hook me up?"

"Well..."

Roman paused before he put on his shoes. *Here it comes. I wonder who in his family needs what and how much it's gonna cost me?* "Well, what, Jorge? What do you have in mind?"

"I do have a place in mind that may work. It's about ten miles south of Miami in Pinecrest. I have a house there I rent out to a few of my, ahhh, ladies of the evening."

Great, a freakin' whorehouse. "Is the place decent, Jorge? I can't have a kid running around finding condoms and naked people in the house."

"You hurt, Jorge! You know me better than that, *amigo*!"

Roman placed his hand over his eyes. "Okay, sorry to doubt you. So what's the deal?"

"Unfortunately, the tenants of my home have been 'requested' to spend a little time in the local correctional facility for nothing more than providing a public service."

"I understand that, but what is it gonna take to make this happen?"

"Well...without my tenants being able to pay the rent..."

"How much is the rent, Jorge? I don't have time to waste. I need this to happen now, and no one is to know."

"Hmmm, for you, I make it five hundred a day, including utilities. And I know how you work. Of course no one knows."

"Five hundred a day! Are you—" He caught himself, knowing that was his only option at the moment. He couldn't risk putting them in a hotel; too many loose ends to tie up. "Okay. When can we do this?"

"Anytime you like! My caretaker will meet you there. I'll e-mail you the address in a minute. As always, good doing business with you!"

"Yeah, you too, Jorge. I'll send your rent money the usual fashion. Later."

Shadow, I'm sendin' your ass an updated bill as soon as I get the e-mail from Jorge. Time for you to dig deeper in your pockets.

He paused and chewed his bottom lip as his mind went back to the phone call to Jeanette from Shadow. *Sounded like he really gave a damn about my safety with that keep-an-eye-on-him crap he told Jeanette.* "This has got to be the strangest damn job I have ever been on." Curiosity about Shadow's true motives ate at him as he gnawed on a fresh toothpick.

Chapter Sixteen

Roman parked the goat a block away from the Royal Investments' building, got out, briefcase in hand and straightened his navy-blue Armani suit. "Ready?"

"Sure." Jeanette closed her door, then opened a side pouch on her Italian leather briefcase, took out a small tube of lotion and walked over to him. "Hold out your hands."

"No thanks, you've already poisoned me once."

"You *really* need to let that go." She set down her briefcase and grabbed his hand. She couldn't wait to see what his reaction would be to the lotion. "This won't hurt, much." Smiling, she squeezed a small amount of the creamy substance into his palm, then nudged the sleeves of her chocolate Chanel pantsuit up and placed a dab of lotion on her palm.

"That outfit looks good on you. You look like a chocolate-covered, caramel candy bar." He set his briefcase down.

She winked at him. "I'm a whole lot sweeter, though."

He brought his hand to his nose and sniffed. "Oil? What the hell is this?" he asked as if asking the date. To anyone watching the surveillance monitors, it would appear they were having a normal conversation.

"Just a little something I cooked up called liquid latex." She massaged the lotion into her hands and forearms. "Once it dries, you don't have to worry about leaving fingerprints for twenty-four hours."

"Really?" He rubbed in the lotion. "That's sweet! You have an extra case or two you can leave with me?" He bounced his eyebrows.

She laughed. "Maybe for Christmas."

They continued along the zinnia-lined walk and through the revolving doors. *Good, just as Roman said, they only have one guard on.* They signed in at the security desk. As they had rehearsed, Roman signed them both *out* as Jeanette distracted the guard by pretending she'd lost a contact lens.

"Oh, I found it, thank you, Peter," she said to the seventy-something Asian guard after Roman signaled he was done. "You were a big help!" She pretended to stow the lens away.

"Very good, Ms. Noble." The blushing guard barely looked at their fake IDs as he handed them back. "Remember, we close in about an hour."

"No problem." Roman picked up his briefcase off the floor. "We'll be out by the time the rest of the employees leave."

Before going back to his newspaper, the guard smiled. "Sounds good." He blatantly admired Jeanette's form. "I doubt you guys will walk off with the building. Just put in the time for me when you sign out, will ya? Just in case I'm out doing my rounds."

That was easy. Too bad Roman didn't know the guard would ask us to sign ourselves out. We could have skipped the dumb contact lens skit. "Thanks again, Peter."

They continued to the elevator bank. Once on the thirteenth floor, the elevator doors opened. To Jeanette's surprise, the scientist she was most interested in, Dr. Wyatt, was waiting to board. His eyes roamed over her appreciatively. She offered a coy smile, stepped off the elevator behind Roman and continued along the hallway. Nearing a corner, she glanced over her shoulder at the doctor. He was watching her, as she knew he would be. She nodded, then rounded the corner.

"What are you trying to do, get him to follow us?" Roman increased his stride.

"Is that jealousy I detect in your tone, Mr. Tate?"
"Of course not."
"Sure it isn't."
"We have to take the stairs the rest of the way."

On the fourteenth floor, after Roman used the "bloodhound" and got them inside, she slipped into the janitorial closet unnoticed, followed by Roman. She reached into her trouser pocket, took out a small flashlight, and trained the light on Roman, who was stiff and pale. Beads of sweat had gathered on his brow.

"Are you okay?" she whispered. "There's not enough room in here for you to be getting sick." She reached for the three-rung ladder she'd seen propped against the wall. From the way Roman avoided closed spaces, she knew the cramped closet had to be hell for him. "Here you go, have a seat."

"I'm good. I just zoned out a second." He remained standing.

She heard a man and woman's voices and footsteps outside the door and tensed up. After the voices and footsteps faded, Jeanette shined the light along the wall again, in hopes of finding a second seat. "I'm glad you're polite," she took a second short ladder off the rack on the wall, "but please sit. I have a seat also now." She doused the light.

"I'm good. Come on, let's get out of here and go to the supply closet. The janitors will be up here soon. I don't need them walking in on us."

"Good idea."

They moved on to a cramped supply room. She was still amazed at how Roman was able to hack into the system. She sat on top of two cases of printer paper while Roman inserted the virus that would shut down the automated-motion-detecting alarms on the fourteenth floor from 8 P.M. until midnight, which would allow plenty of time for them to snoop around as the janitors cleaned up. She smiled. *He is much too good at this.* "Come on, you can sit on one of these cases of paper next to me. I don't bite—very hard."

A few seconds passed before he said, "Oh, really?"

"Yes," she said softly, sweetly, seductively in answer to the promise in his voice. She heard him take his seat.

"If we didn't need to remain quiet, I'd..."

"What?" she purred, to take his mind off the closed space.

She felt his fingers gently caress her face.

"We'd better change the subject before we end up butt naked in this supply room," he said, barely over a whisper.

"I think you're right."

"I still can't believe your daddy is mean-ass Mason. Damn, his hits are legendary."

"Yeah? Well, I'd rather talk about being naked than my family at this moment, if you don't mind."

"He's not coming for you...I'm sorry about that."

She rested her hand on his leg. "Thanks, Roman."

The two remained in comfortable silence for the next few hours. No more conversation was necessary. They both fully understood.

"It's time to explore," Roman said.

Jeanette used the flashlight to find her briefcase.

He switched his watch to stopwatch mode. "We'll have to do this right the first time. We only have forty seconds between the time the camera views this hall and rotates away."

She nodded and watched him remove a small, square mirror on a telescopic rod out of his briefcase. He then stood in the recessed area in front of the supply room's door and eased the mirror out an inch at a time until he had a clear view of the camera.

She slipped off her expensive chocolate pumps and "lotioned" her feet. "I move faster barefoot."

He clicked the stopwatch. "Let's move!"

The camera at the end of the corridor slowly turned away from them. They scurried down the hall. At Dr. Wyatt's office door, Roman fingered the access entry box. "This invisible glove stuff of yours better work."

She watched over his shoulder while he plugged the copper-plated end of his code finder into the slot under the keypad. He checked his watch—twenty-eight seconds left. They watched as the red digital numbers blurred by on the display. With only eleven seconds to spare, the numbers stopped on 7843, then they heard a *click*.

"*Voila...*" He opened the door. "Ladies first."

"Why thank you, kind sir." She curtsied slightly then entered.

Two hours later, she'd viewed just about every file on Dr. Wyatt's computer and Roman had searched through Wyatt's written logs and also taken a jaunt to the lab and snooped around.

"He's not our mad scientist," she mumbled.

He thumbed through the file in his hand. "I don't know. According to this file, they're into human/animal gene splicing, cloning, designer mutants and a bunch of other insane shit." He placed the folder back into the black file cabinet and looked at her. "Let's move out."

They ensured they left the office as they'd found it. She didn't even take a piece of the butterscotch candy from the bowl on the desk. Then, using the same camera timing technique, they returned to their hiding place in the supply room seconds before the janitors were due to clean their floor.

Jeanette flicked on the light and moved the cases of paper out of the way. "I don't know about you, but I'm grabbing a spot on the floor." There wasn't much of a spot to grab in the small room. She took a sheet of plastic out of her briefcase and covered the clean, dry floor, then sat against the cool wall.

"Hit the light for me before the camera returns." She barely got it out before the light was out. The chances of a guard actually watching the monitor that was in the hallway were slim and none, but she didn't want to chance it. "You can share my plastic if you'd like," she teased.

He lowered himself beside her and leaned against the wall. He remained silent and his leg trembled slightly against hers. To take his mind off the close confines and because she wanted to know, she asked, "What happened to you? I mean, I was raised by a broken-hearted man and have two jerks for brothers. This is the only life I've ever known. But you were raised by a loving mother."

A few silent minutes passed. "I guess I'm proof that having a loving home isn't a guarantee against raising psychopaths."

She punched him on the shoulder. "Who you calling psychopath?"

"Definitely not you, Black Widow." He relaxed into a laugh. "I really don't know the reason, but witnessing my cousin's murder…"

"Oh, my God! What happened?"

She heard the plastic crinkle when he adjusted himself against the wall. "When I was seven, my thirteen-year-old cousin Terrell and I got harassed by some gang members while on our way to Terrell's baseball practice. They had been trying to get him to join them for a long time, but he always turned them down."

The thin sliver of light coming from under the door allowed her to see the foot of his extended leg rock slowly from side-to-side. "Did they ask you to join also?"

"No…I guess I was too young." He drew in a long, slow breath. "After Terrell turned them down again, the leader hit Terrell in the chest. Terrell hit him in the mouth, then they chased us down the street, toward the freeway."

She remained silent and watched his foot move faster.

"I tried to keep up with Terrell as we ran across the freeway overpass, but he was a faster runner than me…" It sounded as if he weren't breathing. He paused. "I saw Terrell look back and yell for me to hurry up. When he saw they were almost on me, he came back for me and put me behind him."

During another pause, in the dim light, she watched him repeatedly grip and release material on his trouser leg.

"You don't have to continue, Roman…"

He took another deep breath. "Terrell fought them off the best he could, but there were too many of them. When I tried to help, one of them pushed me down. They beat him until he was barely conscious…He tried to tell me to run, but I wanted to help him." He cleared his throat. "They, uhhh...they picked him up and tossed him over the railing, down onto the freeway...I heard the sound of the cars hitting him...he died instantly."

She placed her hand to her mouth. "Oh, Jesus, no! Oh, Roman..."

"I ran. I ran faster than I ever had in my life. After realizing I was a witness, they chased me. I ran into the neighborhood pawnshop owned by this old Jewish man named Mr. Kramer. Once he saw the other boys chasing me, he let me behind the counter. The boys attempted to come behind the counter to get me. He reached into the umbrella stand behind him and retrieved his pistol-grip, pump shotgun. He pointed it at the boys and told them to get out. They froze, then turned and ran. I never saw them again. After witnessing the power of a weapon, I begged Mr. Kramer to teach me about guns. He said no, but allowed me to hang out at his shop and help him out. I guess this was his way of keeping me out of trouble. Finally, after a year of begging, he gave in. First, he taught me how to *respect* a weapon, and then how to *use* a weapon." He quietly coughed and cleared his throat again. "I paid for his burial five years ago...his plot is not too far from our family plot."

"I'm so sorry, Roman."

"It's been years, but...I can't believe I'm telling you all of this. I've never told anyone."

"Believe me, I'm not used to opening up the way I have either."

~~~~~~

Where the hell did all that sap come from? Roman mentally washed the memory of Terrell's death from his mind, but the memory never washed away completely. *Next thing you know, I'll be tellin' her about the crush I had on my first-grade teacher, Miss Edwards, and how I cried when she got married.*

"Can you shine the light on my watch?" His fingers shook a little as he set his watch alarm to vibrate at eleven-thirty. "We might as well get some rest. We have a good hunk of time to kill before the janitors leave and we can get out of here."

"There's not a whole lot of room in here for comfort." They shared a laugh as they both removed their pistols at the same time and placed them within arm's reach. "Great minds, huh?"

He took off his jacket and folded it into a makeshift pillow. *Bet you're flexible enough to ride me damn good in this cramped room.* He grinned and lay back on his Armani pillow. "Try not to snore too loud, Black Widow."

"Whatever..." She took off her earrings and put them in her jacket pocket. "Keep that up and you'll wake up wrapped in a web."

Since the room was only about four-feet wide and seven-feet long, his claustrophobic demons made their presence felt in a big way. He felt his heart accelerating in his chest as the blackness smothered him. *Pretend you're standing in a wide open field...nothing around but grass and a starless night sky...Breathe...*

He tried to slow his rapid heartbeat, but his mind went back fifteen years ago to when he was in sniper school, out on maneuvers in the snow-covered Rocky Mountains in Denver. He, along with three other "Devil Dogs" of the 3rd Marine Division, got separated from the instructors in the middle of nowhere.

"Mario, are you sure we should try and climb that ridge? There's a whole lot of snow on that ledge up there." Roman pointed at the long, wide sheet of snow, resting on the slightly sloping outcrop of rock.

Mario looked at the wall of snow sitting on the ledge. "Quit being a pussy! That snow ain't gonna move."

Jerome, the know-it-all of the threesome, looked at the other two young snipers. "Yeah, Roman! It's too fuckin' cold out here to be cryin' about a little snow. Man up!"

Roman watched in horror as Jerome un-holstered his pistol and pointed it in the air and yelled, "I'm going to show your scary ass it's okay."

"Don't fire that gun, you stupid fuck!" His warning was too late. Roman watched the pistol flash twice as Jerome fired in the air. To Roman, the world went silent for a nanosecond. After that, he watched as a jagged crack worked its way across the thick panel of snow over their heads. As they tried to run in the knee-deep snow, they felt the rumble of the avalanche cascading down on them.

A moment later, silence and darkness covered Roman. The crushing weight of the ten feet of snow that covered him made it hard to breathe. Fortunately, he was able to move his left arm. He was also lucky to have a small air pocket in front of his face.

"Hellllllllllllllllllllllllllllllp! Help me! Somebody help!"

His cries reverberated in his ears in the cold darkness. In his panic, he tried to dig into the snow with his left hand. More snow fell down on him, further shrinking his air pocket. *Think, think. What do I do?* None of the classroom training he'd undertaken over the past few weeks prepared him for this freezing hell.

Two hours later—which felt like nine-million years to Roman—as his oxygen slowly dissipated, he no longer felt the frozen tears on his face. All he wanted to do was go to sleep. His lungs burned for air when he stopped struggling and closed his eyes.

Ten minutes later, led by the homing beacon in Roman's backpack, the rescue party dug out three dead men. After three jolts from the defibrillator to Roman's chest, Dr. LaBeau of the Search and Rescue team found a weak pulse and helicoptered him to the base hospital.

Roman was the only one of the three who survived.

Just as a massive panic attack prompted by the memory headed his way, he felt Jeanette lay her head on his chest. Again, her touch shifted his mind from the memories and terror of being buried alive to much more pleasant thoughts.

"Don't get it twisted. I just need a pillow."

He offered no response. The feel of her warm body killed his tension. The aroma of her kiwi-scented hair replaced the smell of the printer toner in the tiny room. Whether intentional or not, she effectively calmed him better than any technique *ever* had. *Damn, woman...could sure get used to havin' this kinda comfort.* His subconscious took over as he took a chance and let his arm wrap around her. "Don't get it twisted. I just need someplace to rest my arm."

~~~~~~

Exhausted, Jeanette fell into a sleep filled with nightmares.

As she walked, Jeanette saw children burning up with fever and in agony from open sores on their bodies. She reached down to comfort a small boy, and the scene change. She approached a child's gravesite. A shadowy figure kicked dirt off his grave. Once she reached the grave, the shadowy figure faced her and transformed into her father. He reminded her that she had no ties to anything, anyone.

Suddenly, she was running behind a gang of boys chasing a teen and a boy who appeared to be around seven. Realizing this was Roman and his cousin, she increased her pace. She had to save Terrell. She had to save Roman from entering the life she'd been condemned to. The boys lifted Terrell to toss him over the railing. She reached to snatch Terrell and had him in her grasp when a black cat jumped out of nowhere and clawed at her face.

Terrified, Jeanette woke up. The only thing that stopped her from crying out was Roman's hand over her mouth.

He rocked her. "It's all right, baby." He lowered his hand from her mouth and continued to rock her. More than anything, she wanted to push him away, but the security of being in his arms felt too good. Slowly, her heart rate returned to normal.

"What happened to you?" he whispered. "What are the nightmares about?" He ran his hand along her back.

That he had opened up to her about Terrell meant a lot to her. More than she cared to admit. She fingered the thin scar along her hairline and explained where they had come from and told him about her frequent mad-cat dreams. By the time she finished telling him about this latest nightmare, she knew he'd think she was a nut. She didn't know what had come over her. Ever since she'd met him, it seemed as if she'd had "running mouth" disease. Yes, they were partners, but this was taking it a little bit too far, making it too personal. She wanted him to know everything about her and she wanted to know everything about him too much. This was moving beyond a partnership into something...something she wasn't ready to even consider.

"We've got to get the antidote soon, Roman. Things are worse in Cuba than we're being told."

"We'll find it."

"I want to look at Doctor Wyatt's personal files. Coming here was a bad idea. I doubt he'd keep this type of thing lying around his office."

"But his home? Come on, Jeanette, that's a stretch. If anything, they have a secret lab out in no-man's-land."

"Then maybe I can find out where that lab is if we snoop around his home."

"We? That's a no go. I'll do it."

"Roman, we can't keep breaking into places. I'm sure I can get him to allow me into his house."

"No."

"You're being difficult. You know I'm right. Plus, I want to speak with the doctor, see what his frame of mind is, if he's psychologically capable of creating this toxin. I might be able to get him to slip up and give me insight into the toxin."

"I don't like this."

"It'll work. You'll see. I already have a plan in mind."

The alarm on his watch vibrated. "Fine, but first, let's get the hell out of here. I'm past tired of this closet."

The instant he led her into the maintenance room, he opened his briefcase and removed his laptop and a three-foot length of

Ethernet cable.

"What are you doing now?"

"I'm going to remote into the alarm system, shut off the cameras, so we can take the stairs to the lobby and get the hell out."

She watched him boot up and plug into the jack inside the Third Eye Security panel. "How much time will we have to get out?"

"I'm setting the system reset mode for twenty minutes." He looked down and saw she had put her shoes back on. "You might want to take those off, so we can make it down these fourteen flights of stairs and get out in time."

Hands on her hips, she asked, "Why didn't you do this from the get-go?"

He grinned and put away his laptop. "If I had, I wouldn't have gotten the chance to feel you up in the supply room."

"Freak."

"Yes, I am that. But really, instead of getting into a bunch of technical B.S. about the complexities of this security system, with janitors going in and out, just suffice it to say things got complicated."

Pulling off her shoes, she smirked at him. "Whatever you say, freaky man."

~~~~~~

Mid-afternoon...

Ready to continue his conquest, Roman purchased a phlebotomy kit, latex gloves and a box of surgical masks from Mercy Medical Supplies, then drove the Yukon to a nearby Winn-Dixie grocery store. The radio station played a jazz version of "Jingle Bells." *Thank God Christmas will be over soon.* He parked, went into the Winn Dixie and exited the store with a Styrofoam chest full of ice. *Gotta make this quick. Don't like havin' to leave Jeanette alone at the house, but I can't risk bringin' her this close to the CC gang's turf.*

Following the directions given to him by Jorge, Roman drove into Pinecrest. At number three Chestnut court, he parked the Yukon. A six-foot high redwood fence surrounded the white, two-story house. Trees and shrubs, along with the fence, made it virtually impossible to see the front of the house. With the phlebotomy kit and bag of other supplies in hand, he managed to press the intercom button at the gate and waited. A small camera lens mounted next to the speaker stared at him.

"Hello?" a deep Spanish voice said.

"It's Roman."

"Hold on."

The weight of the pistols in the dual holster underneath his leather jacket was comforting. Two minutes later, a rough-looking Cuban with a long scar across his cheek pulled the gate open. He looked around, stepped aside to let Roman in, then closed the gate. "I need to pat you down."

Roman pulled out one of his silencer-equipped pistols and had it pointed in the man's face before the man could even get close to pulling his own gun. "You still need to pat me down?"

The man broke out in a huge smile and slowly moved his hand away from his waist. "Ah, so you *are* Roman. Jorge told me to expect you to be packing a gun or two. And not to let anyone else enter the house. Welcome! I am Mateo."

Before Roman put away his weapon and offered his hand, he made sure no one else had a gun pointed at him. "Good to meet you, Mateo." He glanced around the spacious yard. "Nice spot."

"Yeah, I like it. I'm the caretaker." He began walking up the cement walkway. "Come. Your guests are waiting."

Surprisingly, the interior of the five-bedroom home was spotless. Although the furnishings were plain, the house had a comfortable feel. He looked around the living room. "Where are they?"

Mateo pointed over Roman's shoulder. "In the kitchen."

Crossing the hardwood floor, he entered the canary-yellow

kitchen. *Awww damn.* He watched a cute, tired-looking little girl nibbling on a graham cracker. Seated across from her was a regal-looking older woman with a worried look on her face. Roman set the phlebotomy kit on the Formica kitchen counter.

"Hi, ma'am. I'm Roman."

The plump woman rose from her seat and grasped Roman's hands in both of hers. "I'm so glad to meet you. My name is Lolita. I was told you're going to make my grandbaby better."

Thanks a lot, Shadow. He managed a smile and buttoned up his jacket to conceal his weapons. "I'll do all I can." He looked at the child. "What's her name?"

"Vanessa."

Roman walked over and kneeled down next to Vanessa's chair. *My God...the blotches on her face and arms...* "How are you doing, Vanessa?"

She wiped crumbs off the front of her Dora the Explorer pajamas. "I'm hot and itchy. Are you...my doctor?"

The look of hope and fatigue in her big brown eyes was almost too much for him to bear. "No, sweetheart. I'm the doctor's assistant. Do you like going to see the doctor?"

"Yes, sometimes...I get a toy for...being a good...girl."

"Is it hard for you to breathe, honey?"

"Sometimes...it makes my inside hurt...to breathe."

Roman traded glances with Lolita. "Vanessa, I need to talk to your grandmother for a minute. Will you be okay until we get back?"

"Yes." She nodded her head slowly. "Can I have...something ...to drink?"

Hiding his gun under his shirt, Mateo walked over to the refrigerator. "I got it, Roman." He took out a carton of orange juice. "You two go talk."

Vanessa frowned. "No...I want...some Kool-Aid."

Lolita shook her head. "You should be tired of drinking that junk. That's all you kids drink at home."

Out on the front porch, Roman faced Lolita and started a conversation in Spanish. "I have to draw blood from your granddaughter. How do you think she'll take it?"

Lolita tucked her shoulder-length hair behind her ear. "She's a good girl. Strong girl. She has had so many shots over the past few weeks, I doubt she will even notice your needle."

Roman read the dread in Lolita's voice. *What happened to the days of just findin' some no-good son-of-a-bitch and putting a bullet in him?* "Okay...well, let's go back inside and get this done."

"What does she have?" Mateo asked.

"I'm not sure."

"Can I watch TV while you give me a shot, mister?" Vanessa asked.

Roman put on blue latex gloves. "You sure can, sweetheart. But call me Roman." He smiled, picked her up and looked at Mateo. "Can you turn on the TV in the living room?

"I'll get her *Dora the Explorer* DVD," Lolita said.

Haven't done this since MASH training. Roman prepared a butterfly needle to insert into her small arm. After swabbing down the crook of her arm, he carefully inserted the needle. Vanessa barely moved as a stream of her blood filled the first vial.

Roman drew a third vial of blood and put all of the vials into the ice chest. "Almost done, thanks for being such a great patient, Vanessa. I have a special Band-Aid for you." He displayed the bandage, Vanna White style.

A huge smile grew on her face. "Wow! Granny! He has...a Dora...Band-Aid!"

After putting the Band-Aid on her arm and removing his gloves, he prepared to leave. Vanessa could barely take her eyes off the bandage. She smiled, got up and hugged him around his leg. "I love you...Doctor Roman! I'm going to...tell Santa...to give you...a...good present! You and...Papa Linc! He is...nice to...me...like you."

An ice pick of emotion jabbed him in the heart as he bent over and hugged her back. "I love you too, hon." He went into the blood-collecting kit, pulled out a sandwich bag containing a grayish gel and kneeled next to Vanessa. *This salve Jeanette made has to work.* "I'm going to put some of this on your sores, okay? It will make them feel better so you can feel better."

"All right...they burn and...itch...sometimes."

After he applied a thin layer on the sores, he closed the bag and cleansed his hands with handi-wipes. He squatted down to her. "Try not to let it rub off, okay?"

"I won't." She kissed him on the cheek.

"Thanks, sweetheart!" Before he got swept up any further, he rubbed her head, grabbed the ice chest and looked at Lolita. "I'll be in touch." He handed her the rest of the salve. "Put a light coat of this on her sores twice a day."

She wiped a tear from the corner of her eye. "Okay...thank you."

He smiled at Vanessa and pulled a dollar bill out his pocket. "Do you wanna see something cool?"

"Yes!"

He transformed the bill into an origami heart ring and slipped it on her finger. "That's for being my best patient!"

The joy in her eyes matched the smile on her thin face. "Wow, Granny!" She wiggled her fingers. "Look!"

Back on the road, he couldn't believe the emotional roller coaster this mission had him on. *You know goddamned well you're not supposed to get emotionally involved. But what if she doesn't make it to see Christmas?*

Just off the freeway, two miles from the house, he spotted a Funland toy store. He cut across three lanes of traffic, evoking a concert of angry horns as he exited the freeway. "Fuck you!" He drove into the Funland parking lot, shut down the engine and rested his head on his hands, on the steering wheel.

Seeing the pictures of the dead children was one thing, but now, having spent time with Vanessa, the vise-like grip he usually had on his emotions was slowly loosening. He sat motionless as the cold reality of death repeatedly pimp-slapped the face of his soul. For the first time since being buried alive, he knocked on the door of the Lord.

Hey, God, it's me...I know it's been a while, but I need to ask you for a favor. Even though I know I definitely won't be welcomed into your kingdom because of my boatload of sins, I beg you to spare Vanessa. She's too young, too sweet, and too innocent to deserve a hellish punishment like this. Let me take the person responsible for this fuckin' plague to hell with me. Amen.

Taking a deep breath, he stepped out and went into the toy store. Half-an-hour later, he, along with three clerks, rolled four shopping carts full of toys to the Yukon. "Thanks for the help, fellas." *I'll be damned if I let that baby miss this Christmas.*

He returned to Pinecrest and surprised Mateo. "Did you come back to get your blood- collecting equipment?"

Roman walked to the back of the Yukon and opened the tailgate. "No. I have a special delivery."

Mateo's eyes widened and he grinned. "You're going to make someone very happy, my friend."

"She deserves it." Roman and Mateo carried in all they could on the first trip. "Where is she?"

"In the backyard, looking at the flowers with Lolita."

"Good. Let's just stack all the stuff here in the living room and surprise her."

"Sounds good." Mateo pushed a button on a Dora doll and it spoke to him. "She's going to really, *really* like this one!"

They piled box after box of *Dora the Explorer* toys, board games, DVDs, video games, books, pajamas, shoes, and other Christmas gifts on the living room floor. He then quickly set up the small, fully decorated, tabletop Christmas tree.

Mateo turned to go get Vanessa.

Roman placed his arm on his shoulder and stopped him. "No, wait until I leave."

Puzzled, Mateo said, "But don't you want to be here when she sees all this stuff?"

Roman adjusted the collar of his jacket. "No...just tell her Santa made a special trip to see her while no one was around because she's been such a good girl. You know, something like that."

A look of respect and admiration crossed Mateo's hard facial features. He offered Roman his hand. "You do God's work, my friend. Happy holidays, *amigo*."

Chapter Seventeen

Colin's patience had worn past thin, and now he had to be trapped in a rinky-dink conference room with several Cuban officials and be reamed out about all the shit America had done to Cuba over the years. Granted, the majority of the items on the list were true, but at this moment there was more important territory to cover.

While he finished allowing them to vent, his mind wandered to Jeanette. She'd been on his mind a lot of late. Not that she wasn't always there, but this seemed more urgent. Like she was going through some turmoil and needed him, her daddy.

Then there was Lincoln. His ass had been able to get in contact with her too quickly. He loved Lincoln and knew he would never do anything to hurt Jeanette, but something was up. Knowing Lincoln, he'd bet he'd already had Jeanette on the case. Hell yeah, he'd had her on the case already. But why hadn't Lincoln just said as much?

With his opportunist ass, he's probably used her in the past. I wouldn't be shocked if she's one of his operatives, but does she know who he is to her? He doubted if any of Lincoln's operatives knew his identity.

Tired of wasting time they didn't have, Colin stood and used his size and powerful voice to take command of the room. "It's time to get to business. Hell yes, the U.S. has done some fucked-up shit in past times, but this isn't one of them. This contaminant won't give a damn about Cubans, Americans or anybody else. It's time to set our differences aside and work together."

Sure he had everyone's undivided attention, he continued, "I have a lead on a few terrorist organizations in the U.S. that may be behind this attack."

"So you agree Americans are behind the plague that is ravaging Cuba?" General Guzman stated more than asked.

Colin glared at the little general who had more medals on his chest than the law allowed. "I have no idea. But I have found viable suspects. Would you like to continue wasting time playing politics or find those responsible?"

"If you know you have terrorists in your country, you should neutralize them, no matter who their target is."

"We have laws we must follow. Plus, if we target the wrong organizations, word will leak and the real organization will go further underground. In the meantime, we have our best scientists working on an antidote."

General Guzman smacked the table. "America has been harboring terrorist organizations for years, and the world needs to be shown. We won't stand by while you blatantly harbor terrorists. It's time for Cuba to strike back." He pushed away from the table.

"Are you threatening us?"

"No, sir. Not threatening. Just stating fact. Cuba will not stand by while you allow your home-bred terrorists to kill our children. Seventy-two hours. You have seventy-two hours to put a stop to this terrorist attack before we fight back!"

~~~~~~

Inside the Nut House coffee shop, Jeanette sipped the citrus goodness of her Earl Grey tea as tanned, last minute Christmas shoppers ventured in and out loaded with packages. Dr. Wyatt would show any minute, and she was ready for him. She watched as the petite Asian server with frosted hair, whom the good doctor reportedly had the hots for, cleared the booth across the room. Her green eye contacts added to her exotic look. Neither petite nor Asian, Jeanette wasn't worried. She could hold her own. The heat she had seen in Dr. Wyatt's eyes had shown her he had a versatile palate.

Heat. The sun had nothing on the heat between her and Roman.

~~~~~~

Running late, Roman checked his watch when he entered the coffee house. He had stayed behind and covertly watched Vanessa's reaction to her Christmas surprise through a gap in the living room window curtains. The moment had been priceless. He groaned, thinking he could never let anyone know his soft spot for children, especially Shadow. But the jerk had been correct. Jeanette couldn't know Vanessa was within her reach. She'd lose too much focus.

Walking past Jeanette as if he didn't know or care to know her, he went to the far corner of the coffee house, reserved for patrons who wanted to take advantage of the Nut House's free wireless Internet connection. He opened his laptop and logged on. From his seat, he had a clear view of Jeanette on the far side of the room as she sipped on her beverage. *All right, Dr. Wyatt, it's past eight. Where are you?* According to the credit card records Roman had hacked, the doctor always stopped at the Nut House on Saturday nights between seven and ten for a cup of over-priced yuppie coffee.

He logged into his home server and went through his information on the doctor's home security system. He didn't like Jeanette's plan. It felt too much like he was tagging along. He looked up and caught a glimpse of Jeanette. Even across the room, her eyes seemed to glow. After her eyes locked onto his, he found it hard to look away. He closed his eyes, sighed, then turned his attention back to his screen. *In another life, maybe we could—* He pulled his Oakland Raiders cap down on his forehead. *No time for that shit, solider...*

He scanned his computer files on the doctor's "Safe Tec" alarm system. *How much you wanna bet Safe Tec hasn't changed the administrator password on their monitoring system lately?*

He'd go along with Jeanette's plan for now, but he still wanted to create a plan B. He went to his file of alarm companies he'd successfully hacked into and logged into Safe Tec's customer database, then began scanning Safe Tec's customer files. *Nice security setup, Doc.*

Roman jotted down the alarm code on the same piece of paper with the doctor's address. The code was actually a series: an eight-digit alphanumeric combination, followed by a five-second wait, then a different eight-digit alpha combination, followed by a three-second wait, then finished with a five-digit numeric combination. If you didn't have the perfect timing, you wouldn't gain access.

He glanced up as a forty-ish man resembling Sting, the former lead singer of The Police, entered the coffee house.

~~~~~~

Jeanette was reading an article on the three R's of DNA: Replication, Repair, and Recombination and trying to ignore Roman when Wyatt entered and glanced around.

The doctor hesitated, but neared her table on his way to place his order. Jeanette looked up. Her eyes grew wide as if she were shocked, then with a smooth, sexy smile and slight nod of the head, she said, "Hello, Doctor Wyatt."

"What a pleasant surprise." He slid into the chair opposite her. "And you would be?"

"Doctor Angelique Deveraux. Pleased to finally meet you."

He tapped the scientific journal. "Do you even know what you're reading," he teased.

"I could probably teach you a thing or two."

"I'll bet you could."

~~~~~~

Roman pulled his cap further down and bent over his laptop as the doctor exchanged words with Jeanette and placed his hand on top of hers.

Why did I agree to her lame plan? Roman logged off, packed up his laptop and left the coffee house.

Wyatt and Jeanette seemed so engrossed in conversation, Roman didn't think they noticed him leave. *Be in and out of his place before she's finished playin' kissy face with him.*

After he got into the Yukon and placed the laptop on the passenger seat, he spotted a black Mercedes with the license plate: DNA MAN. *Just the kind of arrogant asshole who would have a plate like that.* Roman started the Yukon's engine and began the twenty-five-minute drive to Dr. Wilson Wyatt's house.

A few minutes into Roman's drive, his phone rang. "Just the person I need to talk to. This little project is going way over budget. You're gonna have to come up with a lot more cash."

"Well, that's new. This is the first time I can remember you actually *wanting* to talk to me," Shadow replied. "Usually, I get a nice death threat."

"I need to make sure I get paid first. I can't collect from a dead man." He placed a fresh toothpick in his mouth. "What do you want, anyway?"

"I wanted to get an update on Vanessa. How's she holding up? Were you able to get the blood samples for Jeanette?"

"She's doing good...a real little sweetheart."

"Yeah...you should see how funny she is when she's healthy. I tell you, she can melt your heart."

Roman grinned at the memory of how her little face had lit up when she saw the mound of toys he bought for her. "Tell me about it. She didn't even fuss when I drew the blood from her."

Shadow sighed. "We have got to save her, Roman. I don't give a shit who we have to take down or how much it costs. Is there anything else you need?"

This softer, caring Shadow was hard for Roman to hate. "Nah...so far so good. I'll add my out-of-pocket expenses at the end of the operation."

"You know I've got you covered."

At the point where Roman usually hung up after promising Shadow a horrible death, there was a long silence. The importance of the mission overrode their personal issues. "Cool. I'll be in touch."

What's going on with Shadow? He took the exit for Dr. Wyatt's house. *It's not like he hasn't sent me on missions involvin' kids before.* Then he remembered how Shadow had asked Jeanette to look out for Roman. *Are you tryin' to earn your way into Heaven, Shadow?*

Upon arrival at Wyatt's house, he parked in the visitors' parking lot of the Del Sol Golf Club, which was across the street from Dr. Wyatt's exclusive home. *Must be paying you very well, DNA MAN.*

Roman visually assessed the large, Spanish-style home. The high, ivy-covered walls made it difficult to see more than the red, Spanish-tile roof. The palm trees around the perimeter aided in hiding the home. A wide wrought iron gate with the initials "W.W." blocked the entrance to the circular driveway. A similar gate with an alarm code pad, stood at the foot of the walkway, which led to the front door.

Roman took his penlight and black leather gloves out of the glove compartment. *Wish I had some of Jeanette's liquid latex stuff.* He got out the Yukon, made sure he was alone, then walked up to the doctor's gate.

"Let's see how the doctor is livin'." He punched in the alarm code and the green light on the keypad blinked on. He quickly walked up the sandstone walkway and picked the lock on the massive double doors. The four-bedroom house reeked of excess. It looked more like a museum than a home.

He stepped inside, closed the door and listened. The only sound came from the faint hum of the air conditioning system. He whistled and placed his hand on his lucky knife in the side pocket of his cargo shorts. *No dogs, I hope.* Hearing nothing, he turned on his penlight, walked down the marbled entryway and crossed the large living room. He shined the light on the walls.

"Oh shit!" A very good replica of Dali's painting, *Persistence of Memory*, hung on the wall next to replicas of Da Vinci's *Mona Lisa*, Cezanne's *Apples and Oranges* and Fragonard's, *The Reader* as well as additional replicas. A few statuettes sat on shelves scattered around the house. Being a semi art buff, he wished he had more time to inspect Dr. Wyatt's collection.

After trying a few doors, he found one that was locked. *You live alone and you have something so secret you don't even want your maid to see it?* He used the lock-picking tool on his key ring and opened the door. "Nice den." Besides the large metal and glass desk, ergonomic chair and top-of-the-line Apple Computer and gigantic flat-screen monitor, five file cabinets occupied the room. Before searching the room, he explored the rest of the house. Three of the four bedrooms—all on the second floor—looked as though they'd never been used. The ultra-modern kitchen with its large pantry, like a lot of the house, appeared to have been seldom used.

He went back into the den and began his search for clues on the contaminant. He opened the sliding doors on the bookcase behind the doctor's desk. "Goddamn, Doc!" Rows and rows of Asian pornography DVDs filled the shelves. "You are one freaky bastard."

~~~~~~

After hours, the professor had quizzed Jeanette on just about every article in the journal and seemed genuinely impressed that she could answer any question he threw her way. They'd even debated findings on a controversial study on gene splicing. The entire time he flirted and accidentally touched her several times until he finally rested his hand on her thigh and caressed it.

"One last question, why were you in my office?"

"What makes you think I was in your office?"

"Honeysuckle." He combed her hair with his fingers. "Yesterday your hair smelled of honeysuckle. A faint honeysuckle scent greeted me as I entered my office this morning. Did you find what you were looking for?"

"I'm afraid not," she said innocently, ready to kick herself. She'd used the honeysuckle because Roman seemed to like it better than the kiwi. *This man is messing in my game.* "And you should be sure to close your door completely in the evening. Anyone could just walk in there."

He chuckled lightly. "I'll be more careful. Are you ready?"

"For what?"

He pulled his leather wallet from his back Dockers pocket, then tossed thirty bucks onto the table to pay their tab. "A little privacy." He held his hand out for her. "My place is nearby. We can discuss freely what you were looking for."

She placed her hand into his and rose. "Aren't you worried about taking a strange woman into your home?"

"Aren't you worried about being alone with a strange man?" His hand at the small of her back, he gently led her toward his Mercedes.

"Do I need to worry?" she purred.

He backed her against the car. "Smart, beautiful and sexy...a perfect combination."

Jeanette entered the car, wondering where Roman was.

~~~~~~

After searching the doctor's files for nearly an hour, and finding nothing linking him to the Cuban crisis, Roman walked out the den and stretched. He froze in mid-yawn as a pair of headlights pulled into the driveway. "Fuck! I forgot to reset the alarm!" He ran down the hall to the doorway and quickly used the keypad to set the alarm system. He went back to the den, made sure to put everything back the way he found it, then hid in the pantry.

~~~~~~

Jeanette fiddled in her purse yet listened to the tones as Dr. Wyatt entered his code to open the wrought iron gate in front of his home. She knew Roman wouldn't have any difficulty breaching Wyatt's perimeter security, but getting Roman into the house would be a different story. They'd already underestimated the doctor. She kicked herself internally, again, for the honeysuckle scent she'd left behind. No, she knew his private alarm system would have a surprise or two Roman wouldn't expect. Hopefully, the good doctor would have his mind on things other than setting the alarm.

To her dismay, as soon as the front door closed, Wyatt engaged the alarm system. Disgusted but not shocked, she set her purse on the entry table. Before she could turn, Wyatt wrapped his arms around her and pulled her close.

"I almost followed you off the elevator yesterday," he said quietly.

She turned in his arms. "You don't say."

"Who was that man you were with?"

"My brother, Alexander Deveraux." She backed away. "Do you want to continue discussing my family tree?"

"I forgot dangerous. Smart, beautiful, sexy and dangerous."

You have no idea.

He held his hand out for her.

She didn't know if he was crazy or if he thought because he was a man his strength gave him the upper hand. She surely didn't like how he so easily accepted her breaking into his office and was now coming on to her. He was too intelligent to be so easily swayed by the prospect of sex. This felt like a setup. As if he were stalling her.

She allowed him to lead her across the marble floor into the den.

He walked to the bar. "Nothing like this has ever happened to me."

"Like what?" She quickly slipped a capsule under her tongue.

"Day after day my life has been equations and formulas. Then this beautiful woman and her *brother* break into my office." He poured two glasses of Scotch. "But it doesn't stop there. I just happen to run into this same beautiful woman at my favorite coffee house and her *brother* walks out. Then to top it all off she knows biochemistry inside and out."

"Interesting," she said from the sofa.

"Very." He rounded the bar and joined her.

"So why did you bring me here?"

He handed her one of the glasses of Scotch and took a drink from the other. "At first I didn't know what to think. But the more we spoke, the more I realized you really are a scientist. Whatever you're looking for is about the science, not harming me."

"So, again, why did you bring me here?" She set her glass of Scotch on the coffee table.

"That's purely carnal, my dear." He leaned over and gently nibbled along her bottom lip. This was not the first time she'd allowed a man to kiss her for the sake of the job, but this was the first time she felt queasy about it. Like she was cheating...on Roman. *Oh shit! Get that man out of your head!* She bit down on the capsule. Butterscotch flavor filled her mouth.

His tongue slipped into her mouth and laved every drop of the sweetness. He moaned his pleasure and deepened the kiss. His hands roamed over her body, and she felt violated. She pulled away and sipped her Scotch, then swished it around her mouth to rinse out the potion.

"Butterscotch is my favorite candy," he said.

She turned her head away from him and gently spit the now-drugged Scotch back into the glass, then set the glass on the table. The minute amount that would soak into her system would make her drowsy, but she'd still be able to function.

He dropped his Scotch to the floor, then pulled her close and suckled along her neck. She wrapped her arms around him and leaned her head back to give him better access, and counted the seconds until the drug took effect.

Thirty-seven long seconds later, he shook his head. "What have you done to me?" The doctor's eyes began to slowly close.

"Don't fight it. You're just about to take a little nap."

Once Dr. Wyatt drifted off to sleep, she resituated him fully on the couch and set a throw pillow under his head.

"Is that how all your dates end?"

Heart pounding, she spun around. "What the hell are you doing?"

Roman emerged from the dark kitchen. "Don't shoot, Black Widow." He leaned against the kitchen doorjamb and crossed his arms. "If you weren't so caught up in playing kiss-and-lick with Wyatt, maybe you might've heard me coming."

"You scare me like that again, I'll do a hell of a lot worse to you than shoot your ass, that's for damn sure." She drew in a few non-too-calming breaths and released her grip on the Glock in her purse.

He walked over and cupped her face. "You okay?"

"I'm fine." She broke out of his hands. She couldn't look him in the eyes. She felt ashamed and angry with herself for feeling ashamed. They weren't a couple. This was a job. She had no reason to feel guilty or ashamed.

She pushed him away. "Since you're already in, I take it you did the snooping. Did you find anything?"

"He's not the one."

While the ride from the coffeehouse to Wyatt's had been ordinary, the ride to Homestead with Roman was a pain in the ass. Roman kept staring at her instead of keeping his eye on the road. When she complained, he stopped staring, but then proceeded to rag on her about her behavior with the doctor.

She already felt sleazy and didn't need or appreciate his input. He sounded like some sort of jealous lover, instead of her mission partner. If this was anything close to what having a real relationship with a man would be like, she wanted no part of it. Her life was already too complicated.

Chapter Eighteen

"Get away from the door, Roman." Arms folded over her chest, Jeanette stared at the heavy oak front door that rattled under Roman's force. "I'm going for the lovely Glock you gave me. I advise you step away from the door." The banging stopped.

"This is stupid, Jeanette. Let me in."

Stupid indeed. Technically, they weren't even a couple. He had no right to be mad. She could have slept with Wyatt, and Roman would have had no say-so. He wasn't the boss of her, she fumed.

"For what? So you can try to make me feel bad for doing my damn job? Do you actually think I wanted that dirty old man pawing all over me? You think I enjoyed it? Fuck you, Roman. I have lives to save. You won't make me feel like shit for doing what I had to. You can sleep your ass out on the porch, in the garage or wherever the hell you want, except in here."

"Shit."

She heard him lean against the opposite side of the door.

"I'm sorry. I'm really sorry I tripped like that. I was completely out of line."

She remained silent. The sincerity in his voice caused her anger to ebb.

"I'll sleep out here tonight."

How could she stay mad at him when he kept saying and

doing the right things—even when she didn't know what the right things were? And why did he have to be so perfect for her. This was not a good time for her to be falling for anyone. Disgusted, she opened the door and invited him in.

He gently ran his hand along her cheek. "I'm sorry, Jeanette." He rested his forehead on hers and his hands on her hips. "It's just..."

"Just what?"

After a long pause, he drew in and released a deep breath. "I'm an asshole. Always have been." He pulled away. "I must get it from my dead daddy, because my mom is the sweetest person you'll ever meet."

Sorry he broke contact, yet glad he broke contact, she forced her feet to head toward the couch. Neither was ready for whatever was happening between them. "From what I've heard, my mother was almost as bad as my father."

"So you got a double-dose of mean," he teased.

"Don't start." She kicked off her shoes, sat cross-legged on the couch and picked up a scientific journal off the coffee table. "Dr. Wyatt was a complete bust."

"Yeah, but the salve you created might work. I sent the sample you gave me out to my folks. I should be hearing from them soon and..."

"And what? Even if the salve works, creating an injection will take time we don't have. And I need more samples and symptomatic patients." Feeling overwhelmed, she got up and carried the journal she was browsing toward her lab.

"That reminds me. I have something for you." He rushed out.

"I hope it's a cure," she mumbled, sat in her wheeled chair and read about a conference being held in Miami.

Moments later, he re-entered the house and walked into her lab, carrying a cooler and putting the Cheshire cat from *Alice in Wonderland* to shame with his smile.

"Oh, my God." She couldn't believe what she'd just read. "The Dr. Javier Escondido will be at the Better Living Through Chemistry Conference! I've *got* to go." She smacked the journal's two-page spread about the conference. "He's brilliant. I need to ask him to help create the injection."

Smile nowhere to be found, Roman stopped short of her desk. "How do you know he isn't involved? With him being so 'brilliant' and all." He set the cooler in front of her.

Jealous, Roman was actually jealous, which she found cute—this time.

Stone-faced, he said, "I thought you might wanna see what's in here."

"What is it, your leftover lunch?" She opened the cooler and squealed with delight at the sight of three tubes of blood. "Oh—my—GOD! Is this what I think it is?"

"If you think it's blood from a patient with your mysterious illness, yes."

"You're the greatest bodyguard *ever*!" She hugged Roman. "Thank you, thank you, *thank you*." She released him. "Is this really infected blood? How did you get these?"

"Yes it is, and it's a secret." He took the journal from her and began reading the article about the Better Living Through Chemistry Conference. "So you think this Escondido dude can help?"

"I could find the cure, but if he's able to help, the time would be cut drastically. He's a pillar of the community. I've only heard good things about him. I can go to the conference and meet him—"

Roman shook his head. "Hell no. We're not playing that Dr. Wyatt game again. We'll attend the convention together."

"I don't need you tagging along, and I wasn't going to pull a Dr. Wyatt. I need to speak with the man to see if he will help. I don't want you there scaring him half to death."

Roman grumbled something under his breath. "I need to look up more information on Escondido and this convention. I'll make arrangements for *us* to attend. With such short notice, the convention hotel will most likely be booked, so if we can't get connecting suites, we'll have to share a room. Better yet, we'll just share a room and pretend we're married."

"I don't need a bodyguard."

Arms folded over his chest, he said, "Either we do this my way, or you don't go."

"But Roman..."

"No butts. What if Wyatt is there? I'm sure this event will draw his nasty ass."

Granted, she hadn't thought about Wyatt, she'd been too focused on Escondido, but she still could handle herself. She had for years. Then again, it felt good to have someone who actually cared about her well-being.

"You make me sick." Ready for a long night in the lab, she closed the cooler.

"Yeah, I know." He closed the door on the way out.

~~~~~~

What the hell am I doing? Roman took off his cap and threw it across the room. *I'm not focusing like I'm supposed to. Constantly havin' Jeanette on my mind is bad enough, but now Vanessa...*

He took off his twin holsters, put them on the bed and got his laptop. Visions of Jeanette kissing Dr. Wyatt replayed over and over in his mind. Not since boot camp had he had such a hard time concentrating. *Why should I give a shit about who she kisses?* Grimacing, he carried his laptop out to the redwood deck and sat in one of the wooden patio chairs. *Whatever, I have work to do.*

The cool night air helped clear his head—a little. In the quiet of the backyard, he managed to find the information on the conference he needed. Minutes later, he had "Glenn and Monica Noble" registered. He sat back and put his fist to his mouth. A small smile touched his lips. "Yes...I'm gonna do it." A short time later, he had booked them a room at the new Ritz Carlton, half-a-mile from the convention center. "I think we both need a break from this seclusion. Fuck tiptoeing around those Caribbean Connection punks."

His good mood dropped a notch after he used Google maps

and checked the surrounding area. While he watched the image on his screen, he exhaled deeply. *Fate is a cold bitch.* Eight blocks from the convention center stood the Diamond Dust Casino.

The image of Daphne's face momentarily dominated his thoughts until the shadow of a moth dancing around the light over the sliding glass doors distracted him. *Need to find out what Daphne's role is in Heavenly Associates. I know damn well she's not the mastermind. Besides being rich and shrewd as hell, her only other asset is her ass.*

Memories of the three lust-filled days she'd spent with him in Prague two years ago awakened his snake. "Damn, that was one hell of a birthday." The combination of his deep-down desire for Jeanette and the memory of the hot, hot sex and lust he'd shared with Daphne caused him to get up and adjust his crotch lump. *Need something to wear to the conference.*

Online, he searched for clothing stores in the area and settled for the Orange Blossom Mall in Key Biscayne, a predominately affluent area. *Good...not many gang members hang out there.* He shut down his laptop. *Time for me to check in on the genius.*

The sight that greeted him once back inside was pure torture. Jeanette, wearing nothing but an oversized, Wonder Woman T-shirt, had moved her work area from the lab to a pillow-laden area on the living room floor in front of the TV, which was off.

Unable to take his eyes off her, he stood in the doorway between the kitchen and living room, paralyzed with want. *Get a grip and stop staring at her, fool...there's way too much at stake to let your dick overtake your good sense...*

"Roman, would you please pass me the extra pillows off the chair next to you?"

"Hmmm?" His paralysis finally broke. Every drop of semen in his sack begged for release at the sight of her. The oversized T-shirt fit her like the sexiest of miniskirts. It ended at the middle of her long, well-toned, cinnamon-brown thighs. Her calves and perfectly arched feet deserved to be caressed and massaged. Her marimba plum-colored toenails deserved to be kissed and sucked. The way her hair framed her face and rested on her shoulders caused a rush of heat through his every cell. "Uhhh...what you say?"

"I said," she tossed three pillows off the sofa to the floor and slid the coffee table to the side, "can you pass me those two pillows off the chair next to you?"

"Here you go." He tossed them and watched her shirt crawl a couple inches up her thighs as she caught them.

"Thanks." She continued to look at him. "What's wrong with you?"

"Nothing," he lied. "I'm a little hungry."

She gave him an innocent and alluring look, then she eased down on the bed of pillows and pulled the hem of her shirt down. "Are you sure that's what's on your mind?"

He dropped his eyes from hers. "Yeah...Hey, I need something to wear to the conference. We're going clothes shopping tomorrow."

"No can do, bud. I have work to do."

"I'm sorry, you heard me wrong. *We* are going clothes shopping tomorrow. You can't stay on this twenty-four/seven, Jeanette. Take a break and you'll get more done."

She sighed and acquiesced. "Fine. I'm sure I won't get any peace unless I go." She opened a thick book on genetic mutation. "I guess I do need something nice and conservative to wear for the convention."

Slightly miffed that she was more focused on her damn books than on him, he had to remind himself this was strictly business not a seduction rendezvous. His frustration helped him find his focus. "I'm going out for a little while...maybe go scout out the area around the convention center. You want me to bring you back something to eat?"

She waved him off without looking at him. "No, I'm fine. Go do what you have to do."

Before his swelling became too noticeable, he took one last look at her sexy bare legs and went to his room. *Time to strap up.* He put his holsters back on under his leather jacket, checked his pistols, then went outside. Before he left, he did a perimeter check.

On his way to Miami, the Christmas decorations didn't agitate him as much. *Bet Vanessa would love to see all these decorated houses.*

Entering the Miami city limits, his juices began flowing. "I think I'll go see if that punk who snitched me out is working at the convenience store tonight."

A short time later, he entered the gas station and saw a middle-aged, white woman working the counter. *You lucked out, homeboy.* He purchased a black Florida Marlins baseball cap, slapped it on his bald head and left.

"Let's see what the nightlife is like." He peered out the tinted windows. The city crawled with CC members. *Damn, these assholes have damn near completely taken over the streets.* At the convention center, he drove around and made note of all the alleyways, street closures, freeway entrances, one-way streets and other useful getaway information.

At a stop light, an explosion of color reflected off the hood of his truck. He looked to his left and saw the brightly colored marquee of the Diamond Dust Casino. On impulse, he pulled to the curb across from the casino and watched the steady stream of gamblers, hookers and other degenerates go in and out.

Moments later, a shiny black, top-of-the-line Rolls Royce pulled up in front of the casino. "No...that can't be her." He watched a burly black man step out the driver's door and open the rear door. Daphne got out. She was just as lovely as she had been two years ago—the last time they'd seen each other.

Against his better judgment, he pulled around the corner and parked in an alley near the casino. *Horniness is a muthafucka.* Seeing the area clear of gang members, he removed his pistols and put them in the console. "Can't walk around the casino wearin' these." He exited the truck, pulled his cap down over his brow and walked into the casino.

Casually strolling through the casino, he spotted Daphne and her bodyguard talking to a tall, slim pit boss at a blackjack table across the room. Her eyes got big as hubcaps at the sight of her former lover. She immediately walked away from the pit boss, mid-sentence, bodyguard in tow.

"I guess she sees me." He grinned when she spun around, gave the bodyguard a stern look and a few words.

The bodyguard reluctantly backed away and walked off. She hurried over to Roman and wrapped her arms around him. "I don't believe it! How long have you been in town? Why the hell didn't you call me?"

"I just got in. Thought I would surprise you." The feel of her breasts beneath her white fur coat made his heart pound with recognition. The familiar, light scent of her designer perfume bought back sexy memories.

Her eyes reflected his feelings. "You know I love surprises." The smile on her face was almost as brilliant as the ten-carat diamond necklace around her neck. She took his hand. "Let's get out of here."

Roman looked at Daphne's full lips coated in strawberry lipstick and recalled how well she used them. The bodyguard kept a close eye on them from fifty feet away.

Pulling Roman across the room, she stopped at the bodyguard. "Carl, I'll call you if I need you. I'll be entertaining for a little while. If you run into Juan, just tell him I'm still meeting with my associates on the yacht, and I gave you the night off."

Roman could tell by the look in Carl's eyes that he knew his boss was up to no good. "Okay, Ms. Peres." He looked at Roman. "Call me if you need me."

"Okay, bye, Carl." She looked at Roman. "Wait right here. I need to go get something. Don't you disappear on me."

"I'll be by the roulette wheel."

Minutes later, he watched her approach, carrying a large black leather purse. They then went outside the casino and got into the Rolls. "Where are we going, woman?"

She picked up the intercom phone. "Jameson, take us to the Grand Beach hotel."

"Nice spot, I hear."

Her jacket opened up, giving him a nice glimpse of the green, low-cut Christmas elf outfit she said she'd worn to her staff Christmas party earlier that evening. Her two womanly decorations were prominently displayed.

"You can tell me what you think of it in the morning." She then placed her tongue deeply in his mouth.

After booking a room on the fifth floor, she molested Roman all the way up the elevator, making him briefly forget about his claustrophobia. She fondled his junk while kissing his neck.

"Mmmmm, damn, woman..."

Inside the room, she wasted no time. "God, I have waited so long to have you again." She took a few "toys" out of her purse and put them on the nightstand and slowly undressed for him. She stepped out of her red, crotch-less panties.

Wish I could watch Jeanette do this.

Since he was preheated from his longing for Jeanette, he scooped her up and carried her to the bed. After he made love to her—instead of *fucking* her the way she was used to when they hooked up—they lay in the bed in silence.

This was wrong, wrong, wrong! He got out of the bed. "I'm taking a shower."

She rolled over and glared at him. "What happened to you? That's the first time you wouldn't use my cuffs or ball-gag on me. And I *know* I heard you say some other bitch's name when you came."

He glanced at the fur-lined handcuffs and red ball-gag on the nightstand. *Did I really slip up and call Jeanette's name? She's probably lyin', but how the hell did it come to this anyway?* "No...I said your name." He picked his clothes up off the floor. "As far as your using your 'toys' goes, sometimes it's good to mix things up, try something different."

She sat up and continued to glare at him. "That's bullshit, Roman! Even though your dick was inside me, your mind was *definitely* someplace else."

He took a deep breath and picked up his brown Lugz boots.

"What the hell should it matter? We are no more than fuck-buddies anyhow. You knew from the beginning all we ever had was a bedroom relationship...and ain't shit changed since then but the date."

"Take your shower and get the fuck out of my room." She rolled over and pulled the covers up to her neck. "Our business is done for the night, maybe forever..."

"Forever sounds more like it to me."

Chapter Nineteen

"You need me to get you a cab, sir?" the gray-haired doorman asked.

Roman shook his head and put a fresh toothpick in his mouth. "No, thanks. I think I'll walk." Guilt covered him like a suit of lead armor. *I'm not in love with Jeanette!*

Halfway back to the Yukon, he saw a pair of hooded young men loitering at the entrance to an alley. Both had blond-tipped dreadlocks. He tensed up. *This night is just gettin' better and better.*

"Yo, money, you got a cigarette?" the man in the Boston Celtics hoodie asked.

"No, don't smoke."

"You got the time?" the man in the Miami Dolphins hoodie asked.

Roman paused and checked his watch. "Eleven-thirty."

The Boston Celtics fan stepped in front of him and pointed what looked like a gun concealed in his jacket pocket. "You know what this is." He mean-mugged Roman. "Run me ya cash, wallet, *and* that watch!"

His buddy pulled a switchblade out of his pocket and shoved Roman into the alley. "You heard the man! Break ya self!"

Roman calmly looked from one of the black faces to the other. *This is not happening tonight.* He lowered his head and exhaled loudly. "Fellas, I'm a trained assassin. You can either let me go about my business, or I can kill you both. I'll give you ten seconds to make up your minds."

They looked at each other and laughed. The Boston fan pulled his gun out far enough for Roman to see clearly. "Nigga, you crazy as fuck! I don't wanna hear none of that fantasy shit! *I got the gun, muthafucka! I'm* runnin' this shit!"

"...seven, six, five..."

The switchblade holder laughed. "Yo, this cat is actually countin' you down! Cap his monkey ass and let's go."

"...three, two, one." Roman spit out his toothpick. "What's it gonna be, fellas?"

The Boston fan grabbed Roman's left wrist. "Gimme that watch, bitch!"

In the space of a few seconds, Roman grabbed the gunman's wrist—knocking the pistol to the ground—and snapped it. In another quick move, he kicked the knife out of the hand of the other robber before shattering the knee of the gunman with a well-placed kick.

"Ooooooowwwwww fuuuuuuuuckkkk! You broke my shit! You broke my shiiiitttt!"

Roman's hat flew off when he elbowed him in the face, knocking him out cold.

The knifer's face filled with surprise after getting a good look at Roman. He snapped out of his shock, ran over and picked up the gun before Roman could get to it. "Hey, you look like that nigga Marquis told us to watch out for!"

Bang!

"Ahhh, shit!" Roman yelled as a bullet grazed his left bicep. He looked away from his wound just in time to see the man take off running after the cheap pistol jammed on him.

Roman took off. "Fuck! I can't let that fool get to his boys." They ran down Bayshore Drive, though alleyways, dodged traffic and curious pedestrians. Roman briefly lost the man as he narrowly dodged a fire truck.

Where the fuck did he go? He looked at his left hand, saw a drop of blood roll off his wrist, and fall to the sidewalk. He spotted the man running in the alley across the street. He ran across the hood of a limo and chased after the man as the angry limo driver yelled at him. Roman saw his quarry approaching a ten-foot-high chain-link fence.

Gotta stop him now! Damn, if only I hadn't put my guns in the Yukon.

Ten feet behind the man as he hopped on the fence, Roman stopped, grabbed his knife and threw it. It struck the thief deep in the right ass cheek.

"Fuck!" The man dropped off the fence and grabbed his ass. He reached to pull the knife out of his ass with one hand and waved the gun with the other. "Back the fuck off me!" He fired, but the cheap pistol jammed again.

Roman continued his approach. "You picked a *real* bad night to fuck with me." He kicked the gun out the robber's hand. "I have had just about enough of you Caribbean Connection muthafuckas." He grabbed the man's head and twisted. The would-be robber crumpled to the ground with a broken neck. Roman rolled him over, removed his knife and wiped it on the dead man's jacket.

Great, three long blocks out of my way and bleedin' like a stuck pig. He grabbed the dead man's long white T-shirt, cut off a piece and folded it into a thick square. He then quickly removed the shoestring from one of the dead man's shoes and used his teeth and hand to tie the cloth over his wound. "I'm sure that's nice and sterile," he groaned.

A block from the hotel, he walked past an all-night Chinese food restaurant. *She might be hungry by now.* He ordered shrimp egg foo young and chicken chow mein to go. He was amazed, but not surprised that the Asian man who took his order didn't even blink when he saw his bloody bandage. *No way would I want to live in this insane city.*

~~~~~~

Roman entered the house a little after three. He wouldn't

admit it to himself, but he couldn't wait to see Jeanette's face. On the floor, in the middle of a pile of books, papers, and pencils, she lay sound asleep. He crept over and watched her for a moment. *Has she been crying?* He looked around and saw no signs she had eaten anything.

He put the food on the coffee table, went to the bathroom, and inspected his wound. *Not as bad as I thought.* His lead suit of guilt gained a thousand pounds as he retrieved the first-aid kit from under the sink and patched up his four-inch wound. *She's been working on an antidote all night while I was out chasing a piece of ass.* For the first time ever, he felt guilty for having sex with a beautiful woman.

He did not like it.

In her bedroom, he turned the covers down, went back and gently picked her up. The dried tears on her face crushed his heart. *Damn, Jeanette...I'm so sorry, baby...*She stirred in her sleep, then sighed and rested her head on his shoulder, mumbling something about the innocent victims. He tucked her in the bed and turned to go sleep in the chair.

"Roman...please lie with me..."

Her soft plea shocked him. "Okay," he whispered and reluctantly undressed down to his boxers. He didn't want to bring his guilt into the bed with them, but didn't see an alternative. He joined her in the bed and left a foot of space between them. The bed moved as she hitched while weeping. He wrapped his arm around her and spooned her into his body. She continued to cry softly, laced her fingers in his and held his hand tight. He had no idea what words to use to comfort her, so he just held her and rocked her until she calmed down.

"Try and get some sleep, baby," he said softly.

"Thank you, Roman...thanks for being here."

He kissed her on the back of the head. Soon she fell asleep. He stared into the darkness of the room. Even though he had showered in Daphne's hotel room, he felt as filthy as a cesspool. Jeanette had grown on him so much, so quickly, that he could imagine living in this house with their own children to look after. *Damn.*

Many would have seen her crying as a weakness, but he saw it as a strength. She wasn't afraid to feel. He wanted to know why she was crying, but would let her tell him in her own time. He just hoped the time came soon; her sorrow was too painful for his soul.

~~~~~~

Jeanette woke with Roman's arm wrapped around her and their fingers interlaced. An odd sense of security had overtaken her when he carried her to bed. One she enjoyed and didn't want to lose. He was all right, yet all wrong for her. This wasn't what she wanted. No, she wanted to remain unattached and uncaring. She had to.

Crying in front of Roman didn't upset her in the least. What upset her was that she longed to hear his voice, argue with him, laugh with him, open up to him, be held by him, make love with him. People like her weren't supposed to fall in love. And what if he were hurt, murdered? Her father still mourned for her mother. *I don't want that. I don't want this.* But she did. She wanted to love Roman and for him to love her. *Falling in love is not an option for me. I can't, but...*

Last night Papa had called to update her on the situation in Cuba. But before the update, he had slipped into the "protective father" role she hated yet longed for. He had grilled her about Roman and refused to allow her to stay in denial about her feelings. Since Roman hadn't told her the who and why behind the shooting at the club, she'd asked Papa what he knew. After he gave her the details, he updated her on Cuba.

She rolled over and rested her hands on Roman's chest. *This is impossible. We just met.* She looked into his face. *So peaceful. So perfect.* She blew out a deep breath. *How did this happen? Hell, when did I fall in love with you?*

He stirred slightly and pulled her closer. The bandage on his arm grabbed her attention.

*What the...*In need of a distraction, she lifted herself for a better view.

"What are you doing?" he asked and cracked his eyes open.

She fingered the bandage. "What happened?"

"Some asshole shot me last night. I had to put his ass to sleep."

Eyes wide, she asked, "The same guys who were after you at the club?" A momentary flash of guilt lit his eyes. Her brows furrowed.

"At first I thought they were your run-of-the-mill hoodlums out mugging unsuspecting tourists, but then one of them recognized me and…Well, you know how that ends."

She wondered why he'd feel guilty about taking out someone interested in collecting the price on his head, but let it go. She'd be willing to bet he'd chosen that mall out in the boonies, instead of shopping in the city, to avoid the gang. Not that he was afraid for himself. This was his way of keeping her from harm's way. *Who keeps you from harm's way, Roman?* She picked at the adhesive and slowly began lifting. "I'll bet they weren't ready for the Sandman," she said proudly.

He weaved his fingers through her hair. "Are you okay, baby girl?"

Her heart warmed. She liked him calling her baby girl too damn much. "I'll be fine. I just have too much on my mind." She gently uncovered his wound. "This isn't clean and you need stitches."

"Who are you, my nurse?"

"Yes." She pulled him out of the bed, led him into the lab and made him sit on a stool in front of the stainless steel sink.

"What happened, Jeanette?"

She turned on the water and lathered up her hands. "Papa said six more have died." She gently washed his wound. "He wouldn't tell me if they were adults or children, so I knew." She felt herself tearing up again, but didn't care. She grabbed the pull-out faucet and rinsed his arm. "I kept pressing him and made him send me the photos. Babies. Roman…the things I saw…" He wiped her tears away.

"I know this will sound crazy, but the pictures were so vivid I could *hear* their cries of agony."

"Why the hell does he keep sending those damn photos? You've seen the lesions."

"I asked him to send me additional photos." After properly cleansing the wound and sewing him up, she noticed his stitched wound was in the shape of a tilted letter J. A smile tipped her lips. He now permanently carried her mark. She looked through her bag of homemade goodies for a healing poultice. She concentrated on applying the poultice instead of visualizing the babies that would die waiting on her to find the cure. "I can't do this alone, Roman. I need help. They're dying."

"Tell me, Jeanette. What did you see?"

She continued applying the poultice to his arm. "I needed to see lesions at each stage for a clearer view of what we're fighting. You can literally see their skin is decaying. Like they have brown recluse bites all over their body." A lump formed in her throat. "Their internal organs..." She hiccupped. "I saw autopsy photos. The same process is happening internally...I'm failing..."

"Oh shit." He drew her into his arms and rubbed her back. "I'm so sorry, baby girl."

"Why did God put people like us on Earth if not to protect the children?"

He rocked her gently. "We'll stop them, baby. I promise."

"But how many more have to die?"

"Jeanette, listen to me." He lifted her chin and gazed into her eyes. "This is not your fault. You are not some sort of archangel. We'll stop these bastards. But all we can do is our best. Stop beating yourself up for being human."

Logically, she agreed with him. But emotionally...this was too important for her best not to be good enough. "I need Doctor Escondido's help."

"Oh, he'll help." He pressed her head onto his chest. "He'll help."

Chapter Twenty

Bacon, eggs and pancakes had never tasted so good. After breakfast, Roman took the still-brooding Jeanette on a shopping spree in the swanky Orange Blossom Mall. In order to make it back to Miami in time, they had only a couple of hours to shop.

"I need to go to the powder room," she said.

"Meet me in Macy's when you're done."

While Jeanette was in the restroom, he rushed into a jewelry store and purchased a platinum, two-carat diamond engagement ring and two bands.

When he returned to Macy's, he found her in the shoe department. He walked over to her and bent down on his knee.

"What the hell are you doing?"

Taking her by the hand, he stared into her eyes with the most serious look he could muster. "Jeanette, will you marry me?"

Other customers began whispering and pointing.

He pulled a velvet box from behind his back and showed her the two-carat diamond solitaire ring and platinum wedding bands.

Mouth hung open like the entrance to a cave, she stammered, "What? What are you...a *ring*? Roman, are you... *serious?*"

The moment lingered. He read a million emotions in her

face. The same million emotions within him had him regretting this proposal. He wanted it to be real, but it couldn't be. He noticed people waiting for his response. Instead of telling the world, he stood, lovingly wrapped his arms around her and whispered into her ear, "I need you to be my wife for this mission. This will complete the charade."

She stared at the fiery diamond from different angles. Smiled. "Yes, I'll marry you." The gathering crowd began to cheer and clap.

Cheeks rosy, she whispered into his ear. "I hope you know I'm keeping this once the mission is over."

He chuckled. "Sorry, can't do that, ma'am. That goes back in the prize vault."

When the time comes to give her a ring, I'll get her one custom made. He dismissed the thought.

Women who were only spectators before gathered around Jeanette to view the ring.

"I'm sorry to interrupt the show," Roman said, "but may I have my fiancée?" He held his hand out for Jeanette.

"He's always rushing me." She left the shoe department, hand in hand, with Roman.

Jeanette's spirits lifted as he used his black American Express card—in the name of Maxwell Bond—to pay for her new outfits. After purchasing himself a few new fits, Jeanette dragged him into the perfume department.

After the woman at the fragrance counter rang up Jeanette's order, Roman handed her his card.

"Thank you, sir." She smiled at Jeanette. "You are lucky to have such a generous husband."

Jeanette looked him in the eyes. "I know."

A tickly thing in his heart made him blink and turn away from Jeanette. Before leaving, she bought a small digital camera and insisted they take a picture with the mall Santa. Roman scoffed at first, but the strength of her rarely shown sweet side overpowered him. They stood side by side with the bulky Santa while a sexy female elf snapped their picture.

After shopping, Jeanette drove them back toward the hotel to check in. "We still have a little while before the conference starts." She pulled into the parking lot of the Diamond Dust Casino.

"What are you doing?" Roman asked.

"I'm feeling lucky and want to play a little blackjack before we head to the conference."

He tried to talk her out of it. He sure as hell didn't want to chance Daphne seeing them. Even though he and Jeanette had no relationship, it still felt wrong to him.

Dread shrouded him when he walked into the extravagant casino with Jeanette. Roman kept an eye out for Daphne en route to the blackjack tables.

Jeanette elbowed him in the side. "Relax and have some fun for a change. Quit being so tense all the time."

He pulled her chair out for her at a blackjack table and was preparing to sit next to her when he spotted Daphne across the room. She saw him and smiled broadly until Jeanette rubbed him on the shoulder. At that moment, her face soured.

Daphne continued to walk around the casino, eyeballing both Roman and Jeanette—mostly Jeanette. Roman tried to ignore her, hoping like hell she didn't come over and start any shit. He knew she was damn well capable of doing just that with her envious ass. After a while, he actually got into the game and won a few hands, but Jeanette became a little distracted. He blamed her mood change on her losing two hands in a row.

"I need to use the powder room," she whispered in his ear. "I'll be right back."

He nodded his okay. Just as he checked the hand he'd been dealt, he saw Jeanette following a few paces behind Daphne, headed toward the hallway that led to the restrooms.

The predatory look on Jeanette's face worried him. Her eyes had darkened to deadly. He picked up his winnings, forfeited his hand and went after Jeanette as quickly as he could without drawing any attention to himself.

Halfway down the hall, he saw an elevator maintenance

closet door closing. He looked around, saw he was alone and sprinted to the door. The door was locked. He placed his ear against the door and heard angry voices. He grimaced, removed the lock-picking tool on his key ring and unlocked the door.

He rushed inside and found Jeanette tugging on a handful of Daphne's hair and the barrel of the Glock under Daphne's chin.

"Jeanette, baby," he said calmly, "let her go."

"Hell no. Not until she tells me why the hell she's been watching me the entire time I've been in the casino."

"Call your dog off, Roman."

Puzzlement contorted Jeanette's face.

"Are you the one he called for last night?" Daphne snapped out.

Glaring at Roman, Jeanette said, "What the hell's going on?"

Roman sighed and drew his hand down his face. "I know her, but we have no ties to each other."

"That's not what you were saying while you fucked me last night."

Without a word, Jeanette released Daphne, un-cocked her Glock, put it in her purse, adjusted her hair, then walked out. If he didn't already know, the look on Jeanette's face left no doubt he'd royally fucked up.

"What the hell do you think you're doing? Why would you say some shit like that?"

Daphne dusted herself off. "Is that your fucking ring on her finger?"

He glared at her. "Last night was a mistake. A serious mistake that will *never* happen again. Stay the *fuck* away from me and my fiancée."

He rushed after Jeanette and barely caught up to her before she pulled off in the GTO. He knocked on the locked passenger door. She unlocked the door, but didn't say a word.

It also hurt him to have Jeanette think he cared more about getting a piece of ass than her, but how could he explain that though he'd been physically with Daphne, emotionally, he had been making love to Jeanette. He racked his brain to try and figure a way to make things right between them as they headed back to get dressed for the conference.

~~~~~~

Jeanette continued to give Roman the silent treatment as she drove them to the Ritz. Of all the men out there, she had to fall for this arrogant jerk. And it was not like she could just turn her feelings off for him, but she would try to protect her heart from being broken.

She began rationalizing in her mind: He's a single man, we don't have any relationship outside of our odd partnership. Then she remembered how she'd felt when he got jealous over her kissing Dr. Wyatt. Just as she'd said, he had no hold on her, she had no hold on him, but damn, she was still angry with him.

This is stupid. He's not my man.

~~~~~~

This sure as hell wasn't part of the deal. Hope she cools off by the time we go to this dull ass conference. Since he had a little time left to kill, he ordered a sandwich from room service, took his laptop into the living room and logged onto the Interpol database using the Maxwell Bond account he'd created for himself. "Let's see what's up with Javier Escondido."

Twenty minutes and a half-sandwich later, Roman said, "He looks clean. Not even a damn unpaid parking ticket."

"How did you get access to Interpol?" Jeanette pointed at the screen over his shoulder, startling the shit out of him.

"If I tell you, I'd have to kill you." The ring he'd bought her sparkled in his eyes for a moment. It looked too good on her slender finger. *Still can't believe how quietly she creeps up on my ass. Surprised she gives a shit what I'm doing after that Daphne episode.*

"Yeah, right." To his surprise, she picked up the other half of his sandwich and began eating it. "So what did you find out about Escondido?"

Although there was still a heap of tension between them,

their professionalism kicked in and they discussed their strategy for dealing with Professor Escondido.

~~~~~~

How could a rich man be so broke? Bagley asked Marta if she needed anything. He knew she couldn't speak. He just got a kick out of watching her try. He didn't know how much longer he could keep government investigators from looking into his bank's financial records. He needed this money and needed it fast. He'd been visiting Marta since convincing her to stay home until they figured out what this illness was that had come on so quickly.

"Don't try to speak," her mother cut in before her daughter could answer. "Thank you so much, Mr. Bagley. We have everything we need, thanks to you."

"I must admit, it's purely selfish. I want her to be healthy again." He'd never liked Marta's mother. The old bat always looked at him as if he were beneath her daughter.

"I'm sure Marta will bounce back." Sarafina took her daughter's hand. "She will."

I pray to God not! "You're right. We have to stay strong."

He heard those snot-nosed children asking the nurse who had gone to get Marta some fresh water if they could see their mother. He'd instructed the nurse to keep those brats away from him when he was around, so he wasn't worried about having to fake liking them.

"This has all been so hard on the babies," Sarafina said. "She'll bounce back," she repeated. "For the babies, she'll bounce back."

Bagley wished those brats would shut up. He had thinking to do. He needed Marta dead and dead NOW, not days from now.

~~~~~~

Roman tapped on the Yukon driver's side window with his knuckle. "This has *got* to be geek heaven. Nothing but glasses, beards, sensible shoes and pocket protectors as far as the eye can see!"

Jeanette adjusted the collar of her beige Gucci business suit. "If it weren't for us—quote, unquote—geeks, you so called 'normal folks' would be up to your asses in diseases and God knows what else."

Intellectuals of all races walked in the direction of the auditorium as Roman pulled into the parking lot.

"Say what you want, Queen Geek, but I wouldn't trade my 'cool card' in for a pair of horn-rimmed glasses for all the tea in China. Not even if you threw in a piece of white tape to wrap around the bridge of those thick-ass glasses."

She gave him a two-handed, middle finger salute. "And I don't mean this in a good way."

He laughed and smoothed down the lapels of his new loose-fitting, burgundy, two-piece linen suit. He reached behind his back and removed his pistol. "Is that the only sign language you know?" He inspected the gun. "Where's your piece?"

She opened her tan and white Gucci shoulder bag and showed him her pistol. "Please don't embarrass me inside. I sure as hell don't need to have an uncouth *and* trigger-happy *husband* tonight. We have other business."

He bulged his eyes and nodded his head vigorously. "Yes, massah! Toby be *good* nigga!"

She pursed her lips, but he could tell she was attempting to stave off her laughter. "Roman! *Stop it!*"

He put his gun away, exited and rounded the truck, then opened Jeanette's door for her.

"Thank you." She straightened out her suit and adjusted her hair. "This should be a really nice conference. Too bad we don't have time to attend the entire event."

Roman stood next to her. "Thank God we don't have enough time. I don't know if I could stand it."

Jeanette looped her arm around Roman's, and they followed the crowd to the auditorium. Just inside, to their right, sat three college-aged women at a long table. After signing in, they were handed name badges and a copy of the program.

Roman pinned Jeanette's badge on her lapel, then pinned on his and they walked toward the conference seating area. "Are you *sure* this isn't a *Star Trek* convention? I swear I saw a dude with a pair of those fake Spock ears."

She elbowed him in the side. "Don't make me give you a matching bullet wound on your other arm."

Posters from chemical companies around the globe lined the walls. Christmas decorations were sprinkled throughout the venue. Representatives of many of the chemical companies sat at tables handing out literature, key chains, ink pens, note pads and caps advertising the merits of their products. Jeanette accepted a couple of ink pens and a note pad from the representative of a large chemical company.

She opened the program and scanned it. "Professor Escondido should be speaking in a few minutes."

They entered the large seating area and managed to get seats four rows from the stage. Roman leaned over and whispered in her ear, "You didn't say anything about having to actually sit here and listen to this boring shit."

She smiled, let her hand fall on his thigh and pinched hard. "Quiet, dear."

"You're going to pay for that." He rubbed the sting of her pinch out of his thigh.

The master of ceremonies welcomed Javier Escondido to the stage.

"Welcome, my friends! Welcome!" Escondido stood at the podium. An average-sized Spanish man with a ponytail that touched the collar of his dark blue, designer suit jacket, Escondido's white smile and dark eyes gave him the appearance of a Hollywood actor. He played to the crowd like a veteran of the stage. He used a wireless remote and went through his PowerPoint presentation.

"Wow, he's *good*!" Jeanette said ninety minutes later, clapping along with the rest of the crowd.

Roman's enthusiasm was as false as their marriage.

She stood, along with the rest of the crowd, then took

Roman's hand. "Come on. Let's go meet him."

They walked over and stood behind the small crowd of people congratulating Escondido on his work. The professor did a double take once he noticed Jeanette's smile. He shook hands with a grinning fan, then excused himself.

"Hello. Thank you for coming!" He took Jeanette's hand and kissed it.

Jeanette's smile widened. "Thank you, Professor Escondido! Your presentation was fabulous!"

"Please, call me Javier."

Roman did his best to hold his forced smile. *I see we have a wannabe Spanish Romeo.* He offered the professor his hand. "Well done, Professor."

He shook Roman's hand. "Thank you, Mr...?"

"Noble. Glenn Noble." He took Jeanette's hand and gazed into her eyes. "And this is my wife, Monica."

Javier's eyes traveled over her body. "You have a spectacularly beautiful wife."

Can't believe his bullshit has her blushing. "Thanks."

The rest of the crowd went to the refreshment table and began the networking portion of the event. Javier took Jeanette's hand again. "So, Monica, are you here on business or pleasure?"

"A bit of both. By the way, congratulations on leading the Merck team to winning the Presidential Green Chemistry Award. It's quite an honor to win the highest environmental award given in the U.S."

"Thank you, *señora*! It was an honor to be chosen."

Oh, this asshole is acting as if I'm the Invisible Man. Roman listened in as they conversed in Spanish. *Damn, homeboy, when are you gonna let her hand go?*

"So, Professor, do you travel with your family?" Roman asked in Spanish.

He glanced at Roman, then returned his attention to Jeanette. "Ahhh, no...I have no family. My lifestyle has been too hectic for me to settle down."

She smiled at Roman. "The professor also has several breakthroughs in vaccinations and ways of combating pollution, which are revolutionary."

"Interesting," Roman mumbled.

"So, Professor, how is your research going on removing pollutants from chemical spills in natural waterways?"

He chuckled. "I'm not telling until you promise to stop calling me 'Professor'." He took the hand Roman wasn't holding. " Please, call me Javier."

You disrespectful son-of-a-bitch! I don't know how you folks get down over in Spain, but if you keep this shit up, it's gonna be me and you. Roman couldn't tell if Jeanette read the irritation in his face, but he did his best to cover it up. "Let's go get some refreshments and have a seat."

"No thanks, hon, I don't want anything. How about you, Javier?"

"No, no thanks." A slick grin curled Javier's lips. "Why don't you get yourself something while Monica and I find seats for us?"

She looked over Javier's shoulder and nodded toward the refreshment table. "Yes, why don't you do that, dear?" She pulled a notepad out of her purse.

Ain't this a bitch! Roman fought the urge to slam his fist through Javier's jackal-like grin. "Okay...I'll be right back."

He scanned the room for potential bad guys as he placed a few cubes of cheese and slices of ham and turkey on a small plate. He nibbled on the snacks and watched Jeanette scribble notes while smiling at the professor. *Let it go. She's just doing her job. You're acting like a fool in love. And you definitely don't have time for that.* He finished off his snack and tossed the plate in the trash, then rejoined them and took the seat to Jeanette's left. "What did I miss?"

She put her hand on his. "I just asked the professor if he's heard about the mysterious illness in Cuba."

"I was explaining that I was contacted by Cuban authorities a month or so ago. They gave me the *Spark Notes* version of what was happening in a small township. My immediate thought was there must be something wrong with the water, but if so, more people would have been infected. I wanted to travel to Cuba to help figure out what was wrong, but when I tried to get passage, both the U.S. and Spanish governments balked. The Cubans haven't contacted me since. So, Monica, tell me how such a beautiful woman is tied into a few sick people in Cuba?"

Roman and Jeanette exchanged glances. He could tell she wanted to tell Javier what they really wanted with him, but they needed more privacy. Roman looked at the professor. "Javier, can we speak to you outside, privately?"

He gave Roman a curious look. "Privately? What do you mean?"

Jeanette took the fake CIA badge Roman had given her out of her purse, quickly showed it to him, then put it back. "We *really* need to speak with you."

He turned to Roman. "You, too?"

Proud of Jeanette for thinking so fast on her feet, Roman flashed him his badge. "Yes, me too."

The trio went outside and walked a few yards away from the auditorium entrance. After questioning the professor and being satisfied he didn't work for whoever had created the contaminant, they brought him up to speed on the case.

He ran his hand over his head. "Those poor people."

Roman checked the time after noticing most of the nerds were leaving. "So what do you think, Javier?"

"I'd be able to give you better answers if I were able to apply a few tests to a sample of the actual contaminant. What have been the results of the salve?"

Jeanette looked to Roman who answered, "Wait a second and I'll check."

Roman turned from Javier and Jeanette, pulled out his satellite phone and called Mateo for an update on Vanessa. Once he finished his conversation, he returned to Jeanette and the professor. "The patient's wounds have stopped itching and burning, but they can't tell if the lesions are actually healing yet."

"That's wonderful, Roman." Jeanette hugged him, and he didn't want to let her go. "This is the key to the cure. I know it. I can feel it!" She turned toward Javier. "You're in luck. We have samples of the infected blood."

Excitement filled Javier's face. "That's great! Do you have it with you?"

Roman shook his head. "No, it's back at our hotel."

Javier thought for a second. "I'm sure I can borrow a microscope from someone's exhibit and take it with us back to your hotel."

Forty-five minutes later, they entered Roman and Jeanette's suite. Jeanette stepped out of her pumps. "Make yourself comfortable. I'll get the samples."

Roman cleared off the hotel desk and plugged in the heavy white, high-powered microscope. "Is this enough room?"

Javier pulled two Petri dishes out of the pocket of his jacket, along with a few glass slides. "I'm really looking forward to seeing this toxin up close." He removed his jacket and laid it on the arm of the sofa. His eyes opened wide as Roman reached behind his back and removed his black pistol. "Wow! You *are* the real McCoy!"

Roman grinned internally as the smug scientist took a step back. "You could say that."

Jeanette walked into the room with vials in her hands. "Is everything okay?"

"I'm fine." Roman sat on the couch and dismantled his weapon. "You two do your thing." He turned away from her questioning eyes and checked the barrel of his pistol.

She joined Javier at the desk and handed him the vials. "Time to see what makes this bug tick."

For the next few hours, Roman watched TV and downloaded the pictures from Jeanette's cheap digital camera onto his laptop while she and Javier took turns looking in the microscope, jotting down notes and chatting excitedly in Spanish. He gave up trying to keep up with their conversation and looked at the pictures he'd downloaded.

Horrified and thrilled at how Jeanette had coaxed him into wearing Santa's hat, he noticed that Santa had stolen a peek at Jeanette's bosom in that same picture. He chuckled, then e-mailed the pictures to the account he'd set up for Jeanette. He'd never seen someone so intelligent so paranoid about the electronic age. You just needed to take a few safety precautions. He yawned and checked his watch—1:53 A.M.

Javier stretched.

Jeanette yawned. "We made a lot of progress tonight, Javier."

"I'm sure we'll create a cure, either an injection or a pill. You've got a great start here."

"Thank you."

Frown firm on his face, Roman set his laptop on the coffee table and picked up his phone. He looked over at them. "I'll call to have a limo take you home, Javier."

Javier ignored him, took Jeanette's left hand and examined her ring. "This is a very nice prop." He flashed a "knock 'em dead" smile. "Since you're not really married, I was wondering if I could treat you to dinner and a tour of Miami."

Oh, yeah, it's definitely time for you to leave, pimp. Roman looked at Jeanette just in time to see her place her hand on top of Javier's.

"I'm sorry, Javier. Thanks for the offer, but," she casually looked past Javier and into Roman's eyes, "although I'm not married, I am spoken for."

Roman's chest puffed up about ten imaginary sizes. "Yes, she's spoken for. Good night, Javier." He took the professor's jacket off the arm of the sofa and handed it to him. "The limo will be downstairs momentarily. We'll meet you first thing in the morning. Let's say 8 A.M."

Javier bowed slightly. "It will take me a day to thoroughly review Monica's notes and have a lab prepared."

"A day? We don't have a day?" Jeanette said.

"I'm sorry, I know we're in a hurry, but I need time to absorb your work and to run a few tests on my own. I may be able to have everything ready by tomorrow afternoon. I'll work as fast as I can."

"I understand."

Roman didn't like the sorrow in her voice, but he knew the professor was correct. Just as Jeanette had needed time to read through and absorb the information she'd been given before she could do any real work, the professor would need the same thing.

"Call me when you're ready for us, Javier." Roman wrote his number on a piece of paper and handed it to Javier.

Jeanette escorted the professor to the suite door. "Good night."

"Good night."

She closed the door behind the professor, then turned on Roman. "You were entirely too rude. What's wrong with you?" She fully entered the suite.

He grabbed her hand. "He thought you were my wife, yet continually flirted with you. He's lucky I was only rude."

"So, he's a disrespectful ass. He's not the first or last one you'll deal with." She began working. "I'm continuing. We don't have a day to waste. I'm too close to the answer to play into your jealousy."

Gonna be a long night. She might think she could work herself to death, but Roman wouldn't allow it. He didn't care how mad she was with him. And this went beyond his feelings for her. A tired Jeanette couldn't think straight and would make mistakes, mistakes that could lead to death. After stripping down to his pants and T-shirt, he went into Jeanette's suitcase, took out a pair of red boy shorts and a matching tank and set them beside her.

She stopped writing formulas. "No, you can't borrow my clothes."

"Cute. You have until I finish my shower to finish acting like a maniac. Then you'll shower and go to bed."

"I'll shower when I'm damn well ready and not a second

sooner. Same goes for going to bed."

"You know I'll throw your butt in the shower, right?"

"What's wrong with you? I have work to do. I don't have time for this."

"I don't want you killing someone because you screwed up in your calculations 'cause you wouldn't take your ass to bed and take a few hours off to clear your mind."

She snarled, then continued being a maniac until Roman finished his shower and readied himself to carry her into the bathroom.

Chapter Twenty-One

"This is a big waste of time. I should be going over my notes instead of going to a big, stupid, crowded mall." Jeanette abused the keyboard of Roman's laptop. "I had a major breakthrough last night I need to be working on."

She's gotta be on the rag. She's been talkin' shit all day! Roman continued to drive down the highway. They'd checked out of the hotel, but he had other business to take care of before returning to Homestead. "I'm sure it'll be worth it to you once I get you a new Internet card, so you can get back online."

A glint of one of the diamonds in his wedding band got his attention. A cold sweat condensed on his forehead. Wearing the damn thing didn't feel strange to him at all. Pushing the reason to the back of his mind, he focused on Bagley. *Why in the world would a wealthy British banker bother to have a nearly empty office building in Miami? And why does he have a fuckin' lab on the 14th floor?* He sped around a Coke truck with a mural of Santa Claus drinking a bottle of Coke. *If I had been on my game, instead of splitting my attention between Jeanette and the mission, I would've checked his office while I was there. I'm missin' a lead.*

In the mall parking lot, Roman found a spot close to the main entrance. Once he shut the engine off, he heard a ding on his laptop. At the same instant, Jeanette's feverish typing stopped. He felt her eyes on him.

"It's for you." The frosty glare she gave him could have chilled an ice cube.

"What?"

She handed him the laptop. "It's your woman."

Fuckin' Daphne!

He'd forgotten to log off his instant messenger program after chatting with Jorge earlier in the day. He grimaced at the name Sexy D next to a small, topless picture of Daphne. She awaited a response to the message, "We need to talk."

Fuck, roared between his ears. "I don't know why that crazy broad is sending me a message." He quickly logged off without sending a response. "I ain't got shit to say to her ass."

Jeanette said nothing. After giving him one more evil look, she slipped on her dark shades and got out. To him, that was a billion times worse than her cussing him out. He set the laptop on the floor of the backseat, got out and hurried after the Black Widow.

Just inside the main entrance, he found her looking into the window of Uncle Dave's Pet Shop. He walked over and pointed at the five cocker spaniel puppies jumping on the window. "I didn't know you liked dogs."

She walked away. "I thought we came to get something for my laptop? I sure as hell don't need to use yours." She increased her pace.

As they approached the escalator he tensed up; three teenaged members of the CC gang were on the way down. *These muthafuckas are comin' out of the woodwork.* He caught up with Jeanette, gently grabbed her elbow and steered her toward T. J. Electronics just ahead of them. "In here."

She resisted for a moment. "I thought you said they didn't carry what you need for my laptop here?"

His eyes went from her dark shades to the possible menace. "We have company."

As if fully understanding the danger, she acquiesced and entered the store with him. They browsed while the loud-talking gang bangers headed toward the exit. He walked over to the TV display where she watched the news broadcast on display. "Okay, we can get outta here now."

"Good."

He tried to take her hand, but she moved it out of his reach and walked out of the store.

En route to the Best Buy store, she pulled out her BlackBerry and began doing some kind of calculations. Fifty feet from the entrance to the store, she stopped and took a seat on one of the benches reserved for tired shoppers. He looked around, saw no immediate danger and asked, "What are you doing?"

"Working. This is where I'll be until you finish."

He didn't argue with her, instead, he ran his hand down his face. "All right. I'll be right back."

While waiting to pay for her new Internet card and some extra memory for her janky laptop, he saw a *Ms. Magazine* cover that made him chuckle: TROUBLE WITH YOUR RELATIONSHIP? CALL A REFEREE!

He stared at the sexy blonde-haired woman in the black and white referee shirt with the black whistle between her lips on the cover.

After paying for his goods, he stepped outside the store and called Shadow. Jeanette, across the pavilion, scratched her head then went back to her BlackBerry. *All right, Shadow, let's see what you think.*

After two rings, Shadow picked up. "Ahhh, Mr. Sandman, what's going on?"

Roman watched a baldheaded black man wearing a Malcolm X T-shirt and baggy black shorts hand out pieces of paper to some of the mall patrons. "How did you know it was me? My number is programmed not to show up on caller ID."

Shadow chuckled. "There are ways around everything, young man."

Roman paused. "Does that include Spiderwoman's bad attitude?"

"Uh-oh! Did she narrow her eyes and snarl at you?"

"I can't tell. She won't take off her shades."

"Is she speaking to you?"

"No...hell no..."

"Why did she stop talking to you?"

He hesitated, then gave Shadow an abridged version of what had happened with Daphne. "I don't see why she's even upset...it's not like she's my woman." He tugged at the collar of his shirt, which suddenly felt too tight

Shadow laughed. "Son, you're in *trouble!*"

Roman watched the baldheaded man approach Jeanette. "What are you talking about?"

Shadow sighed. "Sandman, it's time for you to face the facts. You and Jeanette are sick in love and don't have clue one how to handle it."

Roman laughed so loud, the balding, effeminate man walking by stopped to see what was going on. "You have never been more wrong!"

"I can prove I'm right about you two."

Roman watched Jeanette shake her head and refuse the piece of paper the bald man offered her. "How? There's nothing to prove."

"Then why did you call me?"

"Because I..." *I wanted to know how to get Jeanette to smile again. Oh, fuck no!*

Shadow chuckled. "Because what? Because you can't stand to see her upset? Because you don't feel right when she doesn't feel right? Because it's tearing your fucking insides apart because you have no clue as to how to fix it when normally you don't give a damn?"

"Man, you are nuts. I could care les—"

"Roman, listen...I know exactly what you're going through."

Jeanette rose from her seat and said something to the man with the pamphlets.

"All right, genius, what's on your mind?"

"I was you before you were you."

"What the hell are you talking about?"

"Before you were born, I was THE number-one assassin. I'm talking from experience, son."

"Okay, so you were a good assassin. What does that have to do with me being in so called 'love'?"

"Let's get one thing straight. I was the *best*...and depending on how you do on this mission, I may still be."

"Oh, is this a challenge, old man?"

"Roman, listen. I lost the only woman I ever loved because I refused to salvage the only part of my soul worth saving...love."

"Man, I am not—"

"Be quiet two damn seconds and listen! I know about the nightmares you must have after all the killin' and death you've seen and done. It affects all of the people in our trade, son."

Roman thought of the nightmare he'd had a few nights ago where he was descending into hell, pulled down by the hands of those he'd killed. A faceless woman tried to pull him out, but he couldn't grasp her hand. "That can't be...I..."

"Roman, she's in a worse position than you. She has no one close, like a mother or sister, to turn to for help with her feelings. She also has to be extra tough being a woman in a man-dominated field. If you choose to ignore what I'm telling you, you will be making a serious mistake. Learn from my mistakes; don't repeat them. Trust me. You don't want to end up a living, loveless ghost like I am..."

Jeanette had apparently heard more than enough from the man. She pointed her finger at him and twisted her neck when she spoke. The man took a step back, but not far enough away for Roman's liking.

"*If* what you're saying is true, wouldn't that weaken a man— or woman—in our trade?"

"You have a lot to learn about the power of love. Think of all the great or tragic things that are happening in the world; all are the result of love—the love of power, love of money, love of another, love of country. What do you love, Roman?"

He looked across the mall at Jeanette. He gulped and his heart jerked in his chest. *What do I love? My mom* *and...*Jeanette pulled a suspicious looking hairpin out of her hair and barked at the man.

"Hey, I gotta go save a life...thanks, old man."

"She likes Snickers and carnations, son, *pink* carnations," Shadow said with laughter in his voice and disconnected.

Roman hurried over, broke through the crowd and stepped in between Jeanette and the man.

"Get out of my way, Roman!"

"Hey, sister," the bald man said from behind Roman. "I'm just trying to save you from your brainwash! You are a victim of the white man's definition of beauty! The same men who raped your ancestors and gave you those light eyes. Get rid of that hair weave and those fake nails. Dress in less revealing clothes, so you can be closer to the true God! Break the chains, sister, break the *chains*!"

People moved away, yet continued to watch.

Roman held Jeanette's wrists and paid real close attention to the hand with the hairpin. He looked into Jeanette's shades. "Easy, baby...easy..."

She yanked her arm to break free of his grip, but he held too tight. "Why are you protecting this self-righteous motherfucker?"

He spotted a security guard speaking into his walkie-talkie while running toward them. Roman looked over his shoulder at the grinning black man. "Get your shit and get the fuck away from my wife before I do something to you!"

The tall white guard ran over and stood next to them, hand on the butt of his pistol. He spoke in a thick Boston accent. "What's going on?"

Roman looked into her shades. "Easy, baby," he said softly. "I'm showing him my badge...Don't do anything, okay?"

She breathed heavily, but didn't reply. Roman let go of the hairpin-free hand and pulled out his fake CIA badge. He nodded toward the bald man. "This man is harassing my wife."

The guard, clearly in awe of Roman's badge, stepped toward the man. "I'll take care of it, sir!" He grabbed the "mind liberator" by the arm and marched him away.

As the crowd dispersed, Jeanette snatched her wrist out of his hand. "I did not need you to interfere with my business." She tucked the pin back in her hair. "I can take care of myself."

"I know you can. I just didn't want you to waste your venom on a piece of shit like him."

She adjusted her shades. "Whatever."

She likes Snickers and carnations, son. Shadow's words reverberated through his head. He held her by the shoulders. "I'll be right back, wait for me."

She stood in silence, but didn't move.

He ran over to the gift shop next to the Best Buy electronics store and picked up a king-sized Snickers bar. *Damn! They don't have any flowers!* He paid for the candy bar, stuffed it in his pocket, ran back and beckoned her to walk with him.

Back in the Yukon, on the way out the mall, he handed her the candy bar. "I got this for you."

"Why?"

He exhaled loudly. "Because I'm cool like that."

She *almost* lost her scowl. "I didn't ask for it."

"It's called being 'thoughtful.'"

She set the candy bar on the armrest and broke out her BlackBerry. "Don't even go there."

Chapter Twenty-Two

Back at Homestead, after a long silent ride from the mall, Roman used the kitchen counter to repair Jeanette's laptop. *Now, it's better than new.* He browsed the Internet on it. *Maybe this upgrade will calm her down a little bit.*

While shutting down her laptop, he caught a glimpse of Bagley, Lipton, and Enrique on the TV screen. "What are they up to?"

By the time he was able to turn up the volume, he had missed most of the story. The three of them were being interviewed at one of Enrique's resorts by a local TV show. They were being questioned about reports of them promising to add job opportunities as their corporation, Heavenly Associates, continued to purchase coastline property allegedly not for sale—including Las Tunas.

Somethin' don't sound right. Roman listened to a slick-looking government official who fed the reporter line after line of bullshit about loopholes in Cuban policy about the selling of private beachfront property.

"That is way too much of a coincidence." He took a seat on the sofa, rebooting Jeanette's laptop and checking the document she'd saved containing the locations of the victims. "First Bagley and his suspect lab. Then all the recent victims of the plague just so happened to be near one of the areas he and his partners are buying."

Out of nowhere, he felt something bounce off the back of his head. "What the fu—"

He picked up the king-sized Snickers bar from the floor. Jeanette stood ten feet behind him. "Who told you, you could read my documents?"

Gotta remember to listen more carefully for her. At least she finally took off those shades. He held up the candy bar. "Is that why you gave me a concussion with this thing?"

"That's one reason." She took the bar from him and tore it open. "What are you working on?"

After he filled her in on his suspicions—leaving Daphne's name out—she sat next to him on the sofa and checked out her tuned-up laptop.

"I agree. There might be something funny going on between those folks and the plague."

He watched her connect her BlackBerry to the laptop. "What are you up to now?"

"I think I've finished the calculations for an antidote inoculation. However, I need to download some data out of my BlackBerry and run it through some of the programs loaded on my laptop."

The feel of her thigh against his was most pleasurable. "You'll notice that your laptop is now twice as fast as it used to be."

"Thanks," she muttered, with a small smile. "Now let me get to work."

Roman's phone rang. He jumped up, ran to his room and answered. "Jorge, what you got?"

"*Hola*! I might have some news you can use, my friend. Through my channels at the Miami hospitals that sometimes 'offer' me items for sale, I was told of an arrogant asshole doctor who bragged about getting ready to buy into a new exclusive resort in Las Tunas through one of the investors he works with."

Roman sat down hard on his bed. "You sure about that? Did you get a name?"

"I did better than that. I had his home searched. My source sent me back lots of pictures of weird stuff in the doctor's home lab like flavor packets for Kool-Aid and tea. Some of the packages had been tampered with."

Kool-Aid? Roman remembered what Vanessa's grandmother had said about the kids drinking Kool-Aid all the time. He jumped to his feet. "Is there any way you can get me one of those tampered packets?"

"You read my mind, *amigo*. My contact has four of the packets. I can work with you to have them delivered."

"Yeah, let's do that. How much is it gonna cost me?"

"This one is on the house...I hope it helps you find the motherfucker that's behind the killing of my people."

"Thank you, Jorge. Did you get the name of that doctor?"

"Snow. Gary Snow. He's lucky to still be alive."

"Why do you say that?"

"He owed friends of mine in Miami a lot of money for his gambling habits. That is, until about two years ago. Just as my collectors were going to pay him a visit, some foreign asshole paid off his seven-figure debt. He's starting to get in deep again, though."

"Thanks, Jorge." Roman grimaced and hung up. Using his laptop, he did a number of searches and found that Snow was a brilliant chemical toxicologist with a serious gambling addiction. After arranging to have Florida Express Couriers pick up the packets and deliver two to Javier and two to Jeanette within the next hour, he ran to Jeanette and told her the good news.

"That could be how he spread it!" she said, thrilled at the breakthrough. "How does your guy know the flavor packets are tainted?"

"We didn't get into all of that. Does it matter? Anyway, I arranged to have two of the packets delivered here and two to Javier."

"I guess not. I'll run tests on them as soon as they arrive."

A breaking news story about a triple homicide a few blocks

from Bagley's office building stole their attention. It was believed to be gang-related. He paid close attention to the story. "Those punks are in the news more and more every day." After the story, he caught Jeanette watching him. Ignoring it, he removed his pistol and decided to clean it. The danger in the area put him back into combat mode. "After you test those packets, it's time to pay a personal visit to Bagley."

~~~~~~

Jeanette went into her lab and called Papa. Now that they knew who was behind the toxin and were on track to stopping future outbreaks, she could relax some.

"What's wrong?" Papa asked.

"What makes you think something's wrong?" She took a seat on a padded stool.

"Because you've never called me before."

"This Caribbean Connection gang is distracting Roman. Who's behind the hit on him?"

"Roman's a big boy and can take care of himself. Your only focus is finding the antidote. Colin says those crazy Cubans are threatening us with dirty bombs if we don't turn over the terrorists responsible for the attack on their country. We can't turn over terrorists we can't identify, but we can give them a cure, as we'd intended on doing anyway."

"I know we've run out of time. I have my priorities straight." She gave him an update on the inoculation and tainted flavor packets, so he could alert the Cuban authorities.

"Good job, Jeanette. Good job."

"Thank you, but Roman found the mode of transmission. I know what my number one mission is, but this gang must also be taught a lesson."

"What lesson is that?"

Even in the lab lighting, her new ring looked spectacular. "That no one fucks with me or what's mine."

"So Roman's yours?"

"He's my partner. Nobody messes with me or mine."

"I've been around a long time, and am too damn old and tired to hear this bullshit."

"I'm not—"

"Be quiet for a few moments and listen. I know our relationship is...odd, but I've always been here for you. It was your choice not to ask me. It was your choice to stay away from your family. We don't have to be enemies. But I owe you an apology."

Completely thrown, Jeanette wondered how the conversation had turned from her and Roman's relationship to Papa apologizing, yet again. First, she'd fallen for Roman, now this.

"With age comes regrets, and I truly regret manipulating you into working for me. I don't expect you to forgive me, but I am on your side. Always have been, whether you believe it or not. Now please stop shoveling shit my way about Roman and tell me the truth."

Her love-hate relationship with Papa couldn't be explained, but she did know he always looked out for her.

"I'm falling for Roman. Hell, have fallen for him, but all he cares about is chasing ass. I'm glad I'll never have to see him again after this mission is over."

"I made a mistake many years ago and gave up on someone, something I shouldn't have because I was scared. Roman is scared shitless right now."

"Suuuuure he is." She paced about the lab.

"He is, and he'll probably do something to push you away, to make you hate him, but not consciously. Men are like that."

"Stupid."

"Yes."

"What did you do to push away the woman you loved?"

"Who said I was in love?"

She chuckled. "Now who's shoveling the shit?"

"Okay, okay, I was in love. And you're right. I was stupid. I ran away to the arms of another woman and got her pregnant. Did what I thought was the right thing and married her, but...But I was in love with someone else."

"You have children?"

"Because I allowed my fear to rule me, I lost my child, my wife and the love of my life. I'm not saying you should allow Roman to continue hurting you. I'm saying call him on his shit."

She laughed. "You're crazy."

"Probably."

"You're right about my family. I chose to stay away, just as my father chose not to come for me."

"It's time for you to go home, Jeanette. Speak with your father."

"I know. I know. But first I have a plague to stop and someone has to teach this gang a lesson."

"You're right. Someone needs to teach this gang a lesson. I'll start making arrangements."

A second call beeped on her phone. She checked the caller ID. "That's Escondido. I need to go, Papa." She switched over to the other line. "Hello?"

"Hello, Monica, it's Javier."

"How did you get my number?"

"Your registration. I hope you don't mind."

"Wait a second." She admired his scientific knowledge, but didn't like him as a person. Roman had introduced her as his wife, yet Escondido kept hitting on her. *Disrespectful ass.* If she weren't angry with Roman, she would have checked him.

She put the phone on mute and went out to Roman. "It's Escondido on the phone."

"I told that bastard to call me when he was ready. When did you give him your number?"

"First off, stop trippin'. Secondly, I didn't give him my number, he took it off the registration form. I actually wanted additional information about future conferences, so I put my real number."

"Jeanette..."

"Don't Jeanette me." She handed him the phone. "It's on mute."

Not interested in cockfights or catfights, like that between herself and the woman at the casino, she returned to her lab closet and grabbed a few items that might come in handy. Now that they were on track with finding the cure, soon it would be time to pay a certain gang leader a visit. But first she needed to track the results of the testing she'd been conducting.

~~~~~~

"Yes!" Jeanette burst out of her lab and gave Roman a big hug. "I've got it! Preliminary testing shows the antidote will work!"

He watched her do her happy, sexy dance and grinned. "I had no doubt you would do it. Good job, chick!"

"I have to tell Papa. I need someone to test it on."

Vanessa jumped into his mind. "I have someone you can test it on."

Surprise filled her face. "What?"

"I have an infected person you can test it on." He stuck his hands in his pockets. "A little girl."

"A child?" She stared into his eyes. "Is she the same person the blood samples you gave me came from?"

He exhaled and chewed on his toothpick. "Yes."

"Why didn't you tell me she was here? I could ha—"

He gripped both her shoulders. "Because if I had, you would have been too distraught to get as much done as you did. Your Papa and I knew that and kept her from you until you discovered a cure." A ripple of emotional conflicts played on her face. Roman recognized that she knew he had done the right thing. "I'll take Javier to give her a dose before I drop him on a flight to Cuba."

She took a deep breath and composed herself. "Did you use the salve on her?"

"Yes." He smiled at her. "I called a little bit ago and found out her lesions are already healing. You did a great job, Professor Meany."

"So did you, Boy Wonder."

His satellite phone sounded. He released the loving grip he

had on her arms. "Now what?" He walked over to the kitchen counter and looked at the caller ID. "*Hola*, Jorge."

"I'm afraid we have a little complication, *amigo*. That slimeball doctor and one of Bagley's bodyguards walked in on the man I had investigating the doctor's house for more evidence. The doctor was killed, but the bodyguard escaped with a bullet wound. I am very sorry, *amigo*."

Ohhhh, fuck! Roman closed his eyes and ran a hand down his face. "How long ago did this happen?"

"About half-an-hour ago."

Damn...I wonder how long I have before Bagley finds out his ass has been tagged. "Don't worry about it, Jorge. Let me make a few calls. I'll be in touch."

Jeanette nibbled on her fingernail. "What's wrong?"

"We might have a small problem."

After Roman briefed her, she furrowed her eyebrows. "If he finds out, he'll be on the first thing smoking out of town."

"Exactly. I need to find Bagley."

She took her car keys out of her pocket and extended them toward Roman. "Take my car. You can get around a lot faster in it, and, of course, you know it's safe."

"Keep it; I already have a copy of your car keys." He handed her the key to the Yukon.

Shaking her head, she took the Yukon key. "You're lucky I have too much to do to get into how you got a copy of my car key."

"What are you up to?"

"A little last minute Christmas shopping is all."

The look in her eyes told Roman she was hiding something, but he had no time to coax it out of her. "Okay, but be careful at whatever you're up to. I'll make sure Vanessa is taken care of." Bagley would have to wait until the little girl was safe.

Chapter Twenty-Three

Jeanette parked the Yukon between two high rises. Both contained office buildings and luxury penthouses and condominiums. Papa had assured her no one, including the police, would bother the truck while she left it in the alley to handle her business. Though it was night, she slipped on her cat-eyed shades, pinned her hair up with a few "specially dipped" pins and walked into the security area of the building.

"Who are you here to visit?" the guard asked.

"The Saint."

"And your name?"

"Monica Noble."

The guard dialed the penthouse. "Excuse me, sir. There's a Monica Noble here to see the Saint...Okay. I'll let her up." He disconnected.

Unbeknownst to the guard, Papa had commandeered the phone lines in the building, so when he called the penthouse for verification, he was actually calling Papa.

"Come with me." The guard led her to the elevator. Once the doors opened, he stepped inside and keyed in the code to give her access to the penthouse.

"Thank you." She stood at the back of the elevator. "Have a Merry Christmas."

"You too, ma'am." As the doors slid closed, she watched him

return to his post.

The elevator stopped at the penthouse of Wycliffe St. Jean—aka the Saint, the albino head of the Caribbean Connection. The members all had to dye the tips of their dreads in honor of the Saint's blond, ropy, Bob Marley-like dreads.

According to Papa, the Saint was in his multi-million dollar penthouse with his top men having their annual "business meeting." *Great, I might as well get this all done at once*, she had thought when he initially told her of the weeklong "meeting."

She smoothed the legs of her black leather pants, straightened her wide, studded black leather belt and unzipped her black leather jacket, which stopped just above the belt and showed a touch of her red top.

The elevator doors opened, and she stepped into the room holding a briefcase as if she owned the place. Two very stunned men stood and looked at each other with utter confusion in their eyes.

Without missing a beat, she said, "Hello, I'm Monica Noble. I'm here to see the Saint."

Both men stammered, but the shorter of the two burly men spoke first. "How did you...The Saint is busy."

The men looked her over from head to toe, still obviously confused yet attracted to her at the same time.

She smiled sweetly. "Do you like my jacket? I made it myself." She did a little turn to ensure they saw the red hourglass on the back with the studded spider web over it. On the back of her sleeves were rows of small silver studs that ran from her shoulder down to her elbow.

The taller man nervously said, "Real cute, but you sure love studs."

She giggled. "In more ways than one." The men's brows raised and their postures straightened even more. "Seriously, though, I got them on sale and felt compelled to use them all. Now are you going to tell the Saint I'm here or not?"

"He's busy, and I'll be sure to kick the guard's butt for

allowing you up."

"Stop jumping to conclusions. How do you know the Saint didn't give me his code?"

"He would have told us, and he never gives out his code. What did you do, watch him key it in?"

"That'll be my little secret. Now, may I see the Saint?"

"No. Leave your name and phone number, and I'll tell him you called."

"He'll want to see me now."

He huffed out in exasperation. "Why?"

Another diabetes-causing smile tipped her lips. "Because I'm the fiancée of the man who murdered his sons." She flashed her ring.

Both men stumbled over themselves with "Daaaaaymmm" and "Hell nawwww" sprinkled in their reaction.

"You sure you want to go back there, little mama?" the shorter one asked.

"Positive."

She followed the shorter man through the penthouse to the dining room where the heads of the gang were seated around one of the most beautiful mahogany dining tables she'd ever seen. Eight men in all, most in their upper-fifties, turned toward the doorway.

She'd only seen the Saint in photos, but since he was the only albino at the table, he was easy to pick out.

"Who the fuck are you?" the Saint directed toward Jeanette. "And why the hell did you bring her back here," he said to his guard.

"This is Monica Noble, the fiancée of that muthafucka who killed your sons." He motioned toward her. "Sorry for the language, ma'am."

"Thank you for your assistance," she said to the guard. He turned and left the room. Now that she had everyone's attention, she walked around to the leader's end of the table and set the briefcase down. Everyone must have still been in shock, because no one said a word or moved.

"You have to call the hit off Roman. It's ridiculous, and I don't have time for ridiculous in my life right now." Standing beside the still-seated Saint, she opened the briefcase and displayed two million dollars. "The hit is for one million. I'll double your price to call it off."

Looking slightly amused, the Saint said, "This isn't about the money. I have more money than I'll ever spend."

"Nonsense, this is business, and the main objective of business is to make money. What's the price?"

"I like you." He chuckled. "Thank you for giving me your fiancé's name. He doesn't know you're here, does he?"

"Hell no." She didn't worry about giving them a name to place with Roman's face, they'd all be dead or ready to do business her way by the end of the night anyway.

Everyone around the table laughed.

"I figured as much." He tapped the money. "This isn't about money, but respect. You can't put a price on that. Roman must die."

The men around the table all nodded and mumbled in agreement.

Hands on her hips, she said, "Y'all watch entirely too many movies. This is real life. Now there has to be some sort of compromise."

"I know you can't understand, but when Roman killed my sons, he started a war. A respect war. To gain full respect back, Roman must die."

"There has to be another way."

He motioned around the room. "The only other way is for Roman to kill everyone in this room, and that shit won't ever happen."

Again, the men nodded and mumbled their agreement.

"Let me get this straight. Money won't end this. The only way is either all of you die or Roman dies. That's more ridiculousness than I care to deal with." She turned to the other men. "Are you honestly willing to continue this war?"

"Roman started it," one man said.

"This won't be the first war we ended or the last," said another.

This was stupid and yet another prime example why she wasn't bothered with people. "No offense, but it's not like your sons were innocent beings. They were drug-dealing murderers." She motioned around the room. "Just like everyone else in here." Lips pursed, she said, "I take that back. I'm not a drug dealer." She smiled, sure her joke had gone over their heads.

The Saint took her by the hand. "Roman chose well. Too well. I can't allow you to leave."

She fully faced him. "I have no intention of staying. It's getting late, and I told Roman I'd meet him," she looked at her watch, "in a little over an hour."

The amused look returned to his face as he stood. "You have a choice to make." He held her by the waist and pulled her close, invading her private space. "If you help draw Roman to us, I'll kill him quickly. If you force me to use you as bait, then I'll kill Roman slowly."

"Oh yeah, y'all watch entirely too many movies." She turned toward the men, and he pulled her backside into him, ensuring she felt his ever-growing presence. *Jerk.* "Have you ever heard about the prickly pear cactus?"

Confusion engulfed the room. One of the men said, "She's as crazy as she is fine."

Seemingly ignoring the chuckling men, she explained, "The tiny thorns on some varieties of the cactus look harmless." She tapped one of the hundreds of studs on her jacket. "They have areas on them that remind me of the studs on this jacket, but instead of holes like these in the studs, there are tiny thorns."

"Oh yeah, those mothers hurt like a real son-of-a-bitch and are hard as hell to get out," one of the men said.

"You got that right. They work their way into anything, except a piece of paper. Isn't that odd?"

The Saint and everyone else continued indulging her, a look of wonder on their faces.

She turned and faced the Saint. He slipped his hands under

her jacket and caressed her sides. "Are you done?"

"Almost. So all of you must die in order for Roman to live? There's nothing I can do to change your minds?

"You give me a son, and I'll reconsider."

With a roll of the eyes, she said, "Ten million. Consider the two as a down payment." She knew she was attractive, but not that attractive. His desire for her to have his children was grounded in completely emasculating Roman.

"You don't get it, do you?" He tapped the money-filled briefcase. "This is mine." He caressed her face. "You're mine, and Roman is a dead man." He paused. "After you have my son, Roman dies." He picked up his cell phone and dialed one of his guards. "Monica will be staying, *permanently*," he said, as if daring her to dispute him. "She'll be sharing my room. She isn't to leave the penthouse or have phone or Internet privileges."

Unable to believe his gall, all she could do was stare. He actually thought he could keep her as if she were a piece of property. And she knew there was no way he had just put her on some sort of no phone/Internet type punishment as if she were a child.

Tired of playing games with this roomful of scum, she turned her back to the table and pressed a large stud on the cuff of her sleeve. Thousands of highly toxic needles darted out of the studs on her jacket back, hitting the gang leaders who were seated around the table.

Not even a split second later, she whipped one of the pins out of her hair, stabbed the Saint in the neck and moved away to allow the fast-acting paralyzing agent to work.

They didn't stand a chance. The men yelped in pain and quickly began dropping. No needles went forward, which was why she had kept her back to the men. Everything within 180-degrees had been sprayed. The Saint was safe until she used the pin on him. He dropped to the floor, temporarily paralyzed.

She heard the guards coming from the front, reacting to the cries they'd heard, and quickly drew her gun from the hidden compartment in her briefcase. She ducked under the table.

The men entered with guns drawn, cussing up a storm.

Just in case the men were wearing body armor, she quickly shot them in the head. Now that everyone except the Saint was dead, it was almost time to leave. She rose to her feet, slipped in her earpiece and called Papa.

"I'm done." She broke out her small digital camera and took pictures of the fallen men.

"Have you eliminated everyone, including his two guards?"

"Yep." She snapped a picture of the guards.

"I have a man on the patio to help you get out. Don't kill him."

"Ha, ha, very funny." She crossed the room and stood over the Saint, who was on the floor struggling to breathe. "Don't worry, you won't die yet."

~~~~~~

"Thanks for flying the professor over to Guantanamo Bay for me, Jeff. I really appreciate this," Roman said to his Navy Seal buddy. After stopping in Pinecrest and having Javier give Vanessa a shot of the antidote, Roman had quickly driven the professor to Fort Lauderdale.

"No sweat, my man. I don't know how you pulled it off, but damn I'm glad you did! You know how much I love to fly these fighters and get out of my plain-Jane courier jet. And I especially love night flights."

Roman turned to Javier. "You okay, Professor?" The look in his eyes said he wasn't okay by a long shot.

"Yes...yes..." he stammered. "It's just that I've never flown in anything like this."

"Don't worry, by the time you begin to freak out, the flight will be over." Roman handed the professor a briefcase. "Everything you need is in here. Remember, you never saw or heard of Agent Spears or Agent Bond. Just say you had the help of an American scientist in finding the cure."

He nodded. "Okay, but are you sure you guys don't want any credit? This is a *major* development and Monica deserves her credit."

Roman checked his watch. "Positive. Now, climb aboard."

Jeff smiled, then handed the professor a helmet. "Don't worry, there are a few barf bags back there for ya."

On his way out of Fort Lauderdale, Roman stopped just before the exit. *Wonder if Shadow's ass is watching me right now. Wish I had time to search this base for him, but I need to get my hands on Bagley—and fast!*

Chapter Twenty-Four

Come on, Santa. I could use a Christmas gift about now. That son-of-a-bitch being at his penthouse is all I want for Christmas. Roman hit triple digits on the highway to Miami, en route to Bagley's building. Once there, he parked in the alley behind the high rise. He removed his duffle bag from the backseat of the car. "I don't have time for finesse—so, time for plan B, with the B standing for brute force."

Since it was Christmas Eve, the city was as dead as a stone. A pair of mongrel dogs scoured the alleyway in search of a meal. Near the end of the alley, Roman saw the main telephone circuit box for the area. He broke into it, checked the grids, then disabled all the Bagley building phones. Now no outgoing calls by phone or by the security system could be made.

At the rear loading dock, he removed one of his pistols. "Let's do this." He picked the lock, pushed the door open, setting off the alarm. "I hope old dude hurries up." Hiding behind a pallet of boxes, he waited for the guard to come investigate the alarm.

Once the guard entered the loading dock area, Roman rushed him before the guard had a chance to go for his weapon. "Easy, grandpa." Roman removed the shocked guard's pistol, tucked it in his waistband and pointed his own gun between the guard's eyes. "I'm sure they don't pay you enough to get shot over some bullshit."

"Hell, no," the sixty-ish black man said. "I like playin' with my grandkids."

"Good." Roman removed the man's cuffs and keys, duct taped his mouth, then cuffed his hands around a water main. Before going in search of Bagley, he took the guard's electronic badge and walkie-talkie. "Are you the only guard on duty tonight? If you lie, you will get your coworker killed. Understand?"

The guard nodded his head feverishly and mumbled a reply.

"I'll take that as a yes that you are alone." The man nodded again.

Running to the elevators, he used the guard's badge and gained access to the off-limits penthouse suite. Roman dropped his duffle bag, moved the aspirin bottle of sand aside, drew both guns and exited the elevator. He listened and heard nothing.

The penthouse floor reflected Bagley's excessive lifestyle. Roman picked up his bag and followed the hallway until he found Bagley's living quarters and searched the suite. "Shit!" He let his pistols dangle at his sides. "That bastard ain't here."

A waterfall screen saver played on Bagley's computer. Out of curiosity, Roman walked over and hit the enter key. The log-on screen appeared. He opened the duffle bag and removed his laptop and a USB cable.

With the help of another of his favorite hacking programs, Batter Ram, he successfully fooled the computer into giving him access through the USB port. "Hmmph, so that's where he is," he said after hacking into Bagley's e-mail account and reading an e-mail from Lipton dated two days ago.

> Merry Christmas, Bags!
> This is just a reminder that my pilot will be picking you up from the casino heliport at noon, on the 24th. This is going to be the most memorable Christmas party you have ever been to. I also look forward to wrapping up the final land purchases after the holidays. I gave instructions to your pilot

on how to get to my private airstrip just outside Miami. You'll have a much easier time flying out of there in the morning instead of the cluster fuck of flying out of a public airport. See you at the party!

"Damn, I wish he'd mentioned where that airstrip is." Roman disconnected from Bagley's computer and put a fresh toothpick in his mouth. On the positive side, Bagley being on Lipton's yacht might buy Roman a little time—if the guard who escaped Jorge's man didn't get word to him yet.

He used his laptop, hacked into the FAA database, then breathed a sigh of relief. According to the flight request logs for the past twenty-four hours, there had been no requests for Lipton's helicopter to fly to the mainland.

After packing up his goods, he picked up a yellow notepad off Bagley's desk. "He must really like this Marta woman." Bagley had scribbled her name a thousand times. That name triggered a memory. "That's Bagley's assistant." He dropped the notepad. "He's probably screwin' her—nasty bastard."

Marta's name bothered him all the way back to the goat. "It's time to go visit a certain little assistant." He started the car. "But first, I need to meet up with a certain spider lady."

~~~~~~

Roman pulled up to the driveway gate and saw Jeanette get out the Yukon and go into the house. "Oh, hell naw! It's almost three in the morning. Why is she just now getting back to the house? I told her it's too damn dangerous to be out this time of night by herself. The CC gang is on red alert."

Parking behind the Yukon, he sprinted to the door, went inside and found Jeanette in the kitchen, drinking a glass of water. "Where the hel—" The sight of her in that outrageously sexy leather suit dried the words up in his mouth.

She set her glass on the counter and smiled at the awestruck assassin. "What were you saying?"

"Where the hell..." he walked closer and gazed at the form-fitting, studded suit, "...have you been? Don't you know how hot the streets are right now?"

"You worry too much, dear." She took him by the hand and led him toward the front door. "I did a little Christmas shopping. Come see what I got for you."

He gave her a skeptical look. "I know better than that. What are you up to, Jeanette?"

The studs on her jacket glowed in the moonlight as she walked him to the Yukon. She grinned, pulled a small, slim digital camera out of her jacket's inside pocket and handed it to him. "Merry Christmas!"

"A camera? I don't mean to be disrespectful, but why are you giving me this cheap-ass camera you bought for yourself?"

"Look at the pictures, Scrooge."

He scrolled through picture after picture of the dead leaders of the CC gang. "What the fuck? How did you do *this*?"

"A girl has to keep some secrets." She gave him a sly smile, took his hand and led him to the back of the Yukon. "Your real present is in there. Go ahead and open it up."

"Well, damn." He stared at a moving mass under the blanket in the back of the Yukon. "Are you sure this is for me?"

"Positive. Open it up."

Underneath the blanket, to his surprise and pleasure, the Saint was bound and gagged. The biggest red ribbon Roman had ever seen was tied around his head. "Ain't this a bitch!" Roman stared into the pale freckled face of the man who had been hunting him down like a dog. "Now I really believe in Santa Claus."

The Saint thrashed around and groaned with wild hatred in his eyes. "Shut the fuck up and keep still," Roman said just before smashing his fist into the Saint's duct-taped mouth.

The groans turned to moans of agony as blood seeped out from underneath the silver tape. Roman recalled how the Saint had called for the execution of an entire family because the father, an assistant district attorney, wouldn't play ball and offer a few CC members a plea they couldn't refuse. The Saint had the man's wife and preteen daughters raped before they were murdered. "I really am having a hard time not putting a few holes in you right now, muthafucka."

Jeanette crossed her arms. "What's stopping you?"

"I have a better idea." He kissed her on the cheek. "I have to make a run with the Saint. I'll be back in a few. Don't leave."

~~~~~~

In a seedy Miami ghetto, Roman pulled to a stop in front of an abandoned apartment complex, a block away from a pair of CC gang members dealing drugs. He got out, went behind the Yukon and yanked the Saint out onto the street. After roughly kicking the Saint over onto his back, he pulled one of his silencer-equipped pistols and looked into that freckled face. "Tell your sons I said Merry Christmas." The Saint frantically tried to roll away. Roman then emptied half the clip into the body of the CC gang leader.

One more thing. He went to the duffle bag on the floor of the passenger side and removed the aspirin bottle full of sand. *Was gonna use this on Shadow, but this piece of shit deserves it.* Back at his dead Christmas gift, he opened the bottle and poured the sand over the Saint's bloody, bullet-riddled body. After pulling out his lucky knife, he cut off one of the Saint's foot-long blond dreads.

Glancing down the street, Roman saw the dope dealers busy making a sale. He got back in the Yukon, held his pistol in one hand and drove down to the gang members. One of them hurried to his window in hopes of making a sale.

"What you ne—" He froze. "Oh shit! It's the million-dollar man!"

Before he could reach for the pistol in his waistband, Roman pointed his gun at him. "Put your fuckin' hand down and shut the fuck up!" The menacing look of the black silencer on Roman's gun made him comply. He tossed the blond dreadlock to the stunned man. "I left the rest of him down the street in front of those abandoned apartments…a gift from the Sandman. Tell all your friends."

Chapter Twenty-Five

Bone-tired, Roman returned to Homestead where he found Jeanette sound asleep on the couch, her hair tied back with the black scarf she seemed to love so much. Sitting on the coffee table, he watched her. *Absolutely beautiful.* He flipped through the images of the dead CC gang leaders on the cheap camera.

A mischievous smile tipped his lips. *She has a good eye for the shot.* How she had accomplished such a feat amazed him. What amazed him even more was she had nothing to gain by getting the gang off his back, yet she had still gone all out for him. The only person who had ever cared for his well-being was his mother. And now he apparently had Shadow and the Black Widow watching his back.

"Jeanette," he said softly.

~~~~~~

Jeanette stretched awake. Now that they'd stopped the Cuban plague before it became an actual plague and Roman was safe, her body was shutting down from exhaustion. "Did Javier call? Is he in Cuba?" Her yawn interrupted his answer.

"It's Marta."

"Marta?"

"Bagley's assistant. I lost him, but think I can find him through her." He explained about the obsessive scribbling of her name he'd found at Bagley's.

She checked her watch. She'd gotten only ten minutes of sleep, but that would have to do. "Let's go."

"That's my girl." He shoved his toothpick about his mouth with his tongue. "But let's take both cars in case he's stupider than I think and is over at her place, and they split up."

"Sounds like a plan."

As Jeanette drove her GTO down Marta's street, she saw flashing blue and red lights of an emergency vehicle. Something in her heart told her the vehicle would be at Marta's before she was close enough to see that the ambulance had indeed parked in Marta's driveway.

Two paramedics were carrying someone out on a stretcher to the ambulance and someone who looked to be a male nurse was holding a hysterical older woman back in the doorway of the house, trying to calm her. *Why the nurse?* She also heard young children crying for their mommy.

Jeanette rushed out of her car as Roman pulled up in the Yukon behind the GTO.

One look at the lesion-covered woman on the stretcher and Jeanette knew she was in the final stages of the Cuban plague. She turned to Roman and lashed out in anger. "That son-of-a-bitch!" Tears streamed down her face. "Why would he do this to her? Why?"

Roman held her in his arms, calming her.

The confused paramedics loaded Marta onto the ambulance. Roman glanced at Marta. "Is it too late?"

"I pray it's not, but I have to go with them. I'm calling Papa and having him reroute the ambulance somewhere where I can do what needs to be done."

"Understood." He nodded toward the house. "What the hell is a nurse doing here? Why wasn't she in the hospital?"

She knew the questions were rhetorical. Bagley's hand was in this deep. He'd probably kept Marta from going to the hospital. "You have to find that bastard and kill his ass now."

"I'm on it, baby. You go do what you have to do. I'm about to find out who the hell that nurse is."

As the paramedics began securing Marta in the back of the ambulance, Jeanette pulled out her cell phone and speed dialed Papa. She walked away from the house, saying, "The Cuban plague is here in Miami. That bastard gave it to his assistant."

"Wha...wha...what? Slow down. Did you say—?"

"Yes," she cut in. "Bagley. It's Bagley and he tested the shit right here on American soil. I need you to work your magic, so I can try to save this woman's life. The ambulance is about to take her to the hospital." She gave him all of the details about the ambulance company. "For all I know, they're in on this, too. There's a male nurse here."

"A male nurse?"

"Yes, but Roman's taking care of that."

"This will take a few minutes. Follow the ambulance."

"I'm on it." Cursing Bagley with everything unholy, she rushed to her car.

She saw Roman enter the house with a very nervous looking nurse. The ambulance pulled out of the driveway. Tears clouded her vision. She adjusted her scarf and wiped the tears from her eyes. The last thing she saw before pulling off were children holding onto the older woman's legs, crying for their mother. "That bastard will die for this. He will die."

A few minutes later, Papa called with instructions on where the ambulance had been re-routed. Turned out the older woman at the house was Marta's mother and had called the paramedics against the "nurse's" instructions and demanded they take her baby to the hospital.

~~~~~~

If that fool's a nurse, then I'm Mary Poppins. Roman approached the tall, lanky Latino male. Roman noticed a small tattoo of a dagger dripping blood on the nurse's hand between his thumb and forefinger—the same as those worn by the *Vaquero Diablos* prison gang, that had originated in Rio Pedras Prison, Puerto Rico, but now operated heavily in the Florida prison system.

After seeing the tattoo, Roman stopped a few feet in front of the nurse, opened his leather jacket enough for the man to see his holstered pistols, pulled out his fake CIA badge and showed it to the nurse. "I'm Agent Bond. I need to have a few words with you."

The nurse stiffened in his baggy blue scrubs. A mask of nervousness darkened his face. "What did I do?"

Roman put his hand on the man's elbow and motioned toward the front door. "I'll explain inside. Now *move*."

Homeboy wants to avoid trouble at all cost, good. Roman followed the man inside the house and took him to the back bedroom, so they could have a private conversation. "What's your name?"

Ten minutes later, Roman found out—after some very intimidating interrogation techniques—the nurse, Pablo, was a former medical student and parolee. He'd spent the last decade in prison for rape and drug charges.

Roman popped a fresh cinnamon-flavored toothpick in his mouth. "So, Pablo, you heard about this job through your parole officer?" He pulled out his satellite phone. "That means if I call him he will verify your story, right?"

A couple of cigarettes jumped out the pack and onto the floor as Pablo nervously tried to tap one out. "Shit!" He pulled a lighter out his pocket, lit his cancer stick and sucked in a cloud of smoke. "Okay, okay, okay. Don't call...he would put my ass back in the slammer in half a second." He gave Roman a pleading look. "Man, all I wanted to do was make a few dollars, so I can move to Kansas and get the hell out of here. I have a girl there and—"

Roman put his hand up. "Enough of the sob story bullshit. Just tell me who hired you and why you didn't take Marta to the hospital."

Pablo lit a new cigarette off the previous one he had smoked down to the butt. "Okay. I'm not being paid enough to risk being sent back to lockup." He sat on the sofa and looked down at his feet. "I owed this doctor friend of mine a favor. He's paying me good money to watch after Marta, but not good enough to go back to jail."

"What's his name?"

Pablo hesitated, but finally said, "Snow, Doctor Gary Snow."

Cursing under his breath, Roman took a few seconds to compose himself for not doing a better job investigating Bagley and all of his connections.

"Who's Snow working for?"

"I...I don't know."

"It's been a long day. Don't make me take it out on your ass."

Pablo's eyes bugged out. "Some dude with a thick British accent named Bagley. He's come by here a few times to check on Marta."

Gotcha!

~~~~~~

Speeding in the Yukon, Roman passed numerous homes full of light as the residents got a predawn start on unwrapping their Christmas gifts. He had to hurry back to the house and see if Lipton's chopper had left for the airstrip yet. He tapped on his earpiece and waited for Jeanette to respond.

"Hey, how is Marta doing?"

"So far so good. I think she's going to make it, but it's too early to be sure. What's the status of Bagley?"

He sped off the Homestead City exit to the house he and Jeanette now occupied. "I found him. He's at a Christmas party on Lipton's yacht."

"Unbelievable."

"Yeah. Partying hard while he lets his assistant die. He's due to be flown from the yacht early this morning to some private airstrip Lipton owns in Miami."

"Great! I want to help you find his ass. I'm on my way after I leave instructions with the doctors here."

"Just head over to Bagley's building." He pulled up to the gate at the house and entered his code. "That's where the chopper will be taking him. He's going to be flying out *real early*."

"Okay. I'll see you there."

"Ah, shit," he said after hacking into the FAA's communication system and discovering Lipton's helicopter had left the yacht a short time ago, headed into Miami. He ran to his room and grabbed his drag bag and two additional boxes of ammo for his pistols. "I hope like hell I can make it to Bagley's building before he leaves for that airstrip."

An hour before sunrise, Roman ran a host of signal lights and stop signs on the way to Bagley's building. A mile from the building, he saw a helicopter leaving the downtown area. "Shit! I hope that's not his chopper."

As Roman approached the front of the building, he saw Bagley get into the back of a black Jaguar with a briefcase cuffed to his wrist. He was adjusting his wireless earpiece. Two large blond men got in the Jag and drove off, passing Roman up on the opposite side of the street.

With no time to make a smooth U-turn, he tested the Yukon's suspension by hooking a hard U-turn, driving over the concrete island. Horns blared.

~~~~~~

"What the hell is all that racket?" Bagley asked of horns he heard blaring.

"People in this country can't drive. Some fool just crossed over the medium back there," said the driver.

Bagley replayed the message from his injured bodyguard who had been in charge of watching Dr. Snow. *Can't believe Drew was almost killed along with Snow. What an incompetent bastard.* He worried the police investigation into the murder would link him to Snow's research on the toxin. *That idiot had better have covered his tracks.*

A ball of pure terror formed in his belly as he closed his briefcase, which, per his buyer's request, contained a jump drive with the final formula for the plague burned onto it, the hard drives and all the notes on the toxin from Dr. Snow. *Have to get this toxin formula to those racist assholes before any other unexpected crap happens. Once I get paid, I don't give a shit what they do with it—I'll be so far away it won't matter.*

"I think the Yukon's following us." The driver slowed just enough to get a glimpse of the driver. "Ah, shit! It's the guy who broke into the building and tied up the security guard! Hang on, sir!"

~~~~~~

"Fuck!" Roman watched the Jag speed off. "They made me." He tapped his earpiece and called Jeanette. "Hey! Where are you?"

"I'm a couple minutes from Bagley's building. What's going on, Roman?"

The signal broke up as he followed the speeding Jag onto I-95. "I'm after Bagley. He's on the way to the freeway! Get on 95 North and *hurry!*"

High beams on, he followed the Jag through light traffic at twice the speed limit, trying to coax more speed out of the SUV. To his right, he saw a yellow Corvette enter the freeway. Seconds later, the Corvette pulled even with him. He risked a quick glance at the car just in time to see a blonde woman point a pistol at him and fire.

"Muthafucka!" He swerved as the bulletproof glass and armored door rebuffed the bullets. "Where the hell did *she* come from?"

The Jag pulled away as Roman got the Yukon back under control. He looked in his mirror and saw a pair of familiar headlights gaining on him fast. He tapped his earpiece and called his partner. "Jeanette! Watch out for that yellow Corvette. It's one of Bagley's folks. Get that bitch while I go after Bagley!"

"Okay, I'll handle it."

In his mirror, he caught a glimpse of Jeanette pulling up behind the Corvette and ramming the rear. The Corvette lost control for a second, then recovered as Jeanette pulled alongside, trying to force it off the highway. *Good girl! Now let me catch Bagley.*

Chapter Twenty-Six

Car chases had always pissed Jeanette off. In her opinion, car chases were for movies and video games, not real life. She picked up her pistol, stuck her arm out the window and fired three shots. The rear window of the Corvette shattered.

She called for Roman, but instead of an answer, she heard static in her wireless earpiece. *So much for technology. We must be out of range.*

The driver of the Corvette exited the freeway and drove along a frontage road, then whipped around a corner onto a one-way street. Jeanette rounded the corner and saw a garbage truck blocking the road. Red brake lights switched to white reverse lights as the driver of the Corvette fired her pistol out the shattered rear window and backed toward Jeanette's GTO.

Jeanette ducked and turned to her left as the Corvette sideswiped the passenger side of her GTO.

The Corvette swerved and went through a cyclone fence onto a lawn, then stalled out.

Jeanette quickly jumped out of her GTO, ran over to the disabled Corvette and pointed her Glock at the driver. The hatred in the driver's blue eyes was palpable. A bead of blood ran from the woman's scalp, just beneath her blonde hair, down her pointy nose and onto her lip as she pointed her TEC-9 pistol at Jeanette.

Just as Jeanette was about to pull the trigger, Roman's frantic voice startled her. "Jeanette!"

"Roman?"

That half a second distraction was all blondie needed. She fired two of the ten rapid-fire rounds from the fully automatic TEC-9 into Jeanette's chest.

Jeanette landed on her side, next to the Corvette's passenger side. The force of the fall knocked the earpiece out of her ear. Though stunned, she was alive, due to Roman's gift of high tech body armor, which she wore under her gray sweat suit jacket. This was a prime example of why she always shot her targets in the head.

She heard the driver struggling to open the door of the Corvette, which was tangled in the cyclone fencing.

Jeanette winced from the dull pain left behind from the impact of the 9mm shells. She heard a chorus of sirens heading her way.

The driver finally stepped out with a grin on her bloody face, surely expecting to see a dead Jeanette on the other side of the Corvette. Lying on the ground, Jeanette watched blondie's feet on the other side of the Corvette. Jeanette scrambled around to the back of the car.

Once on the passenger side of the Corvette, blondie stopped in her tracks, then cautiously crouched down.

Jeanette stepped from behind the Corvette. "Heil Hitler, bitch." She pumped four hot slugs into blondie's shocked face.

~~~~~~

A few more miles into his pursuit of Bagley's Jag, Roman had tapped his earpiece to check on the Black Widow. "Jeanette!"

"Roman," he'd barely heard her say.

"Jeanette!" he'd yelled over the roar of the Yukon's speeding engine. The sound of automatic gunfire, followed by Jeanette's shriek, had made every nerve in his body come alive.

He gripped the wheel and followed the Jag around a curve in the highway. A sea of brake lights greeted them. Half-a-mile ahead, was a stalled big rig.

"Shit!" Roman slammed on the brakes and swerved onto the shoulder, sideswiping the center divider, banging his wounded arm on the door. The agile Jag was able to successfully speed down the shoulder and around the traffic jam.

"Muthafucka!" Roman laid on the horn and flashed his high beams, working his way down the shoulder in hopes of catching the Jag. Back on the highway, past the traffic, the Jag was gone. He slammed his hand on the dash. "Where the fuck did they go?"

A couple miles down the highway, he saw a sign that read, "JML Airfield, two miles."

He jammed down the accelerator. *That's gotta be Lipton's airfield.*

Exiting the freeway, he spotted a small airfield about a mile away. Seconds later, the Yukon lurched to the right violently. "Awww, fuck! Don't tell me I got a damn flat!" He gripped the wheel hard and managed to ease the Yukon over to the side of the road. After getting out, he kicked the deflated driver's side tire. A piece of the fender had cut through the sidewall. *Can't believe Shadow didn't put run-flat tires on this bucket!*

He went into the Yukon, got his binoculars, ran to the chain link fence and looked. He saw the Jag sitting on the tarmac.

Good, the jet's not there yet. He went back to the Yukon, grabbed his drag bag and ran toward an abandoned air traffic control tower, half a football field away from him.

On the tarmac, as the first colors of dawn grew in the east, a G-5 jet touched down and rolled toward the Jag. *Oh shit, there's his ride.*

Roman fired a shot that exploded the padlock on the gate leading to the tower. The ancient lock on the door to the tower followed suit. He ran up the five flights of stairs leading to the control center. Outside the large window, he saw the jet rolling toward the Jag.

Roman had a choice to make: eliminate Bagley now and keep the formula from reaching the hands of the terrorists or allow

Bagley to give the formula to the terrorists, eliminate Bagley, then track down the terrorists. Decision made, the large observation window exploded after he fired two rounds into it. No way would he chance the formula for the plague spreading like a virus on the Internet.

He cleared away shards of broken glass with the sleeve of his leather jacket, unzipped the drag bag and assembled his "magic wand," a .50 caliber sniper rifle. He didn't have time to hook up the laser sight; the door to the jet was opening up. Resting the barrel on the window ledge, he pointed the rifle out the hole in the window. "Gotta do this the old school way, no laser."

Through the scope, he saw both of Bagley's guards step aside as the jet's door opened and the steps lowered. He swung the scope to the rear passenger window of the Jag. "Shit, it's still too dark to get a good look at Bagley."

A blue flash of light in the Jag's window caught his attention. He smirked. *Got your ass now*. He counted until the light flashed again. *Six seconds*.

"Three...two...one." He pulled the trigger. At that distance, about 2400 yards, it took the bullet nearly four seconds to hit its mark. The .50 caliber round shattered Bagley's Bluetooth earpiece and severed his head from his body.

He swung the rifle at the guards. The driver ran to Bagley's door, snatched it open and vomited. Bagley's mangled corpse fell to the ground with the briefcase attached to its wrist. Roman fired at the driver. He dropped with a cantaloupe-size hole in his chest. Shocked, the second bodyguard gawked at his fallen coworker for a second, then ran toward the jet. Roman locked the man's back in the scope's crosshairs and fired. The guard flew off his feet as the bullet destroyed his spine just below his neck. The jet doors closed quickly and its engines revved up, then the jet sped down the runway.

After packing up his rifle and slinging the drag bag over his shoulder, Roman left the tower and ran to the Jag. He went through Bagley's pockets and got the keys to the cuff and briefcase. "You won't be needin' this, asshole." Inside, he found the jump drive, hard drives and paperwork that reminded him of Jeanette's scientific notes. *BINGO!*

~~~~~~

*Jeanette...*Heart heavy, Roman stopped to gas up the Yukon after changing the flat tire. He couldn't bring himself to call Shadow about Jeanette. He just refused to believe she was gone. No, instead, when he arrived home, she'd be standing on the porch, barefoot, waiting for him.

A tiny grey kitten with its head stuck inside an empty potato chip bag drew his attention. "Now how did you find yourself in this position, fella?" He picked up the green-eyed kitten and removed the bag. The scrawny kitten hissed at him, but was too weak to put up much fight. He opened the packet of beef jerky he'd purchased along with the gas, ripped off a piece and put it up to the kitten's mouth. The kitten devoured the treat.

"Damn! Kind of hungry?" Putting the kitten on the passenger floor along with the rest of the beef jerky, he left the gas station for Homestead, praying that Jeanette had somehow made it home.

He sighed as the first rays of the sun shined in his tired eyes. The ringing of his satellite phone barely got his attention. Without checking the caller ID, he answered. "Speak..."

"Roman? Where are you?"

A billion volts of joy shot through his heart. "*Jeanette? Jeanette! Is that you?*"

"Yes, it's me. Are you okay?"

His face could barely support his smile. "Yes, baby, yes! I'm just fine. I thought I had lost..."

"Hmmm? You thought you had lost what?"

"Nothing, never mind." Once again, his fear of loving and being loved forbade him from voicing his true feelings. "Where are you? How are you feelin'? The last I heard was gunfire, then I lost contact with you."

"I'm on my way home, feeling a little sore. But thanks to this sweet body armor, I'm still alive. And you? Did you find

Bagley?"

"Yes...and he won't be home for Christmas."

Chapter Twenty-Seven

Mission accomplished, Jeanette and Roman were so exhausted when they returned to Homestead that they showered—separately—then met in Jeanette's room, climbed in bed together and slept. They'd both been up over twenty-four hours, and the events of their days together had taken their toll on them. There was no reason for them to share a room or even associate with each other any further, but Jeanette felt she belonged in his arms. She knew she couldn't stay, and so did he.

Jeanette woke in Roman's arms and rolled over to watch him sleep, but he was already awake and watching her. Heart warmed, she thought about the first time she'd seen Roman. She'd finally remembered she had been on her way to the Harold Washington Library in Chicago. She'd been crossing the street when their eyes connected. She would bet he didn't remember. Why would he? They didn't know each other at the time.

He held her close. "Merry Christmas."

Jeanette didn't want whatever it was between them to end and could tell he didn't want it to end either, but it had to. This had been the craziest ten days of her life. "Merry Christmas to you, too."

Just as they leaned in to kiss, her cell phone rang Papa's ring tone.

Both acted as if their near-kiss hadn't happen and backed away from each other. He reached over her and took the phone off the nightstand. She wished his arms would stay wrapped around her, but he handed her the phone. After placing it on speaker, she said, "Merry Christmas, Papa."

"Merry Christmas to you, too. Is Roman there?"

"Yeah, I'm here." They both leaned against the headboard.

"For two bad-assed kids, you guys did an excellent job. You made me proud, your country proud."

"Thanks," they said reluctantly. The new and improved Papa would take a bit of getting used to.

"This was it for me. I'm done intruding on both of your lives. It's past time for you both to go home."

Roman chuckled. "You're just afraid we'll come after your ass."

"You got that right," Jeanette added. "But it's all good. Right, Roman?"

He pulled one of his toothpicks out of nowhere. "Yeah. We're good."

"You two enjoy your new home, and Roman, the Yukon is yours. If either of you need me, you know how to reach me."

"What home?" Jeanette asked.

"The one you're in now. I've transferred ownership over to you two. Enjoy. Now you both need to go *home*." He disconnected.

"That was…" she hunched her shoulders, "…odd." Odd, but not as awkward as she felt in bed with Roman. Their mission was over. This was so much harder than it should be. "I…I guess I should head on home."

"Where's home, Black Widow?"

In her heart, her home was with Roman, but Papa was right; it was time to go to her family home. She'd never be able to move forward until she began to repair her relationship with her father. "I'm tired of being a Black Widow. I want my family back. I'm done."

"You're done?" he said with definite doubt in his voice.

Smiling, she amended, "Unless a certain Sandman needs me. It just burns the hell out of me that we don't know who commissioned Bagley for the toxin."

"That makes two of us. I'll keep looking on the side."

"Let me know when it's time to come out of my web. Otherwise, I'm just your everyday scientist."

"You, everyday?" he teased. "Seriously, though, I'm glad you're making that move."

"What about you? You're so good with the camera."

"The Sandman is gonna leave a trail of footprints in the sand of a faraway beach where no one can find him." He paused for a moment in deep thought. "But I do miss my mom. For years I've been blaming Shadow for keeping me from her, but...But I was doing this shit before he came along. I distanced myself from her because of what I've become, not because of Shadow's little threats." He chuckled. "He always pays on time and has assignments I would have taken on myself."

"So what do you do now?"

"I'm going home and see her first. Once I come back as Roman Tate, I think I'll move from the occasional photo shoot to being a freelance photographer full-time."

Chewing on her bottom lip, Jeanette knew they were stalling, but why prolong their misery? "Well, I need to hit the road. I have a lot of ground to cover before the sun comes up."

"Yeah, I like night-driving also. I guess we need to get on out of here."

~~~~~~

At the beat up GTO, Jeanette leaned against the driver's door and faced Roman, but instead of looking into his eyes, she stared at the moon behind him.

He placed his hands on the GTO's roof on either side of her and gazed into her eyes. Nervous, she nibbled her lower lip.

"There's one more thing we need to settle," he whispered. Instead of saying what, he continued looking into her eyes. Heart and mind racing, she was just as trapped as him and didn't want to escape.

He finally backed away and opened the passenger door of the Yukon. He rummaged around and came back with a tiny grey kitten.

It was the cutest little fur ball she had ever seen. She had always loved kittens; it was grown cats she hated. She recalled how less intense her nightmares had become during her and Roman's time together.

"How and when did you get him? He is a he, isn't he?" She took the kitten and checked his behind. "Yep, a he." She hugged the little creature.

"I found him yesterday on the way back from the airstrip and thought he'd be perfect for you. Maybe if you raise it, it'll help you get past your phobia."

"I'd like that. I'd like that a lot." She Eskimo-kissed the kitten, then put him inside the GTO. "He's *adorable*. Thank you, Roman. Thanks for everything."

He brushed his nose along the side of her face, then rested his forehead on hers. Eyes closed, he sighed and whispered, "Anytime…anytime at all, baby."

His touch, always so gentle, always so potent. This was so hard for both of them. She wanted to tell him how she felt, but couldn't voice her feelings. The lives they wanted to leave would hold onto them longer. They both knew this. And those lives did not lend themselves to her acting on her love. Allowing Roman to walk away from her was the hardest thing she'd ever had to do, but she didn't see an alternative.

As he held her left hand and kissed it, they both stared at the diamond ring. "I suppose you want it back now."

He stopped her from removing the ring. "I'll trade you the ring for this." He untied the black bandana holding back her hair and let her hair hang loose.

Without saying good-bye, he stepped back, turned away and got into the Yukon. She understood; she couldn't bring herself to say the simple word herself.

After she watched him drive away, she picked up the kitten

and snuggled it. "I think I'll call you Roman."

~~~~~~

A quarter mile from the house, Roman pulled the battle-damaged Yukon over to the side of the road. He picked her black bandana off the passenger seat and held it as he looked in the rearview mirror at the house in the distance. *Miss you already, Jeanette.*

A sense of loss and longing for her was so deep in his heart, he flirted with the idea of going back and telling her how he really felt, but dismissed the thought. *People like us don't love…we can't. It's not in our makeup.*

Bandana to his nose, he breathed in the aroma of her honeysuckle-scented shampoo, then tied the bandana around his rearview mirror. He smiled and drove off. For the first time since he'd left his mother and joined the military, he felt a true bit of Christmas spirit. He sincerely meant it when he said, "Happy holidays, Black Widow."

A Few Words From L. L. Reaper

A multi-published, award-winning author, I decided to venture away from the much-traveled path of traditional publishing and strike out on my own as my alter ego, L. L. Reaper, with Hourglass Unlimited™.

Thank you for taking a chance on *Black Widow and the Sandman*. I truly hope you enjoyed the beginning of their journey and are ready for further adventures of Roman, Jeanette and the rest of the enigmatic cast. Be sure to sign up for the blog at LLReaper.com and become privy to upcoming release announcements, action-packed vignettes—not included in the novels—and other insider information.

Until we meet again, enjoy the following sneak peek into the next episode.

L. L. Reaper

PREVIEW

Black Widow
and the
Sandman
Hell Hath No Fury

L. L. Reaper

Chapter One

Earpiece snug in her ear, Jeanette sunk into the vanilla-scented bubbles of the oversized claw-foot tub. The last time she had let down her guard and come completely out of her Black Widow persona was...She couldn't remember and honestly didn't care. No matter what, she'd wind down and enjoy life as a normal vacationer for the first time in her life—even if she had to kill someone to do it!

She took a sip of white Zinfandel, then set the wine glass next to the half-eaten personal pepperoni pizza on the bamboo tray connected to the side of the tub.

"You still there, Jeanette?" Roman asked.

"I'm here," came her lazy reply, loving the way her name rolled off his tongue. She hadn't spoken to Roman "The Sandman" Tate in weeks because they'd both been extremely busy with work in different world time zones.

"What are you up to?" he asked.

She kicked the bubbles about with her toes and rested her head on the neck pillow. "Soaking in the tub."

She heard him draw in a sharp intake of air, then clear his throat. A click over the line indicated another call. Seeing it was her father, she chose to ignore the call. "Did I tell you about my dad's new main squeeze he met on the Internet?"

He chuckled. "Only a couple hundred times."

"Forget you." She took another sip of wine. "Well, he went to meet her and after that, he ended up moving us across the world for her."

"Damn! She must have *really* whipped it on him!"

"Shut up! My daddy is *not* whipped. Your mind is forever in the gutter."

"By the way, Virginia to California is across the country, not the world."

"Whatever." She picked up the universal remote from the bamboo tray and turned up the stereo volume. "I'll bet Charlotte isn't even her real name." Her favorite Rissi Palmer song filled the bungalow.

"Oh oh, you've broken out that country music. This must be serious. I see a subject change in our near future."

"That makes two of us. What are you up to?"

"I'm headed back to Cali and would like to visit Junior," he said, referring to the kitten he'd given her to help alleviate her fear of cats. "I wanna see how well you're taking care of him."

Initially, she laughed at how they made up the silliest excuses to see each other, but all humor of their situation had since been lost. "I'm out of town and left Junior with your mom." Roman was still estranged from his mother, but Jeanette had sought the woman out to begin easing Roman back into her life. The two hit it off instantly. Now if she could only convince Roman to come out of hiding from his mom, all would be grand in the world.

He sighed. "How's she doin'?"

"She misses you. You need to contact her."

"We've been through this. I can't. Not with the life I live. It would kill her."

"Not knowing your whereabouts is killing her. First, your father disappeared and now you've basically done the same thing. Do you honestly think the photos you take are enough," she said of his award-winning photojournalism pieces. No response came. "She will always love you. You need to speak with her. But I'll leave you alone on that, for now. She's close to opening up a dance studio called 'White Rose Dance Academy.' She applied for a grant, but I told her I know of an entrepreneur who would be interested in funding the project."

"Oh really, who?"

"You, so you need to create a shell company."

He chuckled. "You are too much, but I like it in you. And I already have a company. I'll have a representative contact her."

Since he wouldn't ask where she was—because of the nature of their career choices—she told him. "You won't believe this, but I'm actually on vacation. I'm in this great secluded bungalow on the beach. I even started reading a novel."

"Lucky you. I could use a vacation myself."

"I was hoping you'd say that. Why don't you? When will you be done with your assignment? I could use a little company."

"Miss me, huh?" he teased. "I'll see what I can do. So why the sudden vacation?"

"I wish I could take credit, but I can't. Javier called me the other day." She heard him grumble. "Play nice, Roman." It had been over a year since they'd seen Professor Javier Escondido, yet Roman still couldn't stand the man. "The Cuban government gave him and the scientist who created the cure for the 'Cuban Plague' that ravaged their country an all-expense- paid vacation at any of their exclusive resorts. Since their government doesn't actually know the Black Widow is the one who created the cure, Javier made arrangements for me."

"*Please* tell me you're not in Cuba."

The dread in his voice worried her. "Yeah, I'm in Cuba. Why?"

"Shit. Jeanette, run!"

Without missing a beat, she hopped out of the tub, skipped toweling dry and stepped into her underpants. "What's going on?" She put on her bra. When she first met Roman, she'd thought he was paranoid, but she soon learned his instincts were always dead on.

"That fucking Daphne. She knows! It's a trap."

She snatched her T-shirt off the dressing bench and pulled it over her head. "Who's Daphne?" She reached for her jeans and heard something crash through the front door of the bungalow and windows breaking in the front room. "Oh shit!" She dropped her pants and rushed for the bathroom window.

"What the fuck's going on?" Roman asked, voice filled with fear.

"They're breaking in." Just as she reached the window to escape, a large object flew through the closed window. She barely had time to turn away as glass flew into the room. She grabbed a piece of the broken glass to use as a weapon.

"Jeanette, what's happening?" Roman asked frantically.

"Busy...I'm busy."

Two men, dressed in black from their masks to their combat boots, burst through the bathroom door. A third man was crawling through the window. In a matter of seconds, she flung the piece of glass toward one of the doormen—direct hit! He screamed, cursed and pulled the glass out of his eye. She yanked the third man all the way through the window and slammed him into the broken glass on the floor, then stomped on his chest and vaulted off him onto the last man whose cold blue eyes reflected shock.

She rammed into who she thought was the last man, but saw several more intruders in the bungalow. "Roman, there are too many of them."

"I'm on my way, baby!"

Now on the floor with the man she'd rammed, she elbowed him in the neck and kneed him in the groin with all her might, all the while wondering why they didn't have weapons. She rose to fight when a sharp pain stabbed her in the side of the neck. A few seconds later, everything went black.